A Rob Wyllie

First published in Great Britain in 2025 b
Kingd

Copyright @ Rob Wyllie 2025

The right of Rob Wyllie to be identified as the author of this work has been asserted by him in accordance with the Copyright, Design and Patents Act 1988

All rights reserved. No part of this publication may be reproduced, stored in a retrieval system, or transmitted. in any form or by any means, electronic, mechanical, photocopying, recording or otherwise, without the prior permission of the copyright owner.

All the characters in this book are fictitious and any resemblance to actual persons, living or dead, is purely coincidental.

robwyllie.com

The Maggie Bainbridge Series

Death After Dinner

The Leonardo Murders

The Aphrodite Suicides

The Ardmore Inheritance

Past Sins

Murder on Salisbury Plain

Presumption of Death

The Loch Lomond Murders

The Royal Mile Murders

Murder on Speyside

Murder in the Cairngorms

Murder at Christmas Lodge

The Argyll Murders

The Argyll Murders

Rob Wyllie

Prologue

The thing was, if you were to go back just a couple of years, nobody other than a handful of sad geeks working for the power generating companies would have had the faintest idea of what a compound energy drought was. But for the last three weeks, it had been the phrase on everybody's lips, the phrase that was dominating the news agenda and the phrase that was causing politicians to squirm as they gurned their obsequious smiles at interviewers who were intent on tearing them apart. Now, even the dumbest five-year old would be able to tell you what a compound energy drought was. Ask little Jack or little Sophia, and he or she would explain it was an extended period when the sun didn't shine and the wind didn't blow, leaving the increasingly renewables-dependent country unable to generate sufficient electricity to keep the lights on. And the sun hadn't shone, nor had the wind gusted, not for nearly thirteen days and counting, this due to some freak weather condition currently locking the UK in its immutable grip. Suddenly there had been talk of power cuts, and after a week of sanctimonious hand-wringing it had been decided that, as a precaution, one of the previously-mothballed gas-fired power stations should be fired up, although apparently there was only enough liquefied petroleum gas in the national storage network to run it for a week at most. Shortly afterwards, and with obvious embarrassment, the government had published a schedule for a programme of country-wide power cuts, should the unusual weather conditions continue. This being late October when the nights had drawn in and the temperature was already struggling to reach double figures, this news hadn't exactly boosted the poll ratings of the governing party. But at least they had gone to great pains to confirm that hospitals and schools would be exempt from the proposed cuts, along with critical industrial facilities such as oil refineries and steelworks that relied on a constant supply of electricity. Furthermore, to save power, all street lighting across the entire country would be switched off, an action that was acknowledged might increase road accident figures and might even cause deaths, but which was regarded as regrettable collateral damage at this time of national emergency. Unsurprisingly, for the subsequent six or seven days the country had been gripped by a mood of depression almost as unmovable as the recalcitrant weather system hovering moodily above the clouds.

And then, this being the British Isles, the weather suddenly changed. Storm Kitty, which had been pottering about aimlessly in the middle of the Atlantic for days, finally decided to get its act together, setting off towards the west coast of Scotland with ever-gathering menace. With winds reaching up to ninety miles an hour, it was inevitable that serious damage to infrastructure would result, and so it proved. All along the coast, a powerful Atlantic swell pounded seawalls and washed away defences, creating chaos and misery along its path. Up in the hills, the storm took down miles of pylons supplying power right across the Western Highlands. Such was the devastation that the electricity company was forecasting it would take at least a fortnight if not more to restore power to every home and business. In remote Argyll, and in particular along the shores of Loch Fyne, homes were without electricity for more than twelve days, causing widespread disruption and inconvenience. And in the little community of Strachur, nestling quietly on the eastern shore of the loch, the consequences were about to become rather more devastating for one particular group of individuals.

Chapter 1

For Maggie, it had been the most incredible period of her life, a period bursting with a happiness that seemed beyond imagination. The arrival of wonderful little Isobel had been the ultimate joy, the baby now a gurgling four-month-old bundle of delight, with whom her lovely husband Frank and their little boy Ollie were of course utterly besotted. So too were her parents, who for much of the time during the preceding months, had exchanged their Yorkshire home for the spare room of Maggie and Frank's Milngavie bungalow. Isobel was so beautiful of course that you couldn't help but fall in love with her, but what was truly astonishing was the remarkable effect the new baby had had on Maggie's ailing father, who had been slipping ever deeper into the horrible quagmire of dementia during the previous two years. At first, he was confused, believing Isobel to be Maggie herself, but gradually the fog seemed to clear and with it the worst symptoms of his illness. Now, and miraculously, he was back to something approaching his old self, and it was a great wonder to see the smile break out on her daughter's face when she heard the mellow tones of her grandfather's voice as he serenaded her with a classic nursery rhyme.

As for Bainbridge Associates, her little private investigations firm had too enjoyed a short maternity break, but with no deleterious effect on its two employees. Her brother-in-law and part-time investigator Jimmy had also welcomed a new baby into his family, a strapping boy who had of course been christened with a Scandinavian forename in deference to the heritage of his lovely mother Frida. Frank had suggested Thor would have been a suitable moniker given the boy had tipped the scales at nearly eleven pounds, but they had chosen Viggo instead, a name that seemed somehow to fit the ever-smiling baby so perfectly that it was impossible to imagine him being called anything else. Jimmy, joint proprietor of a Braemar-based outward-bound business, had cut back on his work schedule to spend as much time as he could with his new son and was only now ramping up his involvement to something approaching full-time. Maggie's other employee, associate investigator Lori Logan, had decamped two doors down Byres Road to the Bikini Barista cafe, her former employer, where she had taken the reins for the summer whilst its owner Stevie took an extended break in the Mediterranean.

But now, it was time to get back to work, if at first only on a part-time basis, such was the agony of being separated from her little daughter for any length of time. Accordingly, she had resolved to take on just one case at a time, and furthermore, only to take on such matters that could be comfortably progressed in no more than twenty hours a week. Lori, however, was returning on a full-time basis, her associate having grown her investigative capability remarkably in the months that she had worked at the agency. Jimmy too was available on a consultancy basis as and when required, so the agency would have more than enough capacity to take on a case of at least moderate complexity. Although, she reflected ruefully, the case she was just about to take on might tax that assertion to the limit.

It was ten in the morning when she pushed open the door of her office, a quick glance around instantly confirming that everything was just as she had left it when they shut up shop six months earlier. Two desks with almost-matching chairs, a small conference table, a coffee machine, a computer printer and a wi-fi router took up all the available space of the single room. And pleasingly, one of the chairs was already occupied by a smiling Lori Logan.

'Hi Maggie,' the girl said effusively. 'Isn't it dead good to be back in the saddle? It was okay working for Stevie, but I'm glad I won't be baking any more scones for a while. I'm sick of the sight and smell of them to be honest.'

Maggie laughed. 'They're very yummy scones though. But yes, it's lovely to be back, although I'm missing Isobel already.'

'You're only fifteen minutes away from home,' her assistant observed. 'You can nip back anytime you want for a wee cuddle. As long as I can come too,' she added, grinning. 'Because she's *so* gorgeous.'

'She is, isn't she? Frank is convinced she looks like him of course, but I'm not sure I agree.'

'She's beautiful like her mum,' Lori said. 'And I'm not just saying that because you're my boss.'

Maggie laughed again. 'Of course you're not. But enough of babies for the moment. Our prospective client will be here any minute. Let's try to get back into detective mode, especially since it looks like the power cuts are finally a thing of the past'

'Aye, thank goodness for that,' Lori said. 'So what's this case all about then?'

'It's a missing person case. Our prospective client's a woman called Ruth Davie and it's her partner who's gone missing. In actual fact, it seems as if he's gone off with another woman, someone he works beside. But apparently there's been no contact since it happened and that's nearly six weeks now.'

'And now she's worried?' Lori said.

'Worried and angry at the same time I would say. And they've got a little girl too, so you can imagine how difficult the situation is. Anyway, this looks like her now.' Maggie said, nodding towards the frosted glass door.

A woman pushed it open and then looked around the office uncertainly. She was around late thirties, Maggie estimated, petite and notably attractive if rather stern-faced, her smart woollen coat, pinned-back hair and carefully made-up face suggesting she would be going to work following the meeting. Maggie stood up to greet her and smiled. 'Hi, I'm guessing you must be Ruth Davie. I'm Maggie, Maggie Bainbridge, and this is Lori Logan, my associate. Please, take a seat,' she added, gesturing towards the vacant chair. 'If you want a coffee, I can brew up the machine or we can get some better stuff in from the cafe along the road. And here, let me take your coat.'

'Nothing for me thank you,' the woman said briskly, slipping off her coat and handing it to Maggie. She sat down then hesitated for a moment before continuing. 'To be honest, I'm really not sure where to start. I never envisaged myself needing the services of a private detective.' She paused again, giving them a look which Maggie thought was mildly suspicious. 'I still don't know if I really do, quite frankly. I'm probably wasting my time. And yours.'

'Well perhaps Ruth, you can let us be the judge of that,' Maggie said in a kindly tone. 'Most of our clients were in exactly the same position as you, where something out of the ordinary or distressing has happened, and they decided they needed some help. It's what we do. We help people when they have a problem.'

The woman gave a thin-lipped smile. 'Okay. Well as I said when I phoned, it's about my partner. I haven't heard from him in nearly six weeks, and I'm very concerned now. And we have a little girl, and she is missing her father of course.' She hesitated again. 'But it's not totally straightforward I'm afraid.'

'What do you mean?' Lori asked.

Ruth shuffled uncomfortably. 'There was something that happened. Before all of this. Something horrible which I don't like to talk about. But I suppose I must,' she added, her distaste obvious.

Maggie nodded, then gave her a sympathetic smile. 'It would be great if you felt able to share what that was. I'm guessing it would be very important for our investigation, should we mutually agree we should take on the case.'

The woman slipped a hand into her bag and took out her phone. 'I'll show you. It's very unsavoury.' She swiped the screen several times then laid the device on the table and pointed to the photograph she had retrieved. *'She's* the woman he's ran off with. And if you read the message, you'll understand what I mean by unsavoury.'

The picture was of a young woman, in fact no more than a girl, Maggie thought, perhaps early twenties, if that. Given that the girl was in her underwear, Maggie had little doubt about what the nature of the text message would be, and affording it a swift glance, she saw immediately that her assumption was correct. Lori too had assimilated the nature of the message and was leaning back in her chair, open mouthed.

'Did the wee cow send that to *you*?' she asked incredulously.

Ruth shook her head. 'No, to Paul's phone. He'd left it lying on the coffee table and I saw the message come through. It wasn't until afterwards that I forwarded it to myself. I was shocked and devastated as you can imagine. And bloody angry as well. In fact, more angry than anything.'

'I guess you had words?' Maggie asked. 'You confronted him I take it?'

She nodded. 'Of course I did. But pathetically, he denied that anything was happening between them. As if you could believe *that*, after seeing a picture like that one,' she added acerbically. 'But of course, Paul has always been so *weak*.'

'But he admitted he knew who she was?' Maggie said.

'Yes, she was a work colleague, an Indian girl who was a contractor like himself. He said there was nothing going on and that he had no idea why she had sent him the text. He said she must have sent it to him by mistake, but I didn't believe him. Especially when I investigated his message history and saw what was there.'

'You kept his phone then?' Lori asked.

She shook her head. 'No, I gave him it back, but only once I'd looked down the message history from *her*. That only took a few seconds, but it was *enough*. There was at least a dozen of them and some a lot more explicit than the one I showed you.' She spat out the words, her face transforming into a sneer. 'And ridiculously, he still tried to deny that anything was happening.'

'How long had it been going on for?' Maggie asked gently.

The woman shrugged. 'I don't know. Four months, six months, something like that. I think he had a kind of mini nervous breakdown after his mother died. At least, that's how I'm explaining it to myself.' she added. 'Or deluding myself more like.'

'And when did this happen?' Maggie asked, interested. 'His mum's death I mean?'

She shrugged again. 'Six months ago, something like that. He took it hard, especially on top of all the family tragedy they'd suffered over the years.'

Maggie was silent, hoping that the woman would elaborate. After a few moments Ruth continued. 'His older brother Jaz died in an accident about ten years ago you see. A drowning, on Loch Fyne. There was only a year between them and Paul took it really hard. And it devastated their parents too, as you can imagine. This was before Paul and I met of course, but it's always been there, hanging in the background. Especially since his father died four years ago. He was really close to both his boys, and he never got over his death. He drunk himself to death in the end. Weak of course, like his son.'

There was a silence, involuntarily caused by the extraordinary callousness of the statement. Then Lori said, 'Aye, well that's a terrible tragedy right enough. It must have been awful for Paul and especially his mum.'

Ruth nodded. 'Yes, after her husband died, Paul's mum was just existing, not living. It's a horrible thing to say, but her death was a blessing in many ways. She was the saddest person I ever met. Although if you want to know the truth, I think she rather enjoyed it in a weird way. It made her the centre of attention. The tragic widow and all that.'

'And you think it's that event that's at the root of all this?' Maggie asked, ignoring the woman's unfeeling remark. 'From what you say, the timings seem to coincide.'

'Yes, they do,' she agreed. 'And I know this might sound strange, but I think it was clearing out his mum's house that really spooked him, rather than the funeral and all of that. He took a week off work to do the clear-out, and afterwards he was just kind of strange, just not himself at all. He seemed to change.'

'In what way?' Lori asked her. 'What was different?'

'Well, he'd been talking about becoming a self-employed contractor for years and years. He's a software developer you see, and there's lots of developers who work that way. The attraction is you can make big money, and we've always been short of it all through our relationship so I was always nagging him to just bloody do it. But as was *typical* for Paul, it was all talk and no action. Deep down he was perfectly satisfied working at his little secure job at the city council, even though the money was pathetic.' She hesitated for a moment. 'He was happy, but I was fed up having to scrimp and scrape for everything. It was demeaning.'

'I'm assuming there wasn't an inheritance when his mum died?' Maggie said. 'No house to be sold or anything like that?'

Ruth shook her head. 'His parents lived in a horrible wee council house. She kept it tidy enough to be fair to her, but of course it was handed back to the housing association when she died. So no, there wasn't any inheritance, not a penny. Not that we expected anything, nice though it would have been.'

Maggie nodded. 'But then he had this big change, when he suddenly decided to leave his job with the council and become a contractor?'

'That's right,' she said. 'Completely out of the blue he handed in his notice and signed up with a couple of recruitment agencies, and after about three or four weeks he got a contract with Torridon Systems here in Glasgow. The money was great of course, and finally I thought he was going to try and make something of himself. I was suddenly quite proud of him.'

Maggie asked, 'Torridon Systems? That's the company started by Alison Christie, the woman who disappeared on a skiing holiday, wasn't it? They're a big firm, one of Scotland's big success stories. They've got that big fancy office down by the Clyde, near the BBC.'

'Yes, that's them,' Ruth said. 'And that's where he met *her*. Maya Mishra, if you must know. Even her name is beautiful,' she added bitterly.

'You said she was Indian?' Maggie said. 'Do you mean actually from India, not just of Asian heritage?'

'Yes, she was from India. She was a contractor like he was. I don't know much about it, but apparently, it's very common to use Indian sub-contractors in the software industry.'

'Yes, I've read about that,' Maggie said. 'They're very well-educated people, and apparently their universities produce hundreds of thousands of IT graduates every year. Lots of firms use them.'

'They're always dead beautiful, these Indian girls,' Lori said wistfully, if not entirely helpfully. Realising what she had done, she quickly uttered an apology. 'Sorry, sorry, I'm an idiot, I shouldn't have said that.'

Ruth gave her a reproachful look. 'Well, Paul obviously agreed with you, didn't he? And I never suspected a thing, more fool me.'

Maggie nodded. 'I sympathise. I went through the same thing myself a few years ago, and yes, you feel a complete fool for not suspecting.' That had been a terrible time, she reflected, but look at her now, basking in the most wonderful happiness you could imagine. She wondered for a moment whether she should share this with Ruth Davie but decided it would be better to keep that for later in their business relationship, should they decide to take on her case. 'So when did you find out he was intending to leave you?' she continued. 'This was, what, six weeks ago you said?'

The woman looked straight back at Maggie, grim-faced. 'Yes, that's when it was. And it was all so *sudden*. One minute he was there, and then he was gone. Quite frankly, I never imagined he had it in him.'

'Perhaps you can take us through exactly how it happened,' Maggie said gently. 'If it's not too painful.'

'Yes, of course,' she said. 'We had been having difficulties in our relationship, naturally enough, with everything that had happened. He had become very angry with me, and he was continuing to deny anything was going on with the girl. He even said that the text messages had been faked somehow and that someone was out to get him. But it was just more of his weird behaviour. I wanted to believe him, but he was just acting crazy.' She hesitated. 'And then one day at work, I got a text that said he was leaving me for Maya, that he was sorry, but he had fallen in love with her, and he had to be with her. I just fell apart.' She paused. 'I know you might find that hard to believe, but I did. And then one of my work colleagues ordered a taxi and took me home. And that's when

I knew it was true. All the drawers and the wardrobe doors in our room had been left open and he had taken our big suitcase. And then he didn't come home that night, so I knew it was true.'

'That's really awful,' Lori said. 'What did you do?'

'I was in a complete daze,' Ruth said. 'I went to the school and picked up Jasmine and then we went to my mum and dad's and then I just got angrier and angrier, vowing all sorts of vengeance on him. My parents were great, and I stayed with them for nearly a week before I managed to get my head back together and started to work out what I should do next. Eventually I got the courage to phone Paul, but he didn't answer. I tried again and again, but still, he wouldn't pick up. It was just so cruel, but at the same time, just so unlike him too. He was devoted to Jasmine, and it was inconceivable he wouldn't want to see her. She was totally devastated as you can imagine.'

'That's understandable,' Maggie said. 'And I believe you've had no contact or response from Paul since that day? Is that right?'

'Nothing,' she said bitterly. 'Not a word. He plays five-a-side football every week with a bunch of friends, and I spoke to a couple of them. But Paul hadn't said anything to them about his intentions and he hadn't said anything about *her* either.'

'And what about work?' Maggie asked. 'Did you speak to anybody at Torridon Systems?'

Ruth nodded. 'I did, and they were incredibly helpful. I had a meeting with their CEO Jack Easton and their head of development, a woman called Sarah Duncan. She was Paul's immediate boss. They confirmed there had been rumours that Paul and Maya were having a relationship, but because they weren't direct employees, it wasn't covered by the company's normal employee terms and conditions. And since it hadn't been affecting their work, they decided they didn't need to take any action.'

'And did they just suddenly walk out of their jobs?' Lori asked.

Ruth shook her head. 'No, they didn't. They gave the company one month's notice, as they were obliged to do under the terms of their contract.' She paused for a moment. 'I got even angrier when I heard that. *Really* angry.'

So, as the woman had obviously realised, this disappearance had been carefully planned, Maggie thought. She said, 'This might be a difficult question, but have you any idea where he might go? A favourite place perhaps?'

Ruth nodded. 'Yes, I did think about that a lot. He was always drawn to a campsite on Loch Fyne, near where his brother died. We used to rent a caravan up there in the summer, and it was lovely, but it always seemed like a sort of pilgrimage too. I spoke to the owners of the campsite and to the landlord of the wee pub we often went to, but they hadn't seen Paul.' She sighed. 'The thing was, I was tracking his phone. Until it went dead, a few days after he left me.' She fell silent, a silence that Maggie allowed to hang in the air, anticipating that something of importance might be about to emerge.

'I tracked him to Heathrow. Three days after he left home. And that was the last location I got for him. Before his phone went dead.'

'Do you think he's gone abroad then?' Maggie said, surprised.

'The girl only had a work visa. She couldn't stay in the country once she'd left her job.'

'What, do you think they've gone to *India*?' Lori asked, at the same time giving Maggie a look that plainly said how are we going to find this guy if *that's* where he's gone?

'I think he might have,' the woman conceded. 'As I said, he'd been acting crazy.'

'That would obviously add a complication,' Maggie said carefully, 'because I don't think my little firm would have the wherewithal to track your partner all the way to India.' She paused for a moment, thinking through their options, before responding. 'I think it would be worth reporting his disappearance to the police.' She raised her hands as she sensed the woman was about to object. 'And yes, I know they may not take it seriously given the background, but they could at least make some speedy official enquiries to the airlines and to the border force to see if either Paul or Maya have left the country. That would at least give my firm something to work with.' She hesitated again. 'Look, my husband Frank is a Detective Chief Inspector working at New

Gorbals police station. I suggest you go down there and tell the desk sergeant that you haven't heard from your partner for over four weeks, and you want to report him as a missing person. They'll take your details, and I'll alert Frank, and maybe he can get one of his team to spend a few hours on the case. Just solely concentrating on whether the pair of them have gone to India, as you suspect. And then we can take it from there.'

'Would you do that for me?' Ruth said, obviously grateful. 'That would be incredible.'

Maggie smiled. 'Yes, of course. I suggest you go straight there and report it, and I'll speak to Frank and tell him to expect you. I'm sure he'll be delighted to help,' she added, shooting Lori a raised-eyebrow look.

Chapter 2

There was no doubt in Frank's mind that being a dad was the greatest thing that had ever happened to him, despite the sleepless nights and the often-overwhelming sense of responsibility for this perfect young life. At forty-five, he knew he was getting on a bit for a first-time dad, but to be fair, on the frequent occasions when he and Maggie proudly propelled Isobel's hi-tech buggy around Milngavie, her equally enthralled big brother Ollie in tow, he couldn't help but observe that he and his wife, though similarly ancient, were certainly not outliers. For many couples, it was the exorbitant cost of buying a home and establishing a solid family base that had caused so many to defer the decision to have children, whereas in his case, it was because it had taken half of his adult life to find the right woman. Still, however tortured and eventful the journey had been, the destination was bloody marvellous as he recognised, not for the first time, that he was a very lucky man. But then his pleasant reflections were interrupted by the stealthy arrival of desk sergeant Wally Jardine at his table in the canteen of New Gorbals police station, where he'd been enjoying a coffee, and, if truth be told, a bit of a snooze.

'Hey Frank, you sleeping?' the sergeant said languidly.

Startled, Frank spun round, stretched, then involuntarily rubbed an eye. 'I was thinking deeply about my extensive caseload, since you ask. And by the way, it's sir or DCI Stewart to you. Although I'll accept guv as well, at a push.'

'Sorry *sir*,' Jardine said, sounding anything but. 'Anyway, there's a woman at the desk. She says she was told to ask for you. By your *wife*.'

'Really? All right, I'll come and have a word. Any idea what it's about?'

'She says her partner's gone missing,' he said. 'Gone off with another woman she says. But I'll tell you what, the guy must be a bit of an arse if that's the case, because this one's a right looker. Sharp-tongued as well, just to warn you. But I tell you, I wouldn't say no.'

Frank shook his head. 'Wally Jardine, forever stuck in the nineteen-seventies,' he said, not hiding his contempt. 'You should have been in that Life on Mars TV program.' He paused. 'But if this guy's gone off with another woman, then he's not missing, is he?'

Jardine shrugged. 'I don't know, you're supposed to be the detective. I'm just telling you what she told me.'

'You're always such a helpful guy Wally, thanks,' Frank said. They made their way back to the front desk without further exchange. 'That's her there,' Jardine said, needlessly nodding through the open hatch as he pressed the button to release the electric door lock. 'Name's Ruth Davie, or so she says.'

'Aye, well she probably knows her own name,' Frank said. He smiled in the woman's direction and said, 'Mrs Davie? I'm DCI Frank Stewart. I believe you met my wife earlier. Follow me and we'll go and get a tea or a coffee, and you can get a bit of breakfast too if you fancy it.' Two minutes later he was back at the table he had occupied earlier, somewhat of a favourite of his because it was butted up against a radiator. Ruth Davie declined his offers of sustenance then began to replay the story she had earlier shared with Maggie. Frank listened intently, adding the occasional *aye, I see* or *yep, that makes sense,* but allowing the narrative to flow uninterrupted as much as possible. When she was finished, he nodded and said, 'Well thanks for that Ruth, that's all very clear to me. And just to be a hundred percent certain, you say you've not had any communication of any type since the day Paul left the house? No phone calls, text messages, emails, even old-school letters or notes. Nothing, is that right?'

She shook her head. 'No. Nothing, and I must have phoned or messaged him a hundred times in the day or two afterwards. And I kept on doing it for days and days, but still nothing. We both had the Find My app set on our phones, and I tried to trace him through that. And as I told your wife, the last sighting of his phone was at Heathrow airport.'

'And when was that exactly?'

'Three days after he left.' She hesitated before continuing. 'I was bloody angry when I saw that. Because I assumed he must have flown off to India with his new girlfriend, without even thinking what that would do to me and especially to our daughter Jasmine. It was just so cruel.'

'But is he a cruel man Ruth?' Frank asked. 'I've only been speaking with you for five minutes, but I'm not getting the impression that he was.'

'No, he's not, he's a weak man,' she said bitterly. 'Obviously I don't know for sure that he's gone to India, but that's just what I assumed.' She paused again. 'Your wife said the police might be able to help with that.' She gave him a hopeful look. 'Is that right? Is that something you could do for me?'

He nodded. 'Aye, it'll be quite straightforward for us to check with the airlines and with the border force guys. They keep records of everyone who's entered or exited the country, so we'll soon know if Paul and this Maya girl have left or not.' He was thoughtful for a moment then said, 'And what about the two or three days *before* his phone was detected at Heathrow? Where was it during that period, do you know?'

She gave him a sharp look. 'I was checking constantly of course, and it was only switched on for a short time. It was on in his office for a short period of time on the day he left, for a couple of hours. In the afternoon, just after he sent me that text.' She hesitated. 'I was an idiot. I should have gone straight down there when I saw that, I know that now, but I just wasn't thinking straight at the time. I was just so shocked and angry, I must have sat on the bed for hours, cuddling Jasmine and trying to hold it together.'

'I think you said he worked at Torridon Systems, down on the riverside there,' Frank said. 'Is that right? That's where you saw him on the Find My app?'

She nodded. 'Yes, he was on a six-month software development contract there. I went round to their offices the next day, and in fact they were the first people I spoke to after

Paul disappeared. They were very helpful, but the phone was switched off again that morning. They took me to see his desk, and we had a look around, but it wasn't there of course. He'd obviously gone off by then and switched it off when he realised I could track him.'

'Aye, maybe,' Frank mused, unconvinced. This man was a father to a seven-year-old girl, and if the guy had even a quarter of the love for his daughter that Frank felt for Isobel, then there was no way he was going to just disappear off the radar without a word. But then again, the man had apparently been acting out of character since the death of his mother six months earlier, and before that, the family had suffered more tragedy than anyone deserved, so maybe he hadn't been capable of thinking straight. But the fact was, it wasn't exactly unknown for a man to fall for a beautiful and alluring woman and end up doing stupid things, things that he later regretted.

But then out of the blue, something came back to him.

'Ruth, didn't you say that Paul had lost his elder brother in a drowning accident a few years back and that it had really affected him and his parents? Where was this accident, can you tell me?'

She nodded. 'It was somewhere on Loch Fyne, not far from Inveraray I think. Paul's brother had been on a team-building exercise with the NHS Trust he worked for at the time. They were out on a sailing boat when Jaz and another man fell overboard and were drowned.'

'Jaz Davie, of *course*,' Frank blurted out. 'The *Three Men in a Boat* case. I was on it back then, in fact, I was the lead investigator. I remember it now. As you say, another man died too. Peter Denny was his name. I remember it only too well.'

She gave him a questioning look. 'The Three Men in a Boat case? I've never heard that before.'

He gave a rueful smile. 'I'm sorry, it was never called that officially but that's what us coppers called it internally. After the book with the same name of course. Although that's a comedy and this case was far from funny.' He paused before explaining. 'There were three of them on the little sailing dinghy. Jaz, Peter and another guy from the team-building course they were on. Three men in a boat you see,' he repeated. 'But only one of them made it back to shore. It was a terrible thing all together, and it did for the reputation of the outward-bound company that was running the course. Because there should have been a course supervisor checking them out before the boat left with the three guys onboard, and there wasn't.'

As he spoke, it all came flooding back to him. He had been a Detective Sergeant at the time but close to promotion to DI, so they'd put him in charge of the matter, which was assumed at the outset to be a straightforward but tragic accident. The role of the police had been simply to collect evidence to present to the official enquiry, where the Fiscal's office was expected to rubber-stamp a verdict of accidental death. But the case had turned out to be rather more involved than that. The supposed facts were that Jaz Davie and his two pals had been drinking that lunchtime and when they were out on the boat, they had been fooling about and Davie and one of the other guys had fallen overboard and drowned. The guy who had survived, whose name he couldn't remember, had been unsurprisingly traumatised by the incident and his account of what had happened had been unreliable to say the least. He couldn't say why Jaz and the other guy hadn't attached their safety carabiners to the boat's perimeter rail, or indeed if they had been secured when they set off but had been later detached. It was understandable that the surviving guy hadn't gone into the water to try and save his course-mates, but neither was he able to explain why it had been at least fifteen minutes before he thought to phone for help. By which time of course, it was too late. But the big question was, why had they set off without the supervisor on board, and indeed why wasn't the supervisor there to stop them getting on the boat in the state they were in? He vaguely recalled that an explanation had been offered for that latter omission, but he couldn't remember exactly what it was. As to why the lads got on the boat, it was because they were drunk and in high spirits and with typical but unwise youthful bravado, didn't see why they needed to wait for the supervisor to show up.

With no way of corroborating the truth or otherwise of what he had been told, Frank had been forced to stand in front of the Sheriff at the Fatal Accident Enquiry and give an unsatisfactory account full of ifs, buts and uncertainties. The report had no option but to conclude that the two men's deaths had been accidental but could possibly have been prevented if the outward-bound company had taken proper procedures to prevent a boat being taken out on the loch without supervision, such as securing it to the jetty with a padlock and chain. The incident had left a mark on Frank for several months afterwards, partly because he had been frustrated that he had probably not got to the truth of what had happened that day, but mainly because it had caused the needless loss of two young lives. But eventually the memory of the case had receded, until today, when it had re-emerged into sharp and unpleasant focus. There was no re-visiting it now, obviously, so he would just have to bear with it until the unsatisfactory recollections of the matter faded away once again.

He smiled at the woman apologetically. 'Sorry about going down that rabbit-hole, but it was just such a coincidence. Of course it was nearly ten years ago, so it probably doesn't have any relevance to your partner's disappearance.' He stood up to indicate their meeting was coming to a conclusion.

'Anyway Ruth, we'll log Paul as a missing person on our database, and that automatically kicks off a number of standard procedures. There'll be some posters printed, so we'll need a recent photograph, and his details will be circulated to every police force in the country. And I'll get one of my officers to check flights and border force records for the day in question. We should be able to get that done tomorrow with any luck.'

'Thank you,' she said, getting to her feet. 'But should I still use Bainbridge Associates, now that I've reported it officially to the police? Because I don't want to waste money unnecessarily.'

It was a question he had been expecting, and a question which he felt deserved a straight answer. Quietly he said, 'Yes, you should. The fact is, hundreds of folks go missing every month and the police have only got limited resources to dedicate to each one. Every one of the missing people is on our radar, but we can only give them a few hours of our time if that.' That was the truth, he reflected, because the statistics showed that ninety-nine percent of them eventually turned up, safe and sound, but many with no intention of returning to their old lives. Regrettable though it was, it was a waste of scare resources to look very hard for the ninety-nine-percenters, a fact that presented a steady stream of lucrative work for the private investigator community. And as for the one percent, once the body was found, they got all the resources they needed and more. But would Paul Davie turn out to be one of that unfortunate group? That was something he fully expected Maggie and her team to discover very quickly, and right now, even with the little knowledge they had, he was putting the odds of that occurrence at somewhere far north of fifty-fifty.

Chapter 3

There was no denying it, Maggie was excited to be back at work after her enjoyable six-month maternity break, and their new case, the puzzling disappearance of software developer Paul Davie, was just the kind of juicy matter she'd hope to return to. To launch the case, she and Lori had decamped to the comfortable surroundings of the Bikini Barista cafe, two doors down from her own Byres Road office, and were awaiting the arrival of the coffee and breakfast rolls they had ordered.

'Good to be back in the old routine Lori, isn't it?' she said brightly. 'I've really missed it, even although I've not exactly been short of things to keep me occupied.'

Her associate laughed. 'Yeah, Stevie's takings have been down fifty percent during your wee shut-down. Anyway, I'm assuming you've decided to take on Ruth Davie's case? Even though she's reported her partner's disappearance to the police?'

Maggie gave a rueful sigh. 'They don't actively look for missing persons, you know that, not unless there's obvious evidence of foul play, and there isn't in this case. As far as the police will be concerned, he's just ran off with his mistress, so they'll give it a couple of hours max and then it'll be forgotten. It's not exactly an unusual occurrence after all.'

'But *you* don't really believe that do you?' Lori said. 'Because he's got a wee daughter. He wouldn't just evaporate into thin air like that, even if he had decided to dump his partner. He would at least have been in touch by now.'

'Yes, you're right, I think. But we'll see. I'm hoping Frank will be able to let us know later today whether Paul and his girlfriend Maya actually did fly off to India, but in the meantime, I suggest we spend some time here doing a bit of a reconstruction of events and then we go down to Torridon Systems and ask some questions.'

'Sounds good to me,' Lori agreed.

'Okay, so what do we know?' Maggie asked rhetorically. 'As far as the Davie relationship was concerned, Ruth had discovered her partner was having an affair with a work colleague, a younger woman called Maya Mishra, another software developer who had come from India to work for Torridon. He had denied the affair, but the evidence was pretty conclusive.'

'That was the dirty texts with pictures of her in underwear,' Lori interjected.

'That's right, very hard to argue with. We also heard from Ruth that both her partner and Maya had given a month's notice as was required under the terms of their contracts, so despite the rapid manner of his leaving, this was obviously something that had been planned.'

Lori nodded. 'And then one day he just did a flit. Took off, just like that, without any warning.'

'Yes, the flit,' Maggie mused. 'I find that the most puzzling part of the matter so far. I mean, he had obviously planned to leave his partner so why didn't he just tell her that was what he was going to do, instead of just sneaking off like he did?'

'That's easily answered,' Lori said. 'Because he's a coward. He just bottled it. He didn't want to face her.'

'Yeah, that's probably what it was, and it doesn't show him in a very good light, does it? Anyway, on the day in question, he must have got up as normal, got ready for work, went into the office, and then knowing his partner was also out at work, he sneaked back to the house, threw some clothes into a suitcase and then went off to meet his lover. Then he sent Ruth a brutal text saying he's leaving her. And he hasn't been heard of since.'

'I've got a couple of points to add,' Lori said. 'First, we don't know for certain that he went into the office after he left that morning. I'm not sure if it's important, but we don't know. He might just have hung about round the corner.'

'Good point.'

'Secondly, do you remember Ruth said she'd tracked Paul's phone in his office *after* she'd got that horrible text from him? So does that mean he went into the office after he'd picked up his stuff? It seems like it.'

Maggie shrugged. 'It's possible I suppose. Maybe that's where he'd arranged to meet his girlfriend, or maybe he had some other stuff to collect, or some work stuff to hand over.'

They were interrupted by the arrival of Stevie with their order. 'Hi guys, here we go, two americanos and two crispy rolls with the square sausage,' he boomed with his customary bonhomie. 'They're on the house by the way. Lori's got a lifetime free pass after looking after the place over the summer. Me and the wife had an amazing time in Ibiza.'

'Out clubbing every night Stevie?' Maggie asked, amused.

He laughed. 'Not exactly. A nice dinner, a cocktail or three and in bed by ten, that was our thing. Absolute heaven. Then sunbathing by the pool all day long with a good book.'

'Sounds delightful. But thank you so much for these Stevie, they're lovely.' She took a gulp from her coffee then said, 'So now young Lori, let's belt down this breakfast then next stop it's Torridon Systems I think.'

***

Maggie had somehow found a spare hour to research the history of the software company, and it had made fascinating reading. The firm had been founded almost eight years ago by a woman called Alison Christie, a former nurse and single mother who had come up with the idea of an online system which allowed nurses to register for extra shifts and allowed hospitals to book them directly, cutting out the expensive agency middlemen. The website, called Nurses Direct, had immediately taken off, slashing the cost to the NHS of temporary staff and at a stroke, rendering the previous rip-off agency business model redundant. Torridon Systems was now a multi-million-pound business and one of Scotland's major success stories, but sadly, its founder was no longer around to see it prosper. Five years ago, she had decided to extend a business trip to the United States to go skiing in Aspen, a trip from which she never returned. Her body had still not been found, and at first it was assumed that she had been caught in the avalanche that had claimed several lives in the mountain one tragic February day. But then stories began to emerge that cast a more critical spotlight on the legend that had been Alison Christie. Not long after her death, the company filed accounts which showed that the company had slumped to a loss in the previous year. Next, in a separate press statement, it was disclosed that Richie Whitmore, the software engineer credited with writing the Nurses Direct app, was considering legal action against Torridon Systems for their failure to honour a royalty agreement he had made with the company. The third and more personal issue was the revelation of the breakdown of her marriage to actor David Stirling, this the result of his alleged affair with the young co-star of his latest TV project. This avalanche of bad news changed the narrative and soon the speculation was that she had taken her own life to escape from the barrage of problems that were crushing in on her. The news also reached the authorities in Aspen, who in the absence of any firm evidence to the details of her demise, concluded that suicide was the most probable cause of death.

Maggie hadn't had time to research what had happened afterwards, particularly the fate of Torridon Systems, but here it was, its glass and chrome headquarters gleaming by the river, seemingly prosperous, outside of which Maggie and Lori now stood.

'Fancy place,' Lori said as they strolled towards the entrance door. 'Very glassy. It kind of reflects the river.'

'I guess that was part of the idea,' Maggie said. 'But I read they've got a huge bank of computers in the basement, and they use the river water to cool them. Apparently the whole facility cost fifteen million to build.'

Lori looked at her, wide-eyed. 'Phew, that's a lot for a big mirror. They must be making a packet.'

She gave her assistant a doubting look. 'Maybe they are now, but they weren't always, not according to what I've read. I suspect they've got a big mortgage on it more like.' A sign directed them to press a button mounted to the left of the double glass doors and warned them that their arrival was being recorded on CCTV. After a short delay, the doors swished open to admit them to a full-height reception area. On the wall behind the receptionist's counter was mounted a giant image of the company's founder.

'That's her then?' Lori asked, nodding up at the image. 'She's a lot younger than I expected somehow. And a lot more glamorous.'

'Yes, and she was only around forty when she died,' Maggie said. 'But she'd done a lot with her life, and I suppose this company is her legacy,' she added. 'Not bad for someone who left school with hardly any qualifications.' She leant her elbows on the high counter and addressed the young woman behind it. 'Hi. We've got an appointment with Sarah Duncan. Maggie Bainbridge and Lori Logan from Bainbridge Associates.'

The woman smiled but didn't look up from her monitor. 'Yes, I see you both on the schedule. I'll just message Sarah to say you've arrived. She should be with you in a few minutes.'

In the event, it was more than ten minutes before the woman came to collect them, arriving in the reception area looking and sounding suitably flustered.

'Sorry, sorry,' she said breathlessly, 'but there's always some crisis in this business. A big London hospital has lost its network connection and they're going nuts because they can't get on to our system. Nothing to do with us of course, but that doesn't stop them shouting their mouths off.' She smiled at them and held out a hand towards Maggie. 'I'm Sarah, head of operations, although sometimes I wish I wasn't. Follow me and we'll find a quiet oasis somewhere with a couple of soft sofas.'

Maggie thought the woman was joking, but it turned out she hadn't been. She swiped them through a security turnstile where an escalator sped them up to the first floor. A vast open-plan office space housed an army of casually-dressed staff, mostly young, beavering away in generous-sized cubicles decorated by an array of pot plants. Running along one side was a mezzanine floor with low glass protective panels overlooking the reception atrium from where they had just come. Every few metres or so was a group of soft furnishings arranged around circular glass-topped tables. 'Our break-out and chill-out areas,' Sarah explained. 'Essential for our sanity. Anyway, grab a seat, please.'

'Thanks Sarah,' Maggie said, removing her coat and laying it down beside her. 'I might not have mentioned this explicitly when we spoke on the phone, but we're helping the police investigate the disappearance of Paul Davie, who worked for you of course.'

'The police?' she said, evidently surprised. 'Why are they involved?'

'Paul's not been heard of since he left your employ, and that's almost six weeks now. His partner Ruth contacted us and when we heard her story, we advised her to formally report him missing, which she did yesterday. My firm has been commissioned directly by Ruth Davie to supplement their investigations. Hence the reason we're here of course,' she added, as if that wasn't already obvious.

'But he left his partner to be with one of our Indian contractors, didn't he? Maya Mishra. They met here and then fell for each other is what I understand.'

'You must have seen that happening,' Lori said. 'Because that kind of thing is usually quite obvious, isn't it? Eyes meeting across a crowded room and all that kind of stuff.'

Sarah shrugged. 'Well perhaps it is, but no, I personally hadn't been aware of the situation until Ruth Davie came to see us a few weeks ago and told us what had happened.'

'But I assume they worked closely together?' Maggie asked. 'I assume that's how it all started?'

'They worked on this floor, yes,' the woman answered, 'but they weren't on the same team. Maya was working on a new product we were developing, and Paul was part of our legacy re-engineering team. They would have seen each other of course, but they weren't working side-by-side. And just because they worked here, that doesn't necessarily mean that's where the relationship started, does it?' she added.

'I suppose not,' Lori conceded. 'Where do they stay anyway, these contractors? Are they in a hotel somewhere?'

Sarah shook her head. 'No, nothing so grand. We've rented a floor of a student hall of residence, just across the river from here. It's very nice accommodation, and it suits our Indian teams very well. It means they can self-cater, which they like. And they're all very young so they soon make friends with the other students.'

'So do you think that's where Paul and this Maya girl were doing it?' Lori asked.

The woman laughed. 'Conceivably, yes. But I don't know and it's none of my business.'

Maggie smiled then said. 'Please forgive me Sarah, because I don't know anything about IT, but you used the phrase legacy re-engineering, I think? It sounds very impressive whatever it is.'

'Yes sorry, jargon alert,' Sarah said apologetically. 'What it is, we have some ancient code at the heart of the product that goes all the way back to when Alison started the company, and to tell you the truth, no-one has a clue what it actually does. For years it was one of these if *it's not broke, don't try to fix it* things. But eventually we decided we had to bite the bullet and replace it with something we actually understood. There was a small team from our Indian sub-contract partner firm working on it, but they were making slow progress so we thought we would bring in another resource to speed things up. Paul Davie showed a great interest in the area after he joined us, so we put him on that team.'

'And he and Maya could have met in the kitchen or in one of these break-out spaces I suppose,' Maggie said, thinking out loud.

'Very easily,' Sarah said. 'And we're not one of these companies who ban relationships between our staff. Providing it's not between a manager and a member of their team, we don't think it's any of our business.'

'I suppose Paul or Maya might have told some of their team members what was going on,' Lori said. 'Maybe we could have a wee word with them afterwards?'

The woman shook her head. 'I'm sorry, but that won't be possible I'm afraid.' She paused for a moment. 'We closed their teams down recently and so the contractors have all gone back to India or moved on to their next contract. It was part of an efficiency review,' she added. 'A routine thing.'

'They've *all* left?' Maggie asked, surprised. 'Perhaps you could explain, because I'm not sure I understand.'

Sarah shrugged. 'As I said, it's the kind of review companies do from time to time. We're a public company now, with shareholders to satisfy and it's important we maintain our margins and profitability.'

'Yes, I read that. The company floated on the stock exchange a couple of years ago, didn't it?'

The woman nodded. 'That's right, on the AIM listing, I think that's what they call it. It's for smaller companies like ours but I'm no expert in the subject. But all the employees were given shares at the time of the listing so we're all very interested in how the firm is doing. Or at least, how the share price is doing,' she added with a laugh.

'And how *is* it doing?' Lori asked.

Sarah shrugged again. 'Okay I suppose, given the business climate. The shares have dropped a bit, but the whole stock market is down, and we've slipped down with it. And we've got competitors now, which we didn't have when Alison started the firm. That's why we must focus so much on efficiency, much more carefully than we ever did before.'

'And that's why you sent your Indian contractors back home?' Maggie asked. 'Including Maya Mishra?'

She nodded. 'The project to build our new product wasn't making the progress we'd hoped for, so we decided to can it for now. It wasn't expected to bring in serious revenue for several years so we decided it was a luxury we couldn't afford. Similarly with replacing the legacy code. The old software was still working okay so we decided in the end it wasn't a priority.'

'So you just sacked these people and sent them back to India?' Lori said. 'That seems a bit harsh if you don't mind me saying so.'

Sarah shook her head. 'No no, you misunderstand, they weren't sacked. They're employed by an Indian company called Bangalore Infotech, and believe me, the services of that company are in great demand around the globe. We simply terminated our contract with their employer, as we were allowed to do under the terms of our agreement.'

'Is it because they're cheap that they're in great demand?' Lori asked. 'I've read all about these Asian sweatshops.'

The woman gave her a sharp look. 'It's not like that in the IT industry, I can assure you of that. Indian software developers are in great demand because one, they are highly-skilled and two, their companies have a huge pool of staff available at short notice. True, their cost rates are attractive, but we employ them because of the flexibility they offer us, not simply to save cost. And by the way, you don't need to feel sorry for our particular team members, because Bangalore had already contracted them out to a Chicago bank. I can tell you that the guys were excited about working in the US. Most of them were going there directly in fact.'

'But what about Paul Davie?' Maggie asked. 'He wasn't in that position, was he? He didn't work for the Bangalore company.'

Sarah paused for a moment. 'Ah, that was a little more difficult.'

'How do you mean?'

'Paul hadn't been contracting for long, and I don't think he was fully tuned into the downside of being self-employed.'

'You mean the fact that he could be let go at any time?' Maggie said.

'Exactly that. In my experience, most contract staff would never go back to having a regular job, but when you're new at it, it can take some time to adjust to a less secure employment situation. And specifically, you need to build up some cash reserves for periods where you might not have a contract. Paul had only been contracting for six months or so, and he'd moved from a very steady position with the council, so it was all very new for him. And I got the feeling that his decision to go self-employed had caused some tensions at home.'

'But wait a minute,' Maggie said, frowning. 'Ruth Davie said that you or Mr Easton told her that Paul and Maya had given notice that they were leaving. From what you are saying, it sounds like it was the other way round.'

Sarah hesitated for a moment, as if thinking how to answer the question. 'Both are true,' she said finally. 'We gave both Bangalore Infotech and Paul Davie three months' notice of our intentions, but both Paul and Maya decided they wanted to go earlier, which they were fully entitled to do. I don't know this for a fact, but I'm speculating that our decision might have forced them to consider where they should take their relationship. Perhaps if we hadn't decided to close down their projects, the relationship would have simply continued as a clandestine affair. But I don't know, I'm only speculating.'

Maggie frowned again. 'But do you really think that was what happened? That they were forced to confront their situation and make a decision on their future?'

She shrugged. 'As I said, I'm only speculating, but it seems a possibility. And he took it quite badly when I told him we were canning the project. He got quite emotional, and it took quite a while for him to calm down. At the time, I thought it was just a natural reaction to losing his job, but later when I found out about the situation with Maya, I thought it might have been the thought of him being forcibly separated from his lover.'

Maggie was silent for a moment as she tried to work out where next to take the conversation. The difficulty was, what Sarah Duncan had told them made perfect sense. If the pair had indeed been deeply in love, then the prospect of an unexpected and forced separation would undoubtedly have focused their minds. But there was one fact that was still deeply puzzling.

'Sarah, Ruth's Find My app showed that Paul was in the office in the afternoon after he told her he was leaving, the day after he had returned home and packed his clothes into a suitcase. That would have been the fifth of September, a Thursday. Why did he come back, do you know? Because I assume it must have been something work-related. Was there something he had forgotten, something he had left in his desk perhaps?'

She frowned, then picked up her phone. 'Let me just check.' She studied the device for a few seconds than said, 'Yes, the day before should have been their last day, the Wednesday. But yes, he might very well have popped in on Thursday to pick up some personal items, I don't know.'

'But you've got one of those fancy access control systems, haven't you?' Lori said. 'I noticed you had to swipe us in through the wee turnstile, and there's one at the front door too, for the staff. He wouldn't have been able to get in without swiping his card, and if he did come back to the office, your computers would have a record of it.'

For a moment the woman seemed unsure how to answer. Finally, she said, 'Yes, that's true. Leave that one with me and I'll get back to you.'

'Actually, could you not just have a wee look whilst we're here?' Lori said. 'All that stuff's online, isn't it? I expect it just takes a few clicks on a keyboard. And we've got plenty of time.'

'I don't have access I'm afraid,' Sarah said.

'Who has then?' Lori said, bluntly enough for Maggie to have to suppress a smile.

The woman hesitated, then said, 'I suppose I could try and find someone in HR. They have access.'

'That would be great Sarah,' Maggie said brightly. 'Obviously I'm not sure if it will help us find him, but sometimes even the smallest details can provide the key to unlock an investigation. Shall we wait here, and you can go off and find someone, or will we hang on in reception after we've finished? Because I think we're just about done anyway,' she added, answering her own question. 'Actually, maybe we'll just wait here for a bit whilst you go and speak to your colleague.'

***

'That was a very clever question Lori,' Maggie whispered, as the two investigators waited for Sarah Duncan to return. 'What made you think to ask it?'

'Something just came into my head. A few years back, I worked in a big office for an insurance company. I hated it and so I only lasted three months, but I had one of those swipe cards too and they took great pains to make sure I handed it back on the day I was leaving. If they do the same here, which I bet they do, then Paul would have handed his card in on the Wednesday, so wouldn't have been able to get into the office the next day.'

'Good point,' Maggie said. 'But did you get the feeling that the question spooked her a bit? There was quite a bit of hesitation before she answered.'

Lori nodded. 'I thought that too. It'll be interesting to hear what she says when she comes back.'

A few minutes later, the woman returned. 'Right, right, I think we've got our answer,' she said, smiling. 'He did come back to the office in the afternoon, but he had handed in his swipe badge the previous day, so the receptionist had to swipe him in. I assume he had left something in his desk and wanted to retrieve it. It happens, doesn't it?'

'And how long did he stay?' Maggie asked.

Sarah shrugged. 'I don't know. He wasn't issued with a pass, he was just swiped through the turnstile like you were, by our receptionist.'

Maggie nodded. 'Okay, so I guess that answers our question as to why Ruth was able to track his phone here that day. Makes sense.' She paused for a moment. 'You've been very helpful Sarah, thank you for that.'

'No problem, glad I was able to help.' She stood up and gestured towards the top of the down escalator. 'I've got lots to do, so I won't escort you down if that's okay. There's a button at the bottom which opens the security gate and the front doors open automatically. And if you have any other questions, please, give me a call anytime.' She got up and walked away, quickly disappearing behind the maze of cubicles.

They took the escalator as instructed, but as they reached the reception area, Maggie said suddenly, 'Wait here a second Lori,' then strode over to converse with the girl behind the counter. A few minutes later, she returned to her colleague wearing a knowing expression.

'Well, *that* was interesting,' she said, raising an eyebrow, 'because she was working that Thursday, and she doesn't remember Paul Davie coming in. In fact, she's certain he wasn't here, neither morning nor afternoon.'

Chapter 4

No matter how hard he tried, Frank was finding that he just could not get the Jaz Davie case out of his head. True, it had always been lurking in the darkest recesses of his mind, trying hard to bury the unsettling fact that it hadn't been his finest hour, but now it seemed it was an itch that demanded to be scratched. Although technically it could be described as a cold case and therefore just about fell within the scope of his small team, there was no new evidence that had emerged to justify it being resurrected, other than his own rekindled curiosity. If the matter was to be investigated, then it would have to be strictly in his own time and strictly unofficial too, unless of course he discovered something major that would allow a change of status. But that wouldn't stop him discussing it with his pal DC Lexy McDonald, and he had already raised the subject as they enjoyed a routine breakfast that morning in the New Gorbals' canteen.

'The thing is Lexy,' he said ruefully, 'I did such a half-arsed job back then. In mitigation, my gaffer wanted me in and out of there as quick as was decent, but looking back, I think I could have done more. *Much* more.'

'It's always easy to beat yourself up with the benefit of hindsight,' she said, taking a sip from her coffee. 'The question is, would you really do it differently, if you had the time again?'

He shrugged. 'I don't know. Perhaps. The problem is, I never once considered that there could have been foul play involved. It looked one hundred percent like a stupid accident, and I was just basically trying to find out if anyone could be blamed for it. That's what they like to see in these Fatal Accident Enquiries, and I just went along with it.'

'So what actually happened that day sir?' Lexy asked.

He shrugged again. 'Three youngish lads on a works jolly got pissed up and it ended in tragedy, that's the gist of it. Two of them ended up drowned, one called Jaz Davie who worked in

IT as I recall, and he turns out to be the brother of a guy who's just been reported as missing. The other guy worked in the admin department, a fella called Peter Denny. The third guy was another admin guy at the hospital where they all worked. The story is they had been in the pub over lunch and had downed a few beers, and then set off on the water, which was not exactly clever.'

'And no-one in charge realised they'd been drinking I suppose?' Lexy mused.

'No, and that was really a big screw-up on the part of the outward-bound company who had organised the thing. Especially when it turned out the lads had taken a bottle of whisky onto the boat as well. And not just any old whisky either. It was a fifteen-year-old malt.' He gave a short laugh. 'Funny I should remember that.'

'Oh god,' Lexy said. 'It really *was* an accident waiting to happen.' She hesitated for a moment. 'But now you're suggesting there might have somehow been foul play?'

'No, I'm not exactly saying that. It's just that I never considered for a moment whether anyone had a motive to do harm to either of the guys who died. Not necessarily that someone wanted them dead, but maybe someone thought it would be a laugh if they ended up in the loch.'

'But I presume you interviewed the other man who was in the boat with him? He would have been the most likely suspect if there had been foul play, surely?'

He nodded. 'Aye, and I seem to recall he said Jaz had been fooling around on the trapeze line, but he and the other guy were blind drunk too. I don't think they had a bloody clue what actually happened that day, not in any detail at least. And do you know what the awful thing is Lexy? I can't remember anything about the guy. Not his name, what he looked like, nothing.' He hesitated. 'Anyway, I told the enquiry that they had all been pissed up and, in all probability, it had been a terrible accident. The Sheriff was satisfied with the explanation and that was the end of the story.'

Lexy smiled. 'Until now.'

'Aye, until now,' he said wryly. 'But don't worry, I won't be asking you to get involved, I know you're up to your eyes with the serious crime squad. But there is one quick thing I wondered if you could do for me? It's to do with Paul Davie, the brother of the missing guy, the one that got me thinking about all of this again.'

'Yes, sure sir. What is it?'

'Ruth Davie detected her partner's phone at Heathrow airport a couple of days after he left her. That made her concerned that he had ran off to India with the woman he was having an affair with. So can you check with the airlines and the border force guys and see if it's true or not? Her name's Maya Mishra.'

'Yes, I can check them out sir,' she said, nodding, 'both the partner and his lover. And you're sure it's India they would have gone to? I mean, if they've gone anywhere at all?'

He shrugged. 'No, I'm not sure, not one hundred percent at least. But the girl's UK visa was only valid whilst she was working, so I think if she was going anywhere, she would have been going home.'

'And what about Davie sir?' Lexy said, as something evidently came to mind. 'I don't know, but do you need a visa to visit India? Because if so, he would have to have applied in advance I guess. Which would suggest some planning was involved.'

'That's a good point. See what you can find out on that score if you would.'

She nodded and gave a thumbs up. 'I'm right on it.'

***

Frank had a bit of time on his hands, with the National Independent Cold-Case Investigations Agency, of which he was the nominal head, still in hiatus. At least now, after several months of uncertain debate, the future of the organisation had been decided. The good news was the recently elected new government were going ahead with the initiative, but the slightly less good news was that because of financial considerations, it wouldn't be re-launched until the start of the next financial year, in April. That was five months distant, which meant that he would continue to be a kind of detective without portfolio, filling in here and there when Police Scotland had a case that needed an experienced officer to take the reins – cases like that super-complicated murder investigation up in Nethy Bridge that he had successfully wrapped up a few months back. Right now, he was helping

Andy McColl, newly promoted to Detective Inspector, to crack an organised luxury car theft network, but other than that, his plate was empty. The truth was, he was a bit bored, but he knew that would change in an instant as soon as a big case emerged, which experience suggested, they always did and always would. And the bonus was that every night he was getting home in time for Isobel's bath, although his participation was strictly as an observer, with Maggie and Ollie expertly running the show. It was wonderful, but already he could see how quickly his lovely wee daughter was changing, making him resolve that no matter the future demands of his job, he wasn't going to miss any of it.

With no pressing demands on his time that day, he decided he was going to indulge himself for a couple of hours by revisiting the drowning of Jaz Davie. He wandered back up to his office, took his A4 notebook and a ballpoint pen out of a drawer, then leafed through the book until he came to the first blank page. Across the top he scribbled *The Davie and Denny Case 2015*, then chewed on his pen, furrow-browed, for several minutes as he replayed the investigation in his mind. There had been about a dozen or so delegates from a big Glasgow hospital on the team-building course, a deliberately chosen mix of job roles which included doctors and nurses as well as backroom staff like Davie and his two sailing buddies. The group had been staying in a lodge a few miles south of Inveraray, right on the shore of picturesque Loch Fyne. The five-day programme, he recalled, had been a mixture of classroom tasks and outdoor exercises and had been designed, according to the organisers, to take delegates out of their comfort zones, where they would be forced to learn the power and importance of teamwork in a crisis situation. To Frank, it sounded bloody awful, but these courses were certainly popular amongst major organisations, as witnessed by the success of his brother's outward-bound firm based up in the Highlands. Scratching his head, he tried to remember who he had interviewed in the course of his investigation. He had spoken to the guy who had survived the accident, certainly, but what was his name again? With growing frustration, he realised he still hadn't got a clue. He'd also spoken at some length to two of the course leaders, one of whom was a woman, he could remember that much, and the other one, a middle-aged guy, who had a thick ginger beard and came from Castle Douglas in the south of Scotland - two random facts that were as much use as a chocolate teapot. Had that been it, he wondered? Because if so, it was no surprise he was looking back at the case with a growing sense of shame. Then he remembered one of his team had talked to the landlady at the pub as well, and it was that woman who had told them about Jaz Davie's lunchtime drinking session with the two other guys. That, he realised with dismay, was the sum total of their knowledge of the matter.

With a sigh, he realised he was going to have to dig into the old files, which would have been long archived and now buried away somewhere in the depths of Police Scotland's crime management database. Once, he'd been given a login and password and had even received some rudimentary training, but that was about a hundred years ago, and then he'd moved to the Met in London, who naturally used a completely different set of systems. It was looking as if he would have to add another job to Lexy McDonald's list when suddenly, he had an idea. Not a *good* idea, he conceded, but an idea nonetheless. He picked up his phone and jabbed a number from his favourites list. It was answered in a few rings.

'Eleanor Campbell, you're back,' he said brightly. 'Maggie and me have been admiring the hundred and ninety photographs of Lulu you've sent us,' he added, laughing. 'She's an absolute beauty and we're looking forward to seeing her in real life sometime soon. But you're back working part-time after your maternity leave, I seem to recall. In Atlee House?'

'Yes to your first question and no to your second,' she replied morosely. *'I'm in the office two-and-a-half days a week but they made me come back to Maida Vale labs. It's like dullsville here.'*

He sighed apologetically. 'I suppose that's all my fault. Our new organisation isn't going to be up and running until April so we're all having to kick our heels for a while. And as you say, it is a bit dullsville.' He reflected with some amusement that despite its grand title, the National Independent Cold-Case Investigations Agency was an organisation that at present had only four employees, those being Frank himself, Eleanor and Lexy, both temporarily back in their old positions, and DC Ronnie French, who had recently retired from the Met but had signalled his willingness to work for them on a case-by-case basis to fund his West Ham United season ticket.

'Well, I was hoping you could do a wee job for me, but unfortunately, I can't promise you anything exciting. In fact, I'm not really sure if it falls into your area of responsibility, but I thought I'd ask you anyway.'

'What is it?' she said sharply. He smiled to himself as he noted that Eleanor's trademark prickliness had seemingly not been dulled by motherhood.

'I need some stuff retrieved from an old Police Scotland crime database. It was a case from ten years ago, so I think they've probably replaced the system a couple of times since then. In fact, I don't know if you can still get to it at all.'

'That's not forensic work,' she said. *'That's office work. It's not what I do.'* There was a silence, which Eleanor made no attempt to fill.

'Aye, you're right,' he conceded finally. 'I shouldn't have asked. I'll just dump it on Lexy, she'll know how to sort it, or at least she'll know someone who does. And again, sorry for asking. And it's not an official case yet anyway. Just something I might have screwed up ten years ago that's suddenly came back into my life.'

He heard her laugh. *'Like, another one?'*

'What do you mean, another one?' he shot back in mock protest. 'I've got an unblemished track record going back twenty years. My track record is as unblemished as... well, something really unblemished.'

She laughed again, which was encouraging, because Eleanor rarely laughed more than once in any conversation, or at least not in any conversation she'd ever had with him. *'Apart from the one you just mentioned,'* she said.

He nodded. 'Apart from that one, aye.'

'So does that mean there's a murderer running loose?'

It was a question he had been reluctant to ask himself, and he was silent for a moment as he pondered it. Then he said, 'To be honest, that's what I'm beginning to worry about. I mean, I'm probably over-reacting, but I admit, I do have that fear. That's why I want to take a wee look back at the case.'

'Alright, I'll do it,' she said, surprising him, *'but only because Lexy's my friend and I don't want you to be horrible to her.'*

'I'm never horrible to Lexy,' he said, genuinely aghast she could think that. 'DC McDonald's my best pal in the force and also happens to be the most brilliant detective I've ever come across, just so you know.'

'That's all right then,' she said. *'Because Lexy's my friend.'*

He was about to quip *yeah, you've said that already*, but managed, just, to check himself. Eleanor was a lovely girl, but she could be awkward and brusque, which had long made him suspect she might not have many friends. It was evident her relationship with Lexy McDonald was important to her, and it was a situation that warmed his heart. He said, 'That's absolutely brilliant Eleanor, I'm really grateful. But I'm afraid I can't remember any of the log-in details I was given. It was a while ago. But Lexy might be able to point you to someone up there who can help you.'

'I won't need them,' she said, matter-of-factly. *'These old systems have rubbish security. So do the new ones,'* she added.

He laughed. 'I probably don't need to know the details of your dodgy methods. And by the way, since this isn't official at the moment, there's no great urgency. Just fit it in when you can.'

'I'll do it now,' she said. *'Once you're off the phone.'*

'I'm hanging up as we speak. And give my love to wee Lulu. Tell her I'll read her a bedtime story when we finally get to meet. I'll have her speaking Scottish before she's old enough to walk. What do you think to that then?'

Anticipating her reply, he hurriedly jabbed the *end call* button.

Chapter 5

Either by coincidence or serendipity – and Maggie wasn't sure she understood the difference – it was approaching five years to the day since entrepreneur Alison Christie, founder of Torridon Systems, had disappeared in the mountains of Colorado, having taken the opportunity to go skiing after a business trip to the United States, apparently to take her own life. This fact had been drawn to her attention by Jimmy, who had noticed an article by their old friend Yash Patel of the Chronicle, written for the paper's Sunday magazine and obviously timed to coincide with the upcoming fifth anniversary of the businesswoman's disappearance. Now she and Lori were, as usual, enjoying a mid-morning caffeine injection at the Bikini Barista cafe, where Jimmy had joined them on a catch-up video call from the office of his outdoor-adventure firm in Braemar.

'I didn't know anything much about Alison Christie before we took on the Davie case,' Maggie was saying, 'I did a bit of research, but nothing like the depths that Yash has gone to. It seems like she was something of a celebrity up here. Yash's article is very interesting. There's a huge amount of stuff in it that I didn't know about.'

'She was a celebrity right enough,' Jimmy said. *'And not just up here in Scotland either. She was seen as a fantastic role model for young women everywhere, and everyone who was anyone wanted to be seen with her. Prime Ministers, actors and rock stars, she knew them all.'*

'She was dead glamorous too, which always helps,' Lori said, slightly sourly.

Maggie nodded. 'And very young to have such huge success too, particularly since she was a single mother. It's a fascinating story, isn't it? According to Yash, she had her daughter Rebecca when she was only sixteen and still at school and has never revealed who the father was. Alison was living in care at the time, so her circumstances weren't the best.'

'That's right,' Jimmy said, *'and I didn't know this, but according to the article there were a couple of guys who came forward and claimed they were Rebecca's dad after Alison became rich and famous. But they were quickly dismissed as chancers.'*

'Hardly surprising,' Maggie said. 'But it seems that the little girl was mainly looked after by nannies and child-minders, whilst Alison went off to Uni to do a nursing degree and then worked at the Queen Elizabeth hospital.'

'Which is where she came up with the idea for her business,' Jimmy said. *'She saw how much the hospital was paying for agency staff and how much of it was going to the agencies themselves and came up with the idea for a website that cut out the middleman.'*

'Yeah, that was how the Nurses Direct website came about. She had a friend who was IT-savvy, and she got him to write a prototype, which she took to the bank and used it to get the funding to start her company. Yash, in typical Yash style, speculated that the guy might have been a bit more than a friend.' Maggie added. 'Although he didn't produce any real evidence for that as far as I could see.'

'*It was really interesting that he tracked the guy down,*' Jimmy said. '*And what's more interesting, and sad too, is that the chap was sectioned a few years ago and now lives in a home down in Helensburgh. Richie Whitmore's his name, and he suffers from a severe form of autism according to Yash's article.*'

'This might be a wild generalisation,' Maggie mused, 'but isn't it often true that people with that affliction are brilliant at solving mathematical and logical problems? Which makes them amazing software developers.'

'Well, whatever the case, Alison exploited that and then she shafted him,' Lori interjected. 'Good and proper.'

Maggie nodded. 'Or so Yash alleges. Apparently when she started her company, she was determined that she should own it one hundred percent. What Yash says is, instead of offering Whitmore a substantial share in the company, she offered him a measly two percent and some type of royalty agreement on top. At which point, she apparently ended their relationship.'

'Yeah, she chucked him,' Lori said. 'Just like that,' she added, making a throat-slashing gesture with her hand. 'I wonder if that contributed to the poor guy's mental breakdown?'

'Yes, perhaps it did,' Maggie said. 'And what about her husband David Stirling? Yash said he has refused to speak to him. But he and Alison weren't married very long, were they? Three years I think.'

'I think she only married him because he was quite famous and they looked good in a photo together,' Lori speculated. 'But then he dumped her for an actress who's fifteen years younger than him. Which is what actors do all the time,' she added, with evident authority. 'Because now he's dumped *that* one for his Stornoway co-star.'

'And all of that led to the speculation that Alison had actually committed suicide on that Colorado mountain, that it wasn't an accident,' Maggie mused. 'But it doesn't seem in character, does it?' she added. 'Alison was such a go-getter.'

Jimmy shrugged. *'I think she'd grown addicted to all the adulation linked to her success. Maybe she couldn't face the fact that it was all about to collapse in a heap. That's what Yash thinks anyway.'*

'Perhaps,' Maggie said, sounding doubtful. 'I guess we'll never know for certain.' She paused for a moment. 'I was really interested in finding out what happened to Torridon Systems afterwards, but Yash says that's going to be the subject of next week's article. But he does talk about a deal they were doing with an American company. That was interesting.'

Jimmy nodded. *'Aye, it was. The article is suggesting that what really drove Alison was the need to be someone. He says she was drunk on the fame that her success brought her, which he says explained her driving desire to conquer America and then the world.'*

'If I understand correctly, the idea was to take over a firm in the States that did the same thing as Torridon, then merge the operations, with Alison moving to New York to become Chief Executive.'

'That's right. The firm was called Hudson Medical Staffing, and they were based in New York State, and they were in fact bigger than Torridon, so it was going to be what they call a reverse takeover. And I don't have a clue what one of them is before you ask,' he added, laughing.

'But how could they afford it?' Lori asked. 'Because didn't we find out after her death that their profitability had all been a sham?'

Jimmy shrugged. *'I don't understand all of that kind of thing, but Yash does a good job of trying to explain it. Apparently, it was going to be a highly-leveraged buyout.'*

'Naturally,' Maggie said, tongue-in-cheek. 'I've read about these before. It's when a bank lends a company a humongous sum of money which then gets paid back out of the profits. The banks love them because they can charge a massive arrangement fee upfront and the interest rates are sky-high as well. It's risky though,' she added.

'Yeah, that's what Yash says in his piece,' Jimmy agreed. *'You have to be sure the company continues to grow, otherwise it all collapses in a heap of debt.'*

'But she died before the deal went through,' Lori said. 'It was all irrelevant in the end, wasn't it?'

'Yes, it was very bad timing,' Maggie said, 'and yes, I know, that sounds like a terrible thing to say. But it *was* bad timing, from the point of view of the takeover. Yash's article says that Alison and Jack Easton had flown to New York State, to a place called White Plains, which was where Hudson Medical were based. They met with the founder of the company and some of his senior staff to tidy up the final points of the deal, and by all accounts it went well. A price of ninety-five million dollars was agreed and everyone hoped that the contracts could be drawn up and finalised within three months. They shook hands on the deal, and then Jack Easton flew back to Glasgow and Alison went to Colorado for a few days' skiing. Apparently, she was a real ski nut and took every opportunity she could to get on the slopes. But this time it seemed her motivation was much darker.'

'And that was the last time she was seen?' Lori asked. 'At that meeting in New York State?'

Maggie shook her head. 'No, she was seen several times after that. The airline confirmed she had taken a flight from Westchester County airport to Aspen, flying via Chicago. Then, a ski shop in Aspen reported that she had rented equipment and bought a three-day lift pass, and then finally, she was seen several times by a ski-lift attendant. *That* was the last time she was seen. When she didn't return home as expected, her daughter raised the alarm with both the police and the mountain rescue services in Aspen.'

'But she was never found,' Lori said.

'No, she wasn't. As Yash said, the initial assumption was she had been caught in an avalanche or had perhaps fallen over a ledge. That was before all the bad news had begun to emerge and suicide came into the picture. But as you say Lori, her body has never been found.'

Jimmy nodded. *'And her disappearance obviously screwed up the takeover deal. For a start, it wasn't clear who would take ownership of Torridon Systems after Alison's death. And of course, with no body being found, and her disappearance happening in the US, then the whole legal situation was horrendously complicated.'* He paused and then laughed. *'Did you see that Yash signed off by saying he's got a very interesting revelation to make in that regard, which he'll be unveiling in next week's article.'*

'Yes, and that was really annoying,' Maggie said, grinning. 'I was desperate to find out what he was referring to. Actually, I think I'll give him a call. Maybe he'll tell me if I ask him.'

'Good luck with that,' Jimmy said doubtfully. *'I'd be surprised if he wanted to share his big scoop with anyone, not even you.'*

'No, maybe not,' she conceded. 'But thanks for the info on Alison Christie, it was interesting. Although I suppose it's only obliquely connected to our new case. Which brings me to your involvement,' she added, twisting her lip.

He laughed. *'I'm not wanted, is that what you're going to tell me?'*

'More or less,' she grinned. 'You know we love you Jimmy, but there's not really anything for you to do on this case. Not right now at least.'

'Which is just as well, because me and Stew are fully booked right through November and into December. I'm not even sure if I can make our family weekend on Loch Fyne.'

She gave him a sharp look. 'What family weekend's that?'

He laughed again. *'Oops, Frank's obviously not told you yet.'* He paused. *'What is it with this old case of his anyway Maggie? He's gone all weird and obsessed, which isn't like him at all.'*

She nodded. 'Yes, he has. He thinks he made a mess of things all those years ago and it really seems to have got to him. But I didn't know he'd been talking to you about it too.'

'He asked me what I knew about the outward-bound outfit who had been running the course where that guy drowned. He wanted to know if I knew anyone who worked for them, through my industry contacts. I didn't, as it happened, but now it seems he wants to see for himself where the incident happened. He thought we could hire a lodge for a long weekend, somewhere near Inveraray, which is a lovely wee town by the way. And to be fair, it would be great to have us all together before Christmas. We could put the wee babies in back carriers and go for lots of walks. Frida is dying to see you again, and I bet Ollie would absolutely love it.'

'It does sound lovely I must admit,' she conceded. 'Although I'm not sure about the weather, *and* I thought they'd had days and days without electricity. That, I *don't* fancy.'

'Aye, that was awful,' he said, *'but they've fixed the pylons and it's been back up and running for the last couple of days, so we'll be fine. And Frank's already found a place for us to stay so he says, and it's in the grounds of a pub. But a really nice pub he tells me, right on the loch,'* he added, laughing.

'That sounds *very* Frank. But yes, it'll be fantastic to see Frida and Viggo again. He really is *such* a big boy.'

He laughed again. *'Aye, the boy's one hundred percent Viking. Mind you, Frida's dad's the size of a house, so I'm not surprised his grandson's the same. Anyway, if I'm not needed, I need to get up on that mountain. I'll see you at the weekend on the beautiful shores of Loch Fyne. Bye for now.'*

***

'You're really lucky you know,' Lori said unexpectedly after the call had ended. 'Frank's lovely and Jimmy's lovely and your family's got two beautiful new babies, and you've got your lovely wee son Ollie too.'

'I know,' Maggie said, 'and I bless every minute, believe me.' She thought she knew what had prompted her assistant to bring up the subject, so continued, 'And you're a lovely girl too Miss Logan, and I'm not just saying that. You're special, and one day when you're least expecting it, you'll bump into a boy who'll be special to you. I don't think I've ever told you the story, but that's what exactly happened to me just four years ago, and well, look at me now.' And it was true, she'd never told Lori any details of what had happened to her back then, when her life had reached its lowest point and she could see no way out of it, when she had been desperate enough to contemplate taking her own life, and unthinkably, that of her wonderful Ollie. Exactly at that lowest point in her life, she had met Jimmy Stewart and from that coincidental encounter, something completely wonderful had blossomed.

'Anyway, let's get our thinking caps on and decide where we go next with the Davie case shall we?'

'Aye, let's,' Lori grinned. 'But before we start, any news from the police on whether Paul Davie and his girlfriend *did* disappear off to India? Lexy was looking at that I think you said?'

Maggie shook her head. 'I've not heard back from her yet, so I don't know. For the time being, let's work on the assumption that they didn't leave the country, and see what our big brains make of that. And talking of brains, how about another coffee to get the grey cells functioning at optimum efficiency?'

Her assistant laughed. 'Definitely. I'll try snapping my fingers and see if it brings Stevie over.'

'He'll do nearly anything for you, but I wouldn't push it too far,' Maggie said, giving her a wry look. 'So, bear with me Lori whilst I whizz through what we know so far, or at least what we might be able to deduce.'

Lori gave a thumbs up. 'Sure, go ahead boss.'

'Right. So firstly, let's go back six months or so, when Paul Davie suddenly decided to give up his cushy job with the council to become a self-employed contractor. Why did he do that, do we think? Because it does seem a little bit out of character.'

'I don't know if that's necessarily the case,' Lori said. 'He might have been bored out of his head working for the council and finally decided to do something about it. Sure, it was a risk, but he stood to make two or three times what he had been making before, so maybe he decided it was a risk worth taking.'

'Perhaps,' Maggie said, sounding dubious. 'But I also got the feeling that Ruth was frustrated about his lack of ambition. Maybe he finally decided to do something about her nagging, because he couldn't stand it anymore.'

'Or maybe she told him he'd better shape up or she was out of there?' Lori suggested. 'I thought she seemed quite a hard-nosed bitch, to be honest. And I know that's not a nice word,' she added apologetically, 'but that was the impression I got from her.'

Maggie nodded. 'Yes, I got a bit of that too, I must admit. But my feeling is that it's more likely that his job change was related in some way to the fact that his mother had just died. Ruth said it affected him badly, especially after all the tragedy his family had suffered, with his brother dying then his father basically drinking himself to death. Maybe he just felt he needed a change in his life, almost like a clean slate if you will.'

'And he fancied getting a new woman at the same time, did he?' Lori said, not hiding her scepticism. 'To be honest Maggie, that's something that isn't sitting right with me. What I mean is, maybe Ruth Davie isn't the nicest of women, but she's very good-looking, and not just in a pretty sort of way, although she *is* pretty, don't get me wrong.' She hesitated before continuing. 'I thought she had a load of what they used to call sex appeal, and before you jump at me, aye, I know that's a seriously weird thing to say. But I notice these things, so I do, and I bet Ruth is the kind of woman that every man can't help looking at, and the kind of woman every man would want for themselves, if only in their dreams.' She paused again. 'Which is a long-winded way of saying that if you had a woman like that, there's no way you be messing about with anyone else. Especially not some skinny wee Indian lassie.'

Maggie gave her assistant an appreciative look. 'You certainly make a good case Lori. But no-one knows what goes on behind the closed doors of a relationship, do they? For what it's worth, I can well imagine how a man might not take too kindly to his partner nagging him to make something of himself, no matter how beautiful she is. Maybe beneath the surface he hated her, we don't know. And what about the texts? How do you explain them?'

Lori shrugged. 'This Maya girl sent them, sure, but it doesn't mean that Paul wanted them. Maybe he was telling the truth when he said nothing was going on.'

Maggie sighed. 'It's very confusing. Because if the girl had made an unwelcome approach, surely Paul would have just warned her off and that would have been the end of it? But there's no evidence that he did that. He told Ruth that he didn't know why the girl had sent him the texts, and yet he didn't seem to have confronted her about them.'

Lori nodded. 'Aye, you're right. Although we only have Ruth's word that he *didn't* confront her. Or more to the point, we only know that Ruth didn't mention it to us. It doesn't mean Paul *didn't* warn the girl off.'

Maggie furrowed her brow then grinned. 'Yes, I *think* I follow what you're saying. But you see what I mean about it being confusing?' She paused. 'And there's another thing, isn't there? Remember Ruth suggested that it might have been the clearing out of his mum's house that triggered his sudden decision to quit his job? I've been thinking about that, but I couldn't for the life of me figure out what he might have found that could prompt such a drastic action. I guess you find old photographs and letters and toys from your childhood and stuff like that, and it would make you feel seriously nostalgic and maybe even a bit sad. But I'm not sure it would make you go and chuck your job.'

'Maybe he just didn't want to end up like his parents,' Lori suggested. 'They lived in a horrible wee council house, that's what Ruth said, didn't she?'

' I thought that was a nasty comment. But yes, perhaps it did inspire him.'

There was a pause as they both marshalled their thoughts. Then Lori said, 'So what about the thing with his phone? The fact that Sarah Duncan says he came back into the office on the day he left his partner, but the receptionist says he didn't. What should we make of that?'

'That's a tough one,' Maggie said. 'We know that his *phone* was in the office, because Ruth saw it on the Find My app. But it doesn't necessarily mean he was there. He might have left his phone behind.'

'And we only have Ruth's word for that as well, don't forget,' Lori said. 'She could easily have been lying.'

Maggie gave her a searching look. 'You're really not sure about the woman, are you?'

Her assistant shrugged. 'No, I just didn't take to her somehow. And don't forget, when someone disappears and then is found dead, nine times out of ten it's the other half who has done it. Just saying,' she added sagely.

'God, you *really* don't like Ruth Davie,' Maggie said, laughing. 'And they've not even found a body yet. But my instinct is she wasn't lying about seeing his phone in the office. Don't forget that Sarah Duncan corroborated that fact, or at least Torridon Systems' access control system did.'

'Except the receptionist said he didn't,' Lori pointed out. 'You spoke to the girl yourself, remember?'

Maggie sighed again. 'I did, didn't I? But now you see what I mean when I say this case is complicated. It already seems that someone is lying, but we don't know who and we don't know why.'

'But that's good, isn't it? Because already we've identified that either Ruth Davie, Sarah Duncan or that receptionist is hiding something. So I think we should start with Ruth and visit her at her own house. We tell her we want to look at any stuff that Paul brought back from his mother's house - and we do want to do that by the way - but we can ask her a few questions as well, see if she lets anything slip.'

'Assuming she has anything to let slip,' Maggie cautioned. 'But yeah, that sounds like a great plan young Lori.' She paused then grimaced. 'But before that, I have to figure out what the blazes you need to pack for a baby's first holiday.'

Lori looked at her deadpan. 'Everything. I'd pack everything.'

Chapter 6

Having been unsure how Maggie might react to the prospect of a weekend on the shores of Loch Fyne in the middle of a bleak Scottish November, he had been relieved to discover that Jimmy had already broken the news to her and that rather than being sceptical of its merits, his wife was in fact bubbling with enthusiasm for the trip. There had been one rather significant obstacle however and that was the discovery – and this was not exactly rocket science - that it was impossible to pack all the kit needed for two adults, a little boy and a six-month-old baby into Maggie's faithful but compact twelve-year-old hatchback. In the event the problem had been brilliantly solved by his brother, who had purloined the huge and rugged 10-seater SUV that he and his business partner Stew employed to ferry their outward-bound clients up into the heart of the Cairngorm mountains. Jimmy, Frida and baby Viggo had stayed the night with them in Milngavie, and the next morning before setting off, Frank and Maggie added substantially to the giant pile of baby paraphernalia that had been transported down from Braemar the previous day.

The two-hour trip had been magical, shadowed by an autumn sun peering above the horizon, framed by a clear blue sky. Frank had sat up front with his brother Jimmy, Maggie had sat with Ollie and little Isobel, in her car seat, on the next row, with Frida and not-so-little Viggo occupying the third row, an arrangement that still left heaps of room in the vehicle for a mountain of luggage. There had been singing and silly jokes and laughter, and multiple stops on-route, first for coffee and then for nappy changes and then more nappy changes. But in what seemed no time at all they had reached their destination, an attractive holiday complex situated a few miles south of the town of Inveraray

'Here we are,' Frank said brightly as his brother swung the big Land Rover into the car park. 'I'll nip into reception and get the keys and then we'll get settled.'

Jimmy laughed. 'Aye, it'll take us about two hours to unload all our stuff. We might just get it done before it gets dark, if we're lucky.'

A few minutes later Frank returned, grinning. 'It's quiet at this time of year, so the lassie's upgraded us to the fanciest lodge at no extra charge. We've got a Jacuzzi and a sauna and a big log fire, and a fifty-five-inch telly too. Oh, and she said apologies, but the site shop isn't open at this time of year, but there's a good convenience store in Inveraray. But the good news is the bar *is* open tonight and tomorrow night, and she says they have live folk music on to bring in the crowds.'

Jimmy laughed. 'A crowd up here means one guy with his dug. But that sounds great. We'll just need to draw lots for babysitting duties.'

'You and Frank can go if you fancy a pint, and I'm sure Ollie would love to go too,' Maggie said, giving her nine-year-old a fond look. 'But I think Frida and I will be settling down in front of the fire with a glass of wine once we've got Isobel and Viggo tucked up in their cots.'

'I won't argue with that,' Frida said. 'Anyway, let's get inside, it's freezing.'

As Jimmy had predicted, it took them nearly two hours to get settled, which included a frustrating forty-five minutes of Frank struggling to assemble a travel cot they had purchased specially for this weekend away, the task accompanied by notably fruity language. But eventually they were in, their wine glasses charged and the luxury supermarket lasagne in the oven.

'So, what's the plan for tomorrow?' Maggie said, then grinned. 'Because we all know why you chose this place Frank, lovely though it is.'

He gave her a wry look. 'Aye, my cunning plan is finally exposed.'

'So is this the actual place where it all happened?' Jimmy asked.

'It is,' Frank admitted. 'They run outdoor activity courses here in the summer. They've got a classroom and two big dormitories to cater for it, separate ones for men and women obviously. The accommodation is a bit like a youth hostel I think, comfortable but basic. It's all supposedly part of the team-building thing. You know, eat, sleep and work together. I don't fancy it myself, but I can see why it's popular.'

'And this is where that NHS group were staying?' Maggie asked.

He nodded. 'Yep, and the bar's the bar where the three lads got pissed up, and the jetty's the jetty where they set off towards Ardnagown on the south-east bank of the loch. And out there is the loch where two of them drowned.'

'It was damn stupid,' Jimmy interjected, 'letting three novices out on the loch in a dinghy, even if they were meant to be supervised. That's why my wee firm will never go anywhere near water. It's just crazily dangerous.'

Frank nodded. 'You're right, it is, and it did for the reputation of the company who ran the course, big time. They had to close down for six months after the court gave its verdict, and they were damning about the guy who was running the course too, and quite right as well.'

Aye, that was the guy who should have been out on the boat with the three course members that day, Frank thought. He had seemingly been delayed for some reason, but what had been the excuse he'd given? Try as he might, it wouldn't come back to him. Maggie had evidently noticed his furrowed brow and reacted by administering a playful poke in his ribs with her index finger. 'It's Friday and it's nearly five o'clock, so let's park the case until tomorrow, shall we? And before you say anything, I know, I'm one to talk,' she added. 'When a case grabs you, you just can't leave it alone, can you?'

He gave a wry smile. 'Exactly, you can't. But you're right, I should leave it until tomorrow. Let's enjoy our lovely dinner then get the babies bathed, and then me and Jimmy will pop across to the Noble Stag for a game of pool with Ollie. That's what the bar's called,' he added, 'I suppose because there's loads of deer roaming the hills behind here.'

'Good to know,' Maggie said, deadpan, then smiled at Ollie. 'And make sure you give me a kiss before you go darling. And don't have too many cokes, we don't want you up all night.'

'Okay mummy, I won't,' he said, beaming a smile.

'And me and Jimmy will go easy on the beers too,' Frank said, sounding less convincing.

***

He hadn't shared the fact with the group, but Frank had discovered the present landlady had run the pub since it opened twenty years ago, and so there was every chance she had been behind the bar on the day that Jaz Davie and his pals had set out on the loch on their ill-fated adventure. He was hoping he would get the opportunity at some point over the weekend for a wee chat with her, whilst recognising it would be close to a miracle if she remembered anything after the passage of nearly ten years. On the other hand, it had turned out to be a tragic day, and these types of days tended to stick in the mind.

The place was busier than he had expected, presumably a testament to the popularity of the folk group, who, as the receptionist had trailed, were set up at one end of the room. Above the bar, the head of a magnificently-antlered stag was mounted alongside a mirror on a polished wooden plinth.

'Is that a real one Uncle Frank?' Ollie asked, staring up at the beast open-mouthed.

'Nah, it's fibre glass,' he said uncertainly. 'But it's very realistic, isn't it?'

On the low stage, a full-bearded youngish guy wearing a red lumberjack shirt and wielding a mandolin was addressing the microphone. 'Right, we've got three or four more tunes for you before we take a wee break for a bevvy or two. So, feel free to join in or get up and dance or preferably both. Here we go. One...two...three...four.' On the count, the band burst into a raucous upbeat number that made conversation impossible.

'They must think they're Led Zeppelin or something,' Jimmy grimaced. 'That noise would blow your head off.'

'Aye,' Frank shouted back, 'but I see the pool table is in the next room, thank goodness.' He smiled at Ollie, putting an arm round him. 'Let's go through, and then you and me will take on your Uncle Jimmy. He's rubbish at it, so we'll definitely win the match, no bother.'

'I've seen you play Uncle Frank,' Ollie said in a serious voice. 'Can I not be on Uncle Jimmy's team instead?'

Jimmy laughed. 'The boy recognises class when he sees it. Of *course* you can be on my team Ollie, and we'll show Uncle Frank a thing or two about pool, won't we?'

An enjoyable half-an-hour followed, with Ollie easily matching the talentless Stewart brothers when it came to competence with a pool cue. But then, Frank noticed that the music had stopped.

'It must be their interval, thank God,' he said to his brother. 'Would you mind taking Ollie back to the lodge now? I just want to have a wee word with the landlady.'

'Oh, do I *have* to go?' the boy protested. 'We've only played three games.'

Frank laughed. 'What are you complaining about, it's three-nil to you already. But yes mate, you do have to go. Your mummy will be missing you and Isobel will be waiting for her goodnight kiss. We can come back tomorrow, and you can batter us again.' That seemed to satisfy him, Ollie leaving without further protest. Frank wandered back through to the other room, then waited patiently whilst the landlady worked her way through a queue of thirsty customers. Finally, the bar cleared, and he took his opportunity.

'It's Kathy, isn't it? Kathy Sinclair,' he said, smiling at her. 'I saw your name on the website. I'm Frank Stewart. I'm a Detective Chief Inspector with the police, but I'm not here on official business. Can you spare me a couple of minutes before the next wave of customers arrive?'

'If you're quick,' she said in a pleasant tone.

'Thanks, I'll be as brief as I can. I wondered, do you remember that about ten years ago, two men drowned in a wee boat after they'd been drinking in here one lunchtime?'

Her eyes narrowed. 'Yes, of course. It's not something you would forget in a hurry.'

'And were you here yourself that day, can you remember, or was it one of your staff?'

She looked at him again, this time with a hint of suspicion. 'No, I was here. Why are you asking?'

He shrugged. 'There's just something that's come up that means we might be looking at the matter again. But it's probably nothing.'

'I talked to the police at the time,' she interjected. 'The lads had had a few drinks, and they were in good spirits. But I didn't know they were taking a boat out, and even if I did, it wouldn't have been my responsibility to say anything. They weren't being rowdy or troubling any other customers, and I knew they were staying here on the site so they weren't driving or anything.'

'No, it wasn't your responsibility,' Frank said, only half agreeing with her. 'They were just three lads on a jolly from work, enjoying themselves the way lads do.'

'There were four of them actually,' she corrected. 'The three in the boat, and then the guy whose birthday they were celebrating.'

'What?' Frank said, surprised. 'There were *four* of them?' Why hadn't he known that, he chided himself. And then he remembered. He had sent a DC to interview the landlady, and now it appeared this DC, whose name he couldn't remember, had done the same half-arsed job with the interview that he, Frank Stewart, had done with the rest of the case.

'Yes, four,' the woman confirmed. 'As I said, it was the other chap's birthday, and they were celebrating. I remember he gave me his credit card and said I could open an eighty-pound tab.'

'Eighty quid? And who was this generous guy? Was he someone else on the course?'

She shook her head. 'No, I think he was a friend of one of the guys. He'd come over specially, I think. From Glasgow. A bit of an oddball I recall, but nice enough.'

'Aye, sounds like it,' he said wryly. 'But do you remember anything else about him? His name, for example?'

She sighed. 'I didn't get his name. But I remember he did buy them a bottle of whisky. When he was settling up at the end, I told him there was still twenty pounds or so left on the tab, and so he bought a bottle of single malt and made up the difference.'

'I remember they'd taken a bottle of whisky onto the boat,' he said. 'It was a fifteen-year-old single malt. Glenfiddich, I think. How much would you normally charge for something as fancy as that?'

She gave him an uncomfortable look. 'Not much over retail, ninety pounds maybe. I can't remember exactly. Not after all this time.'

He nodded. 'No, I understand. And thanks Kathy, you've been really helpful.'

Over on the small stage, the band was re-assembling. Out of the blue, the singer bellowed *one-two-testing* into his microphone, causing Frank to jump.

'Looks like they're going back on then?' he said, nodding in the band's direction.

'Yes, it's their second set. Do you like folk music?' she asked.

He gave her a wry look. 'I used to.'

***

The reason he had been so anxious to speak to the landlady on the day of their arrival was the simple fact that if he hadn't done *something*, he wouldn't have been able to sleep that night, such was the way the case had wriggled its way into his every waking moment. But as he might have been able to deduce had he thought about it more carefully, what he'd discovered from Kathy Sinclair had only served to make matters worse. So now it turned out there had been a fourth person drinking with the course-members, and this person had been splashing the cash, purportedly in celebration of his birthday. It was this unknown person who had provided the finance to get the three men in a boat seriously pissed before they took to the loch. And yet the existence of this guy, obviously a key person of interest in the case, had completely escaped the attention of the original enquiry. *His* enquiry, he was forced to remind himself, with growing dismay. For the first time in his career as a digger-up of other cops' investigatory cock-ups, he had dug up a case for which he himself had been solely responsible. It had been a massive oversight, an oversight which had succeeded in keeping him awake half the night. The first hour or so had been full of self-recrimination, as he cursed himself for delegating the original interview with Sinclair to a junior DC. The fact was, they didn't know the first thing about this cash-splashing guy, not even that he existed at all, and yet he was obviously critical to the matter. *What a screw-up it had been.* But then, at about two in the morning, his thinking process took a more positive turn. There had to be a strong possibility that this guy, whoever he was, had set out deliberately to get the three course delegates drunk. It certainly looked that way and the question now was, *why?* Was it directed at all three of the men, or was it focussed on one or two of them in particular? And then what about the course supervisor who should have been on that boat with them, but had been supposedly delayed? At least they knew who *he* was, because Frank had interviewed him himself, even although right now he couldn't remember the guy's name. That didn't matter, because it would be in the file, and Eleanor Campbell would soon present him with a dossier containing everything they had discovered back then. But was there something suspicious about the guy's no-show, he wondered? Back then his excuse, whatever it had been, must have seemed plausible, but now, with the emergence of this new information, did it still stand up to scrutiny? By four in the morning, he'd mentally put together an outline plan of action, which was enough to allow him to finally drift off to sleep.

Breakfast was a pleasant but chaotic affair, with two crotchety babies and a ravenous nine-year-old to be fed, on top of which they had collectively decided on a full Scottish for the adults, which kept the frying pan and grill in constant use. But the feast included both potato scones and Stornoway black pudding, a sublime luxury that, in Frank's opinion, launched the day in incomparable fashion.

'Just as well we're all going for a walk this morning,' Jimmy said, patting his stomach as they cleared away the dishes. 'And just as well the weather looks set fair too. A nice late autumn morning.'

'Yeah, what's the plan?' Maggie asked. 'And more to the point, how long is this so-called wee walk you've planned Jimmy? Because I know what you're like when you get a map and compass in your hand.'

'It's about a five-mile round trip, according to my calculations,' he said. 'Just one or two hills, and none of them too steep. And there's a wee jetty at the half-way point, and there's a cafe not far from it where we can stop for refreshments. If it proves too much for anyone, Frank can sprint back to the lodge and fetch the car.'

'Aye, right,' his brother said, laughing. 'I've checked, and the good news is there's a bus, The bad news is, it only runs once a week.'

The walk hugged the rocky shore of the loch for most of its length, with the occasional foray into the woods. With Frank and Jimmy each carrying their surprisingly heavy babies in backpacks and a nine-year-old who wanted to skim stones at every opportunity, progress was pleasant but leisurely. It was more than an hour before they reached the cafe, the path emerging from a thicket of trees into which they had temporarily disappeared. The scene that greeted them was not at all what they had expected.

'What's happening?' Maggie said, catching her first sight of the flashing blue lights. 'Has there been an accident?' Across the road, two police cars were parked in a lay-by next to a gate that opened onto the path to the jetty. A small fishing boat was moored on one side of the pier, and three policemen in high-visibility jackets were bending down, evidently examining an object that lay on the wooden planking of the structure.

'This doesn't look good,' Frank said. 'You lot wait on this side of the road, and I'll go and see what's happening.'

'Let me take Isobel then,' Maggie said.

'Oh aye, I forgot I had her.' Carefully he took off his backpack and gently passed it to his wife, then glancing left and right, he sprinted across the road and pushed open the gate. As he did so, one of the officers spotted him, jumping to his feet and shouting, 'Wait there sir, please.'

'I'm police,' Frank responded. 'DCI Frank Stewart, out of New Gorbals in Glasgow.' He fumbled in an inside pocket for his wallet then taking out his warrant card to show to the officer. 'What's happening here?'

The officer nodded towards the fishing boat. 'This lad was out on the loch this morning and dragged up a body in his nets sir. It's a woman we think, but the body is tightly wrapped in polythene so it's not easy to tell. We weren't sure what to do so we've just called it in. They're sending some guys over from Glasgow.'

'Okay,' Frank said, nodding. 'You just secure the scene and make sure no-one touches anything until the scene-of-crime guys arrive, got that? And talk to the guy with the boat, make sure you take a note of where he picked up the body.'

'Are you taking charge of the scene now sir?' the officer asked, sounding hopeful.

'Afraid not son,' he said. 'I'm on my holidays. But the chances are, I'll be back,' he added ruefully.

Chapter 7

Their weekend away on Loch Fyne had been eventful to say the least, but it had been delightful too, if a little hectic, with all the little Stewart cousins being together for the first time. The Sunday media had of course given extensive coverage to the discovery of the woman's body, which had now been moved to a Glasgow pathology laboratory for further examination. During breakfast, Frank had been in receipt of a text from Detective Chief Superintendent Charlie Maxwell, breaking the news that, as he had half-expected, he was to take on this new murder case as Senior Investigating Officer. But Maggie had her own case to worry about, which was why she was back in her Byres Road office with her associate Lori Logan, preparing for the morning's meeting with their client Ruth Davie. And as part of that preparation, she had some news to share.

'Lexy McDonald messaged me half an hour ago,' she said, 'about Paul and his girlfriend and whether or not they've skipped off to India.'

'And?' her assistant asked eagerly. 'Have they?'

Maggie made a face. 'And it's a *maybe*. Firstly, it turns out that two tickets in the names of Paul Davie and Maya Mishra were indeed booked for an Air India flight from Heathrow to Bangalore on the day Paul's mobile was detected at the airport. Secondly, both Davie and Mishra booked in for that flight online. But disappointingly, there's no record of them passing through passport control on that day.'

'That's not a maybe then, is it?' Lori said. 'About them leaving the country I mean. They booked the tickets and checked in, but then didn't turn up and they didn't go. That's it in a nutshell.'

'Yes, that's the most likely scenario,' Maggie admitted. 'But why *did* he go to the airport if he didn't intend to get on his flight?'

Lori shrugged. 'There could be hundreds of answers to that question, but I'll give you just a few of them. One, he had cold feet at the last minute and refused to get on the plane. Two, he turned up as arranged, but his girlfriend wasn't there. Three, one of them had forgotten their passports so they couldn't get through passport control. Four, his phone was there but he wasn't. Five, he ...'

Maggie laughed. 'Okay Miss Logan, I get the picture. But if they didn't leave, where are they now, that's the question?'

'And that's the question we're being paid to answer,' her assistant pointed out. 'I assume we're going to tell Mrs Davie about this development?' she added.

'Well, yes, although whether it's any help to her or us right now is open to question.'

'But it *is* progress,' Lori said. 'It almost definitely means he's still in the country somewhere.'

Yes, dead or alive, Maggie was about to say before checking herself, it being too early in the case to make such a definitive assertion. Instead, she said, 'The good news is, Lexy is going to do a bit more work on it for us. They've got CCTV with facial recognition software installed all over the airport, so she's going to check if either Paul or his girlfriend were captured on the day in question. So yes, it is progress. And don't forget about that strange business at Torridon Systems, when he supposedly went back into the office on the day he left his partner. Despite having handed in his access card on the previous day.'

'Yeah, I had forgotten about that,' Lori admitted. 'That was a bit weird, wasn't it? And I'll tell you what else is weird,' she continued, obviously thinking out loud, 'and that's the fact that there was then a two-day gap before the phone turned up again at Heathrow airport.'

Maggie was silent for a moment. 'Yes, definitely odd. Although I suppose he might have turned it off to avoid detection after he left Ruth but then needed to switch it on at the airport to meet up with his girlfriend. They're big places you know.' She looked at her assistant, whose face now wore a dubious expression. 'I can see you're unconvinced,' she added, 'but it's the best we've got for now.' She glanced at her watch. 'Anyway, look at the time. We'd better think about going.'

'It's good of her to take the morning off for us,' Lori said. 'Because I think she's got quite an important job up the town.'

'She'll be working from home I expect,' Maggie said. 'If you believe what you read in the papers, hardly anyone goes into the office these days. Not that I'm one to talk, given my current working arrangements,' she added. 'But don't forget,

Ruth's little girl has lost her daddy. That must be so difficult for her.'

Lori nodded. 'You're right. So what's the plan for this morning then boss?'

'Well obviously, we'll start by telling her about our breaking news from Lexy, and then it's a two-pronged attack, I think. The main job is to see if anything that Paul found when he was clearing out his mum's house might have prompted him to suddenly change the trajectory of his life. And before you say anything, then no, I've no idea what we're looking for. Possibly a photograph, or a letter or something like that. Something that must have shocked or surprised him when he uncovered it.'

Lori nodded. 'Maybe some dark hidden secret, like his mum had a secret lover and it was the quiet guy next door?'

Maggie laughed. 'Yes, something like that. The second prong is to find out a little more about the true state of the Davie's relationship, and I mean mainly before Paul's mother died. Because as we said, maybe his uncharacteristic behaviour had nothing to do with his mum dying. Maybe he was just sick of his partner and wanted a complete change of life.'

'Okay,' Lori said. 'And what about him going back to the office the day after he left? Or didn't, as the case may be. Are we telling her about that?'

Maggie thought for a moment then said, 'No, I think we'll keep that to ourselves for the time being. And as to who's doing what, perhaps you can look through the stuff that he cleared out of his mum's whilst I have a chat with Ruth. She might open up more to someone who has had similar relationship difficulties as she had. And who's had to cope with a child who's lost their father, like I had to do with Ollie.'

'Makes sense,' her assistant said. 'But just one question before we go. Do you seriously think she could be involved in this herself?'

'That would mean making the assumption that her partner is dead, which I don't think we're in a position to say right now,' Maggie cautioned. 'But as we've already said, statistically it's often the other half who's the murderer. So yes, she could have been involved.'

'But why would she come to us if she'd done away with him herself?' Lori asked.

'What choice would she have? If your partner has disappeared, it would look distinctly odd if you didn't report it. Especially if and when the body turns up.'

Lori nodded. 'True, I hadn't thought of that. We'd better be careful then, if Ruth Davie's a murderer.'

Maggie laughed. 'I think we'll have safety in numbers. Anyway, you said she lives quite near here, didn't you?'

'That's right, they've got a flat up in Hyndland, on Clarence Drive. The estate agents call it a highly sought-after locale. And it's only ten minutes' drive away from here.'

The Davie flat was on the second floor of an attractive modern block, set high above the road. A small car park at the front offered designated spaces for the residents, together with four spaces for visitors, one of which was thankfully free when they arrived. The communal doorway was secured by a push-button intercom system that allowed visitors to request access from the householder they were coming to see. Maggie stuck out a finger and prodded the button for Ruth Davie's flat. Immediately there was a buzz as the lock was released.

'Up we go then,' Lori said, pulling a funny face. 'Into the murderess's lair.'

Ruth Davie was waiting for them at her door, greeting them with a smile that Maggie thought was tinged with wariness. 'Come in, please,' she said. 'We'll go straight through to the living room.' The room was bright and airy, although the near-white carpet struck Maggie as seriously impractical when a small child was part of the family. At the far end, a bay window offered panoramic views in three directions. 'Please, take a seat,' their host directed, extending a hand in the direction of a blue velour sofa.

'Thank you,' Maggie said. 'As I mentioned on the phone Ruth, we wondered if we could take a look at the items that Paul cleared out of his mum's house. You thought that event perhaps might have contributed or even directly sparked the uncharacteristic changes in his behaviour, didn't you?'

The woman shrugged. 'Yes, perhaps.'

'But he didn't mention any item in particular?' Lori asked.

'No, he didn't. But he was upset afterwards.' Then she hesitated. 'Actually, I'm not sure if that's quite the right word. Troubled perhaps, or maybe even confused. I don't know exactly. But there was something.'

Lori nodded. 'And did you not ask him what it was?'

'I did, of course I did. But he just said it was nothing. It was obvious he wasn't going to elaborate so I just left it at that.'

'Where is the stuff?' Lori asked. 'And I'll go and take a quick look through it, if you don't mind.'

'It's in a cupboard in our bedroom,' the woman answered. 'I'll take you through now, but there's not that much of it. Two or three box files and some toys and things from the boys' childhood. Oh yes, and there's an old laptop. Paul brought it back because he hoped there might be some family photographs on it, but I don't think it works. Anyway, let me take you through.' She got up and led Lori along the hall to a bedroom, returning a couple of minutes later.

'Would you like a cup of tea?' she asked.

Maggie nodded. 'That would be lovely thanks. I'll come through to the kitchen with you if you don't mind. And Lori will probably have a coffee.'

Whilst Ruth prepared their drinks, Maggie brought her up to speed with DC Lexy McDonald's discoveries. 'I don't know what this means,' the woman said, looking confused. 'Does it mean he went to the airport but didn't get on the flight? Even although he and his... his *girlfriend* had booked them?'

'It seems that way, yes,' Maggie said. 'But the only proof we have of Paul being there is your sighting of his phone. And just to be clear, that was the last signal you got from it? After that, it went dead?'

She nodded. 'Yes, that's right. Nothing since then.'

'That's obviously a concern,' Maggie said. 'But the police are going to check the airport CCTV as part of their investigation, so that might help us understand what happened at Heathrow. But I've been wondering if there might have been anything else that could have explained Paul's uncharacteristic behaviour?' She paused. 'What I'm wondering is, how were things between you both, I mean before his mum's death? The only reason I ask was I got the feeling at our first meeting that perhaps his reluctance to advance his career might have created some tensions between you. But please forgive me if I read that wrongly,' she added apologetically.

'We were fine, absolutely fine,' Ruth replied sharply. 'I admit that I wished he was a little more ambitious, but there weren't any *tensions* as you put it.' There was a pause. 'The thing was, I wanted to have another baby, and I suppose I would have quite liked to give up work for a while too. But we couldn't get by on Paul's council salary. I suppose I was a bit frustrated about that.' It sounded as if it was the first time she had admitted it to herself.

'I can understand that,' Maggie said. 'And you don't think it was how you felt about the situation that led him to give up his job and go contracting? Because it would be a logical explanation, wouldn't it?'

She shook her head. 'No, it wasn't that. We'd had the discussion many times, but he was very stubborn about it. He was perfectly content with his nice secure job at the council and wouldn't change his mind no matter what I said.'

'Until suddenly he did.'

'Yes, until suddenly he did,' Ruth said in a sad tone.

They were interrupted by the return of Lori, clutching a large brown envelope. 'There wasn't much, just a few photographs that interested me.' She upended the envelope and let the pictures spill out onto the worktop. 'I don't know if you can help me identify who's who in any of these?' she asked Ruth.

The woman shuffled through them, then smiled fondly. 'This one is Paul and Jaz when they were wee boys. It looks like they've just got new bikes. They certainly look pleased as punch.'

'They were very alike when they were small,' Maggie commented.

'Yes, there was only a year between them of course,' Ruth said. 'It such a shame I never got to meet Jaz. Paul was so fond of him and missed him terribly.'

As well as the pictures of the boys as children, there were a few of Jaz as a grown-up, showing him with a couple of mates in a pub somewhere. In one, he was holding a pint glass aloft, the other arm draped around the shoulders of one of the friends, the glaze in each of their eyes betraying a state of obvious inebriation.

'I don't suppose you know who these guys are?' Maggie asked, examining the photograph.

She shook her head. 'I don't recognise any of them I'm afraid. Maybe one of the guys in Paul's five-a-side football team might know,' she ventured. 'The same lads have been playing together for years, and Jaz and Paul were in the same team back then.'

'That's a useful steer Ruth,' Maggie said. 'We'll definitely follow that up, thank you.'

'There's a laptop too,' Lori interjected. 'I tried to start it up, but the battery was dead, and I couldn't find the power supply. I just wondered if there might have been something on it, like some more photographs or some other stuff that might be of interest.'

Ruth shrugged. 'Like I said, I don't think it works.'

'Could we borrow it for a little while?' Maggie asked. 'We could perhaps ask our police friends if they could look at it. They've got access to all sorts of technical experts who might be able to bring it back to life.' Including one Eleanor Campbell, she thought, smiling to herself as she pictured Frank once more trying to persuade the notoriously temperamental forensic officer to help him with yet another slightly dubious request. But then she remembered that Paul Davie was on the official missing persons' register, so there would be nothing dubious about this particular ask.

'Sure, take it,' the woman said, 'It's no good to me. And the photographs, you can take them too. Just let me keep the one with them on their bikes please. It's lovely.'

'Of course,' Maggie said. 'It's been a very useful meeting, thank you. But just so you know, we'll be working on the assumption that Paul didn't go to India, so our focus will be on finding out where he did go after his visit to Heathrow. Hopefully the police review of the CCTV will uncover some clues and that will give us another line of enquiry.'

'I'm still checking his phone every day,' she said, 'but there's been nothing since then. I'm beside myself with worry you know. I'm just desperate to know what's happened to him.' She looked at them with sad eyes. 'I have to tell you, I'm fearing the worst now. But I just have to know, whatever's happened to him.'

'Don't give up hope,' Maggie said gently. 'The statistics are in your favour you know. Ninety-five percent of missing people are eventually found safe and well.' It was what you always said in these situations, but you and they knew that they were just empty words. 'We'll do everything we can to find your partner, trust me.' And they would of course, leaving no stone unturned in their quest for the truth. But Maggie knew deep in her gut that Paul Davie was already dead, though discovering who had killed him, and where, and how, and above all, why, looked at this moment like an unsurmountable challenge. But then suddenly, something struck her, something in that picture of Jaz Davie and his two pals that she should have noticed right away, and something that sent a shiver of excitement through her whole body.

Because the fact was, there couldn't be too many pubs in Scotland that proudly displayed the mounted head of a stag above the bar. Now she couldn't wait to phone Frank with her news.

Chapter 8

The atmosphere at New Gorbals police station was febrile, as the feelings of apprehension that always accompanied a new murder case began to take hold. It was perhaps media scrutiny above all that was responsible for this state of unease, felt most acutely by the brass, who in this age of the twenty-four-by-seven news cycle, were under constant pressure to demonstrate continual progress in every investigation. Three days in to this one, that pressure was focussed on the identification of the victim, a task made infinitely more difficult by the fact that there had been no recent reports of any missing persons that remotely matched both the time of death or the age or gender profile of the body that now lay in a Glasgow police pathology lab. The victim was Caucasian and female, around forty years of age, the cause of death being strangulation. The fact that the polythene-wrapped body had been submerged in Loch Fyne for some days had made the forensics exponentially more complicated, but the best guess was that the victim had been killed perhaps five to ten days before discovery, and that she had been dead several days before being dumped in the loch. Now Frank was in one of the station's major incident rooms with his skeleton murder team, which so far consisted only of DI Andy McColl and DC Lexy McDonald.

'So, no missing persons matching the profile in the last three months then?' he was asking.

Andy McColl shook his head. 'No sir, not in Scotland at least, not in that time period. We'll extend that to UK-wide and see if that brings anything up. If not, we'll have to go back in time, maybe a year to start with.'

'And fingerprints and DNA have drawn a blank I assume?' he asked Lexy.

'That's right sir. It seems our victim hasn't got a criminal record.'

'And there was nothing in what she was wearing that could help to identify her?'

'She was naked sir,' Lexy said. 'So no, nothing. The forensic team are still examining her body for other clues, but they've not flagged anything up so far.'

He nodded. 'We're obviously a bit limited in what we can do until we've got an identification, but perhaps we can roll back from the discovery of the body and see if we can at least put some sort of framework in place.'

'You were actually there when she was discovered, weren't you sir?' Lexy said.

'Aye, sheer coincidence that. We were all on holiday up there. A guy had been out fishing in his boat which he moors at a jetty a couple of miles from where we were staying. He realised right away when something big was caught in his net because apparently there are strain gauges on the mechanism that flag up an alarm in these circumstances. It's so that the ropes don't snap under the weight, because these nets are bloody expensive.'

'I guess he knows where this happened then sir?' Andy asked.

'He does, exactly. He says it happened about fifty meters off the eastern shore, near a wee place called Strachur. There's a little sheltered inlet near there, which is apparently where some of the shoals congregate, if that's the right term, so it's where he always starts his trawl. And he says the currents are less strong there because of the sheltering effect, which must mean the body was dumped nearby. That's just his opinion mind you, but he's been fishing the loch for more than twenty years, so I think we can trust his judgement. It seems very likely that's where the body was dumped in the water.'

'Shall we have a look at the map sir?' Andy said. 'I'll get it on my laptop, and we can stick it up on the big screen so we all can look at it.'

'A cunning plan,' Frank said, turning to look at the wall-mounted screen. He was immediately disheartened by what he saw. 'Damn, I forgot the main road runs right through the village,' he said mournfully. 'Two main roads join up there in fact. Which means the body could have come from anywhere.'

'That's true sir,' Lexy replied, 'but it's still a good place to start our enquiries. The body would probably have been taken to the lochside in a vehicle, even if the murder took place in the village. We can go door-to-door and see if anyone noticed anything suspicious. For a start, I bet there's dozens of dog-walkers in the place,' she added. 'And they're out at all hours.'

'And look, there's a number plate recognition camera on the junction of the two main roads,' Andy said, pointing at the map.

'But with dozens of vehicles going by it every day,' Frank added, then, realising his tone and been unnecessarily sceptical, he added, 'which will be a great help if we have to prove that someone was in the area on a particular day and time.' He paused for a moment. 'Right then Andy, how are we doing at getting bums on seats? Anything to report? Because I don't think we're going to solve this murder with just the three of us.'

He gave Frank a rueful look. 'Some sort of progress sir. We've got a couple of DC's coming off the case that Lexy was working on, and I've been promised three or four uniforms on top of that. Oh yes, and we can probably requisition the two officers they've got at the wee police station in Inveraray. That should give us enough to start the door-to-doors by the end of the week, given a fair wind.'

'That'll do for a start,' Frank said. 'We'll allow the forensic team a couple of more days to work on the body and then we'll need to get our arty guys to do a drawing of the poor woman to circulate to the media. Because even this early in proceedings, I'm getting the feeling that might be the only way to find out who she is.'

***

The fact was, Frank had already been thinking about how he could supplement his threadbare team, and naturally there was one name that immediately sprung to mind. DC Ronnie

French was the laziest copper he had ever worked with in his twenty-five-year-old career, and he had a take on the world that made Wally Jardine seem woke by comparison, but he was also capable of providing acute insight into any case he was working on. He was a good man to have on any team, but he was also recently retired, although whether he was enjoying it or not was still to be ascertained. Frank suspected that the novelty of having Frenchie at home would already have worn off on his wife, whom he had met on a couple of occasions. In both appearance and demeanour, Mrs French was the exact opposite of how Frank had imagined any wife of the corpulent DC to be. She was sweet-natured and attractive in equal measure, qualities that Ronnie fully appreciated even if he was not always adept at showing it.

He took out his phone and swiped down to French's number.

'ello Ronnie me old fruit gum,' he said, his mock Cockney as excruciatingly bad as ever. 'Glad I've caught you on the old dog and bone.'

'You feeling all right guv? You sound as if you've got a cold or something,' French said, laughing. *'I was just waiting for my Lily to bring me another cup of tea when your bleeding call interrupted my little snooze.'*

'Your Lily is a veritable goddess if she does that for you. But anyway, I thought I'd let you know that Police Scotland have inexplicably made me SIO on a murder case, and there's a vacancy in the team if you fancy a few extra quid for your already massive pension pot. A nice job it is too, on beautiful

Loch Fyne. You might even be able to do a bit of fishing on your day off.'

'It's bleeding November guv,' the DC said, sounding distinctly unimpressed by Frank's proposition. *'It'll be ten below zero up there.'*

'You obviously didn't do geography at school,' Frank said. 'Because if you had, you'd have heard of the Gulf Stream. It makes Argyllshire positively balmy all year round. Nearly tropical in fact.'

'Ain't that the place that was without electricity for nearly a fortnight?' French said. *'And before you give me any bull, I know it was. It was all over the news.'*

Frank laughed. 'All sorted now. I was there myself at the weekend and the lights were shining brightly. But seriously, I could do with your help for a few days if you can spare the time.'

'Yeah, might be able to squeeze that into my busy schedule guv. What's the brief?'

'The poor victim's body was dumped in the loch off a place called Strachur. It's just a small village with a couple of hundred houses maximum. We'll be running a door-to-door in a couple of days, and I need you to co-ordinate the exercise and follow up on anything that might need further investigation. It's probably a long shot, but there's a chance that the murder could have been committed in the village. The shorter odds are that someone drove to the lochside from God knows where to dispose of the body out of a vehicle. But even if that was the case, maybe someone in the village saw something, you never know. Anyway, that's the mission if you wish to accept it.'

'Yeah, that sounds okay guv, I'll give it a go if you want,' French said. *'When do you want me up there?'*

'Soon as you can Frenchie. It's only an hour and a half's drive from Glasgow airport on a good day so if you leave the Smoke first thing you'll be here in time for lunch.' He hesitated for a moment. 'And just so you know, I might have another wee job for you whilst you're up here.'

Frank had been mentally wrestling with himself ever since his return from his weekend away, but in the end, he realised he had no choice in the matter if he was to maintain any measure of self-respect. He felt more than ever that he had fouled up badly on the Three Men in a Boat case, and now some fresh evidence had emerged that compelled it to be reopened. Moreover, a photograph had now emerged of the three men drinking in the Noble Stag pub, a photograph that almost certainly captured the scene just an hour or so before they set out on their ill-fated voyage. It seemed that the stars were aligning in his favour, giving him no choice but to dive into the investigation head-first. In the temporary absence of a direct boss from whom he could seek authorisation for a new cold case, he'd talked the matter through with DCS Charlie Maxwell, the most senior officer at New Gorbals. Maxwell's view was entirely as Frank had predicted it would be. *As far as he could see, there had been no obvious miscarriage of justice in so much as no-one had been banged up for a crime that they hadn't committed, nor indeed was there any compelling evidence that there had been any crime at all. The force had enough on its hands, especially with this new murder case landing on their doorsteps, and had neither the time nor resources to go off on speculative wild goose chases just because some DCI felt bad about his performance on a ten-year old incident, which, Maxwell repeated, had never been classified as a crime and never would be.* The message was clear. Frank must devote one hundred percent of his time and attention to the murder of the as-yet unidentified woman, which, he conceded, was exactly what he would have said himself had he been in Maxwell's position. But on the other hand, the DCS had no jurisdiction over retired ex-Metropolitan Police Detective Constables, and so long as Frank's personal involvement was no more than the odd ten minutes here and there, the Boat case could proceed under the radar.

'What other wee job is this?' French said, interrupting his boss's thoughts.

'Just an embryonic cold case from about ten years ago. We need to track down two or three guys and get statements from them about what happened back then. It's just routine, and it'll probably come to nothing. Eleanor Campbell's putting together a dossier on the case as we speak, so you'll have everything you need to get up and running.'

'Fair enough guv,' French said amiably. *'Right then, I'd better go and make my travel plans, then I'll tell Lily the good news.'*

'She'll be cracking open the prosecco and inviting all her girlfriends round for a party,' Frank laughed. 'Anyway, give her my regards and with any luck I'll see you in a couple of days.'

Chapter 9

As far as both Maggie and Lori were concerned, their visit with Ruth Davie had been no more than a moderate success. On the one hand, the singular nature of the items her partner Paul had retrieved from his mother's house strongly suggested that he, like Frank, had been beginning to doubt the explanation for his brother's death that had been laid down in the fatal accident enquiry all these years ago. In support of this view, there was a paucity of family photographs – he had selected none of his mother or father for example, and just that one shot of him with his brother when they were children, the only item of sentimental value he seemed to have taken. No, the only items that had seemingly elicited his interest were those half-dozen pictures of his brother in the Loch Fyne bar, and the supposedly non-working laptop. Lori had been unable to locate the power cable for that latter item, so it was not possible to say whether it was unserviceable or if the battery was simply flat. However, a replacement cable, soon to be purchased from the computer store at the end of the road, would swiftly resolve that issue.

On the other hand, they hadn't made huge progress in establishing whether the state of the Davie relationship had been a motivation for him leaving his steady job, nor had they made any progress on the thornier problem as to whether Ruth Davie might have had any direct involvement in her partner's disappearance. There was one bright spot though, and that was the remarkable reaction it had generated when Maggie showed one of the pictures to Frank. He had told her earlier about the mystery man who had bankrolled Jaz

Davie's drinking session that fateful day, and now it seemed likely that it was this unidentified person who had been behind the camera when the pictures were taken. Encouraging though all of this might be, the question was, where to go from here? It was that very question they were currently discussing as they sat enjoying a coffee in the Bikini Barista cafe. And at that precise moment in time, it was a question for which no immediate answers were forthcoming.

'I must admit, I'm feeling as if we're up against a brick wall,' Lori said, frowning. 'Besides seeing if there's anything on that laptop, I've no idea what we should do next.'

'Yes, I feel a bit the same way,' Maggie conceded. 'But I think the laptop must be important, so let's not lose heart until we've made some progress with it.'

'I was thinking about that. The guy who runs the computer shop up the road is one hundred percent geek, but I was going to take it along to him and see if he can get it up and running.'

'Yes, that's a good option. And failing that, perhaps we can get Eleanor Campbell to look at it. Now that our man has been officially reported missing, it's probably something Frank might be able to arrange for us.'

Lori was silent for a moment, evidently deep in thought. Finally she said, 'See, that's the problem we've got compared to the police. They've got access to all these fancy databases and apps and stuff, and all we've got is Google.'

Maggie laughed. 'That's true, but what we do have in our favour is that we devote one hundred percent of our time and our brainpower to a case, whereas the police are stretched all over the place. Our ability to focus goes a long way to making up for the things we can't do.'

'I suppose,' Lori said, sounding unconvinced. 'But remember on our last case you got us access to the phone records system and the numberplate camera system and the bank records too, didn't you? Why can't we get access to all that stuff again? In fact, why can't we get access to it all the time?'

She gave her assistant a rueful look. 'That would be useful, but you know as well as I do that the laws of privacy are very strict, and they don't want every Tom, Dick or Harry having access to those applications. Last time was a special case, where we were engaged as subcontractors to Frank's independent cold case unit.'

'So why can't we do that again?' Lori persisted. 'I remember Frank telling us that a lot of that basic search work is done by civilian staff, not police officers. And we're civilians, aren't we?'

'They're direct employees, it's not the same. But I hear what you're saying. Maybe I'll ask.' As she looked at Lori, she became aware that her assistant wasn't listening.

'Am I boring you?' Maggie said, laughing.

'You can do it on *any* smartphone,' Lori blurted out. 'Tracking I mean. I remember Jimmy telling me that they sometimes use the feature when they're doing a mountain rescue. Can we call him, *please*?'

'You don't need to ask me,' she grinned. 'Come on, let's get him on video call right now.'

He answered promptly, smiling broadly at his colleagues as he recognised who had called him. *'Always great to chat to you guys, but I thought you didn't need me on this case?'* he said. He was wearing a bright red ski-jacket, sunglasses and a navy woolly hat that was pulled down so far that it almost touched his eyebrows.

'You look as if you're halfway up a mountain, and is that a dusting of snow I see in the background?' Maggie said.

'Roger to both. Me and Stew do a regular stint with Braemar mountain rescue, and we've got a wee training exercise going on today. Bright sky overhead hence the shades, but it's bloody freezing. Three below zero if you're interested, and forecast to get colder.'

'Brr, that is cold, 'Maggie said, giving an involuntary shiver. 'But funny you should mention mountain rescue, because Lori's got a question to ask you in that regard.'

'That's right,' Lori said. 'Didn't you tell me once that you can use a standard smartphone to track the history of someone's movements? Over quite a long period of time?'

He nodded. *'Yep, that's correct, as long as you've given permission in your settings, and you've got the person's login details. We encourage everyone going into the mountains to use it. It could save your life. I can show you how to access it if you want,'* he added. *'It's easy. It's using Google Maps timeline function, and almost everybody's got that on their phones, even if they don't know it. And yeah, I think it goes back right to the time you first switched it on. Years I suppose, although I'm not totally sure about that.'*

'It would be brilliant if you could show me,' Lori said.

'Nae bother. I'll send you a message when we're done. Anyway, I better go. They've buried some poor guy up on Braeriach and we'd better find him before he freezes to death. Over and out.'

'This sounds incredible,' Maggie said. 'So does this mean we can track Paul Davie's movements going back ad infinitum? It certainly sounds like it.'

Lori gave her a blank look. 'I'm not sure I know what ad-whatever means, but yeah, it sounds as if you can go back for just about ever.'

'And do we need Ruth's phone to do it?'

'Nope. Find My and Google Timeline are two separate apps. We can do the Google thing on our own computers, as long as Ruth knows her other half's log-in details. We would be signing on as if we were him. It'll probably send a security message to his email when we try, but if Ruth has these details too, then we'll be able to get in.'

'That's amazing. We'd better get on to her right away, and make sure she's okay with it too. Although I don't know why she wouldn't be.'

But then suddenly, something occurred to Maggie. 'I'll tell you what I think doesn't stack up in this case,' she said, 'and that's the answer to the question of why he didn't switch all of this stuff off? Because if you were cheating on your other half, surely that's the very first thing you would do. But Paul Davie didn't.' She paused, 'I bet when we see his movements over the last six months, it'll tell us a whole different story.'

***

They had called Ruth Davie at her office and within ten minutes she had provided them with the logon credentials for her partner's Google account. Five minutes later, they had logged on using Maggie's laptop and were ready to start.

'So, what's the plan?' Lori asked. 'What I mean is, how far back in time should we go?'

Maggie shrugged. 'Probably no more than six months, when he moved jobs to Torridon Systems. And we don't need to look at every single day, not right now. I suggest we pick a couple of random weeks to get some idea of his routine, and then we focus in on the couple of days when he left his partner.'

Lori nodded. 'Or better still, why don't we start with these last days first? Because that's where the real puzzle is, isn't it? Did he or didn't he go back to the office the day after he left? I'm dying to find that out.'

'Yes, I think that'll be very interesting, no question,' she agreed. 'But I'd like to get a general picture of his day-to-day schedule before we do that. After that, we can home in on his final movements. It'll make it exciting, like anticipating Christmas day.'

Her assistant smiled briefly, then, suddenly serious, said, 'You said his final movements. Are you now thinking that's what they are? Do you think he's dead?'

Maggie nodded. 'I'm not certain, of course I'm not, but I still can't imagine why a cautious man with a beautiful partner and a much-adored daughter would wilfully just disappear. I think I said it before, but it just seems so out of character.'

'What did happen to him then?'

'That's what we need to find out. Anyway, do you have any idea how this Google thingy works?'

'Jimmy sent me instructions,' Lori said, tapping her phone. 'It doesn't look too difficult. Here, slide over your laptop and I'll have a look whilst you order us a couple more coffees. And a cake,' she added. 'No, scratch that. A roll and sausage please.'

Maggie laughed. 'Yes, sure boss.' She raised a hand to signal Stevie over to their table and gave him their order, which the proprietor scribbled down whilst chattering away in his customary genial manner, before disappearing into the kitchen. 'Right then Miss Logan,' she said, 'start clicking.'

She watched intently as the cursor ranged across the street map of Glasgow which Lori had called up, before hovering over the Clarence Drive home of Paul and Ruth Davie. 'This is showing him leaving home at about half-past seven in the morning, presumably to go to work. What day is this?'

'A Tuesday, about three months ago. That's his five-a-side football day, remember? He takes the car into the office that day rather than cycling, which is what he normally does.'

Maggie watched as Lori scrolled forward on the timeline. 'There, he gets into the office car park at about eight,' her assistant said, 'and it looks like he stays in the office until he leaves at....' Lori screwed up her eyes to read the small type. '...yeah, at six-thirty. And then just before seven, he arrives *here*.' She jabbed the screen to indicate the location of a sports centre in the Jordanhill district. 'He's there for just over an hour and a half, which stacks up, assuming he plays for an hour plus the changing time before and after the game.' She scrolled forward again. 'And then he goes home. Doesn't even go to the pub afterwards.'

Maggie nodded. 'No, and he doesn't sneak off to meet with a lover either,' she mused. 'So far, so boring. Not that there's anything wrong with boring,' she added hastily. 'Right, so I know it'll be a bit of a slog, but let's get another dozen or so random samples of his movements. One for every day of the week at least. Actually, we probably need a couple of dozen. Maybe more.' She smiled at her assistant, who looked as if she was about to protest. 'And then we'll get to the good bit, I promise.'

Lori laughed. 'Fair enough. I suppose we'd better get started.'

They worked diligently for an hour, Lori operating the mouse and Maggie taking notes and looking for any exceptions to Paul Davie's steady routine, none of which seemed to have emerged thus far. But as she studied her notebook, a thought came to her.

'Lori, I assume we can search by location, can we?'

Her assistant nodded. 'Yeah sure, why?'

'Let's look at that student accommodation that Sarah Duncan mentioned to us. You know, the place where Maya Mishra and the other contractors were living. It's at the bottom of Byres Road, that's what she said. I think I've seen them, a block of nice modern flats.'

Lori dragged her mouse to the location and clicked *search*. 'Nothing, not a sausage,' she said, giving Maggie a knowing look. 'He never went there. Not once.'

'No, he didn't,' Maggie said, 'and that's because he wasn't having an affair with Maya Mishra, or anybody else for that matter.' She paused and tapped her notebook with her pen. 'This is a guy who basically goes to work then comes home, except on a Tuesday, when he plays five-a-side football, then goes home. Sure, there were a couple of visits to pubs after work, presumably with workmates, but he generally only stayed an hour or so.'

'And then he went home?' Lori supplied.

'Yeah, and then he went home. There is one thing that's interesting though.' She paused and examined her notebook. 'We happen to have captured his movements on three separate Fridays, and on each occasion, he was in the office to nearly eight o'clock at night. Which is odd, because that's the day when most folks knock off early for the weekend. And yet, he's not one of them.'

'He stays late whilst everyone else has gone home,' Lori said, cottoning on. 'Maybe he was looking for something, something he didn't want anyone else to see him doing.'

'Exactly,' Maggie agreed. 'Specifically, maybe he was doing something on his computer that he didn't want anyone to see. Because don't you remember from our visit? Torridon Systems' office is organised in cubicles and the staff sit facing inwards, looking at one of the dividing panels, with their backs facing outwards. If someone approaches your cubicle, firstly, you don't see them, and secondly, they are automatically looking over your shoulder, which lets them see what's on your screen. And because they're behind you, you've no time to blank it out or call something else up.'

They sat in silence for a moment, taking in the implications of what they had just deduced. Then Lori said, 'This is huge, isn't it? Because Paul Davie wasn't having an affair. He was looking for something or trying to find something out. And maybe someone discovered what he was doing and didn't like it.'

Maggie didn't answer at first, her mind still churning furiously. 'So, does this mean that someone went to considerable trouble to manufacture fake evidence that he was having an affair with a co-worker?'

'You mean these texts?'

'Exactly, the texts. But the question is, why would someone want to do that?'

Lori shrugged. 'We don't know if someone actually did that. But if they did, maybe they thought Ruth would give him an ultimatum if she discovered them. Tell him he has to quit his job or she'll leave him. Something like that.'

Maggie nodded. 'Yes, I think that must have been their plan, whoever *they* are. They hoped he would quit, but he didn't. Which means whatever it was he was looking for, or whatever it was he was trying to do, must have been desperately important to him.'

'Aye, and to them too,' Lori said. 'But as you say, we don't know who *them* are. If they actually exist at all, remember.'

'No, we don't,' Maggie agreed. 'But let's look now at his movements around the time of his disappearance, because that should be very interesting.' She was already pretty sure what they would find as she watched Lori manipulate the mouse, and five minutes later, the supposition had turned into fact.

'He didn't go home to get his stuff that day,' her assistant said, open-mouthed with astonishment. 'His phone was in the office all the time, according to this. Look.'

Maggie studied the screen then nodded. 'You're right. So does that mean someone let themselves into his flat and packed a suitcase with his clothes, and then that same someone composed a text to Ruth to cruelly tell her he was leaving her?'

'Maybe,' Lori said. 'Or maybe he just forgot to take his phone with him when he went back to the house.'

'No way,' Maggie said. 'If you were planning to take off with your girlfriend, you would definitely take your phone. Because the first thing you would do once you'd collected your stuff would be to text her or phone her to tell her the deed was done.'

'Yeah, I think you're right. So that means someone used his phone to compose that message. And then he was never seen or heard from again.'

Maggie considered the point for a moment then said, 'Actually, that might or might not be true.'

'What do you mean?'

'Well not only was the phone in the Torridon offices on the day he left his wife, it was also there the following day too. This is where we have a different version of events between Sarah Duncan and the receptionist, remember? Because Duncan says he did come back...'

'But the receptionist said he didn't.'

'That's right,' Maggie said. 'And then of course his phone turned up at Heathrow three days later. *That* actually was the last confirmed sighting by Ruth.'

'Of the phone, but not necessarily of him,' Lori pointed out.

Maggie sighed. 'Of course. And maybe I'm stating the obvious, but it's definitely the events of these last three or four days that are the key to solving this mystery.' She drew breath and gave her assistant a serious look. 'You asked me earlier if I thought Paul Davie was dead,' she said. 'Then, I wasn't sure, but I am now.'

Chapter 10

The first he heard about the leak was when his phone rang at quarter past seven on Sunday morning, jerking him out of a deep slumber. He and Maggie had already been up half the night soothing a teething Isobel, and it had been barely an hour since they had been able to get their lovely baby daughter back to sleep, so the interruption was unwelcome to say the least. DCS Charlie Maxwell's opening sentence contained a selection of the finest Anglo-Saxon swearwords, alerting Frank to the fact that this was serious.

'Have you seen the bloody Chronicle?' his senior officer was saying. *'Sources within Police Scotland, it says. What bloody sources Frank? What sources are they, when they're at home?'*

'Sorry sir, I've not seen it,' he said, simultaneously stifling a yawn and scratching his head. 'Let me get their app up on my phone and I'll take a look.'

'Aye, you bloody do that, and I'll hang on while you do,' Maxwell barked.

Frank fumbled for his phone then clicked on the Chronicle's app. Instantly, he saw why Maxwell was making such a fuss. The story had commandeered the front page, with a sensational headline precision-engineered to grab attention. *Loch Fyne Body is Missing Businesswoman.* The article, written of course by Yash Patel, went on to clarify that whilst it was purely speculation at this stage, sources were saying that the dead woman bore an uncanny physical resemblance to Alison Christie, founder and former Chief Executive of Torridon Systems.

Struggling to know how to react, Frank said, 'This is bollocks sir. We've not issued a photofit yet and we've no DNA or any other physical evidence to make an identification. And Alison Christie died in a skiing accident in America nearly five years ago, so unless she had a twin sister or she's suddenly been raised from the dead, then this is just tabloid clickbait.'

'Aye, well I bloody hope so,' Maxwell said. *'Let me kindly suggest you get your arse out of bed and go and find out who's leaked this so I can get the Chief Constable off my back. And then get on to that bloody journalist pal of yours and give him a statement.'* Abruptly he hung up, with no goodbye and before Frank could respond.

Now wide awake, he quietly slipped out of bed, leaving Maggie still asleep, and wandered through to the kitchen, cursing Patel under his breath. He filled the kettle then sat down at the table and swiped down to the reporter's number. As expected, there was no answer, so he rattled off a text. *PHONE ME NOW!* He didn't expect a reply to that either but at least Patel would be left in no doubt how Frank felt about the matter. After a moment's thought, he composed another text. *Hi Lexy, I know it's Sunday, but if you've got a wee minute, give me a buzz. No rush.* After a few seconds' consideration, he pressed *send*.

He was just pouring the boiling water into the cafetière when his phone rang.

'Hi Lexy,' he said. 'And sorry to disturb you on a Sunday, but have you seen the Chronicle?'

'Afraid so sir,' she said. *'And before you ask, I don't know who's been speaking to them but I'm guessing it must have been one of the artists in the forensic team. I'll find out first who took the photographs of the body, and we'll join the dots from there. But I don't think the actual computer-generated image has been leaked. It's just that someone's obviously seen it and decided to blab to the media.'*

'Somebody's probably looked over the artist's shoulder when they were putting the finishing touches to it,' he speculated. But what was beginning to worry him was that the likeness must have been bloody striking to make that somebody immediately rush to tell the media.

'I'll follow it up first thing tomorrow,' Lexy said. *'But then maybe you could go down to the labs and read the riot act. It might make someone scared enough to confess.'*

Frank laughed. 'Don't worry about that Lexy, I'm going to beat it out of Patel when I catch up with the wee bugger. No, what I'm really worrying about is that the chief super says I've to make a statement, but he didn't tell me what he wanted me to say.'

'You just say the whole idea's crazy, and that Alison Christie died five years ago in America,' Lexy said. *'Simple as that.'*

'Aye, you're probably right,' he agreed. 'She died five years ago.'

So why was there a voice whispering away in his ear, a voice that seemed determined to be heard? A voice that was shouting *what if she didn't?*

***

Frank woke the next day to find that every media outlet in the English-speaking world had picked up on Yash Patel's sensational if speculative story. As he had expected, the journalist had gone to ground, returning neither phone calls nor text messages, but Patel was soon going to discover the folly of that tactic. DCS Maxwell had ordered that Frank make a statement to the press, so he was going to do that, but that statement would be made to the Globe, not Patel's Chronicle, an act of petty spite for which he would feel no remorse. On the contrary, just one minute earlier he had despatched a message to Patel informing him of his intention, signing off with a broad-smiling emoji and a single-finger motif which he recognised as both juvenile but pleasing at the same time. His call to Amanda Lavington of the Globe was necessarily vague, simply stating that as yet there was no forensic evidence to identify the body and that a computer-generated image of the woman would be released in a day or two. He went on to say that the media speculation as to her identity was not helpful and certainly was not based on any scientific analysis or evidence. He knew of course that it wouldn't stop the speculation, but he'd done what Maxwell had asked him to do and that was a tick in the box.

But he'd woke up with an idea in his head, an idea that required the assistance of Eleanor Campbell to pursue. He picked up his phone again, noting with a smile of wicked if infantile satisfaction that his text to Patel had generated four missed calls and three messages from the journalist whilst he had been talking to the Globe. Eleanor too could be tricky to get a hold of, but this morning she answered promptly with her trademark *'what?'*, indicating she had looked to see who was calling her.

'Nice to speak to you too,' he laughed. 'Listen, thank you for doing that dossier on the three men in a boat case. It popped into my inbox earlier and I've already forwarded it to Ronnie French.'

'Have you read it?'

'Not yet,' he admitted. 'It's on my to-do list.'

'You don't keep a to-do list,' she answered acerbically, before continuing. *'It's short, just four pages. It wasn't a very detailed investigation.'*

'Don't remind me. But that wasn't why I called you.' He knew there was no point in asking Eleanor if she'd seen the stories in the media because she wasn't interested in the news. Instead, getting straight to the point, he said, 'It's a technical question that I've got. What I want to know is, can you use facial recognition technology to identify a dead person? Because I think when you once explained to me how it worked, it was all about angles and geometry and facial points like that, and I guess that stays the same even if you're dead. '

'I don't know, but it's interesting,' she said, an answer that surprised him, since he'd been expecting the usual mixture of

derision and dismissal that was her normal response when their conversation strayed into technical matters. *'Why do you need to know?'*

'Well, I want to *not* identify someone, if that makes sense,' he responded.

'It doesn't.'

'I want to be able to say that a body *isn't* someone, and I need to do it really quick,' he elaborated. 'Today if possible. Because the press has got hold of a crazy story, and I need to damp it down before it gets any more out of control.'

'Ah right,' she said, evidently cottoning on. *'Yeah, I can do that. I need a photograph of the dead person and a photograph when they weren't dead. Like when they were alive, I mean.'*

'Yep, I can organise that,' he said, trying not to laugh at her last comment. 'And how long will it take you to do it once you have them?'

'About a nanosecond, once I have the pictures. Just as long as they're good quality.'

This time he couldn't suppress his laugh. 'That'll be quick enough. I'll go and get some nice photos sorted as fast as I can, and thanks in advance for your help. Speak to you soon.'

He already had some photographs of the dead woman, supplied by the forensic pathologist to the investigation team, and a quick search of the web revealed no shortage of images of the living Alison Christie. The businesswoman had been seriously photogenic and evidently publicity-hungry too, making her a media favourite during her life and meaning there were literally hundreds of pictures to choose from. In the end, he selected a couple of formal shots which had seemingly been used in an annual financial report of Torridon Systems, the last one in fact before she died. With a couple of inexpert swipes and jabs, he had forwarded the images to Eleanor. Whilst he waited for her response, he browsed through the statement Christie had made in that annual report, in which she congratulated the company for another year of financial success, and laid out plans for the acquisition of the US firm Hudson Medical Staffing and the subsequent move of the company's headquarters to White Plains, New York. It was this deal she had been working on when she had disappeared on the ski-slopes of Aspen Colorado, her death initially attributed to a skiing accident before being swiftly revised to a probable suicide as the true state of both the company's finances and her own personal life began to emerge. Scanning a few more news articles at random, Frank found that irrespective of whether they were written before or after her death, the articles invariably started with a summary of Alison's inauspicious beginnings, the fact that she had been abandoned by her alcoholic mother at the age of twelve and taken into care, and that she was pregnant at fifteen and a mother at sixteen. Of the daughter, not much was known, other than she was called Rebecca and that she now lived in Australia. There had, briefly, been a husband too, an actor called David Stirling of whom Frank knew little, other than he was Scottish and the star of a popular crime drama called

Stornoway. It was all very interesting, but of peripheral importance to his investigation.

That was, until Eleanor phoned him with some frankly unbelievable news.

Chapter 11

It was bloody impossible of course, because how could it be the body of Alison Christie, when she had gone missing in Aspen in Colorado, almost five years ago to the day? That's what Frank had said, quite forcibly, to Eleanor Campbell, when she'd called with her news, and she had responded, more forcibly still, that her highly-sophisticated facial recognition software had found an eighty-seven percent match between the two photographs he had sent her, and with fifty-one percent being normally enough for a definitive unequivocal identification, there was no doubt it was her. *So that was it then.* Unquestionably the body which had been literally fished out of Loch Fyne was that of the celebrated Scottish businesswoman, leaving Frank with the immediate and thorny problem of what to tell the media. As far as he was aware, facial recognition technology couldn't be used to identify a body officially - either someone who had known her had to look at it and say *yes, that's her,* or you needed to take a DNA sample from a close relative and prove that there was a match. That was the technical side of the matter, but more important was the human side, that horrible moment when a uniformed officer had to knock on the door of the victim's closest relative and relay the terrible news. Someone was going to have to do that, and as soon as possible. But as far as they knew, Alison had only one close blood relative, and that was her daughter Rebecca who lived somewhere in Australia. That probably meant that it would be her actor husband, from whom she had seemingly been estranged at the time of her disappearance, who would be asked to do the visual identification. All of this and more was being kicked around the major incident room immediately after Frank had shared the astonishing development with his embryonic team.

'Right guys,' he said. 'The two priorities are first, to track down the daughter and the ex-husband, or whatever he is, and bring them up to speed with what's happened. Second, and directly related to that, is to expedite the formal identification, and we'll go two-pronged with that. We'll ask the Australian police to take a DNA sample from Rebecca Christie and we'll try and round up the actor guy and ask him if he will go and see the body.'

'That's David Stirling, the guy who's in that cop show based up in the Hebrides?' DI Andy McColl clarified.

'Aye, that's right. If he can't or won't do it, or if we can't find him quickly, we'll ask someone at the Torridon company instead. Maybe the finance guy who took the trip to the US with her.'

'He's still working there,' Lexy McDonald said. 'He's the chief executive now I think I read.' She paused for a moment. 'But it's definitely her, is it? It's Alison?'

Frank shrugged. 'According to Eleanor, and she's the expert. So unless the formal stuff tells us anything different, then we have to assume it's her.'

There was another pause, and then Andy said, 'Forgive me if I'm stating the bleeding obvious sir, but this means that she couldn't have died in America and that she must have come back to the UK at some point after her trip.'

Lexy grinned. 'You are stating the bleeding obvious Andy, but it does mean that we should be able to get onto the border force guys and find out when she got back. All movements in and out of the country are tracked on a big database so she'll be on there somewhere.'

'Unless she was somehow smuggled in,' Andy mused.

Frank shook his head. 'No, that's unlikely in my opinion, because it's not an easy thing to do. All the legitimate routes are very heavily controlled, which explains why we have all those problems with the migrants in the small boats trying to cross the Channel. And you can't very well come across the Atlantic on a wee rubber boat,' he added wryly. 'Like I say, she'll be on the database somewhere.'

'Okay, I'll speak to them as a matter of priority,' Lexy said.

'And I'll pop over to Sydney and have a chat to the Australian cops,' Andy said, laughing. 'No, I'll speak to Torridon Systems first and see if anyone has an address for the daughter, and if not, the police over there will be able to track her down through their immigration authorities or their electoral roll.'

'I'm surprised she's not already been in touch with us,' Lexy commented, 'because I bet the story made the news over there as well.'

Frank nodded. 'True. But maybe she doesn't follow the media. Not everyone does.' He paused. 'Anyway, now that we've got a victim, we need to start thinking about suspects. Luckily, we've got a big pack of post-it notes to stick on our whiteboard, and now we need a few names to write on them.' He nodded towards the board. 'We need a good half-dozen stickers up there in short order so that the DCS's got something colourful to look at next time he drops by.'

'Don't we need to come up with a few scenarios as to what we think might have happened?' Lexy asked. 'And yes, I accept we don't really know very much at the moment. But this is such a mad case, we need to start making some sense of it.'

'Definitely,' he agreed. 'For what it's worth, here's my summary of the situation.' He wandered over to the white board and picked up a marker pen. 'I'll go through my ideas, and you two can chip in with any observations, or better still, let us have any alternative scenarios if you've thought of any.' He paused for a second. 'So, as far as we know, Alison Christie was last seen on the ski-slopes of Aspen Colorado the day after she'd been in somewhere called White Plains, where she had been finalising a takeover or merger or something like that with a US company.'

'Hudson Medical Staffing,' Lexy supplied.

'That's right. She went there with her company's finance director, a guy called Jack Easton. After the meeting, he flew straight back to the UK and Alison took a flight to Aspen, where she rented some ski equipment, bought a lift pass and took to the slopes. Apparently, she was a fanatical skier and liked to do it every chance she had.'

'And wasn't seen again,' Andy said. 'At first it was suggested she'd had an accident, but then it turned out that her golden image of success wasn't so golden after all. With a crumbling marriage and the business in trouble, the story changed to her not being able to face the failure so she took her own life.'

Frank laughed. 'This is meant to be my story Andy, but yes, you're right.' He paused again as something came to mind. 'We need to check the presumption of death laws over in the States, because I assume at some stage, she would have been declared officially dead, but I've no idea how long it takes over there. It's seven years in England and Wales and I guess the same in Scotland.'

'But we now know she didn't die over there,' Lexy said, wearing a puzzled expression. 'So where has she been for all these years, and why did she go into hiding?'

He shrugged. 'As far as the why is concerned, perhaps she simply couldn't face the shame of being seen as a failure in the eyes of the public. Because it seemed to be the fame that drove her more than anything, wasn't it? As to the where, well that's a total mystery. But we might get some better idea about that when we find out when she came back to Scotland.'

'I bet she wishes she hadn't,' Lexy mused, 'because then somebody killed her. Strangled her first, wrapped her up in polythene then threw her in the loch.'

'That's what it looks like, aye,' Frank said.

'But why did she come back when she did?' Andy asked. 'According to the forensics, she'd only been dead a few days at the most when her body was thrown in the lake, and they're also saying she'd only been in the water a week or so at the very most.'

'She could have come back anytime between when she disappeared and when her body was found,' Lexy pointed out. 'She may have been living somewhere in the UK. Anywhere in fact.'

'Aye, maybe,' Frank said. 'But if so, where was she hiding, and why the hell was she doing it?' He sighed and then shook his head. 'You know what? There's absolutely no point in us continuing with this until we know when she got back. So Lexy, you'd better get onto it right this minute.'

***

Ronnie French had been successful in negotiating a pass-out from his wife and so had now made the arrangements for a five-day stay up on Loch Fyne. Accordingly, Frank had arranged to meet the DC at Glasgow Airport where he would brief him on the latest developments in the Alison Christie case and find out what he made of the Jaz Davie affair. Eleanor Campbell had sent out her dossier of that investigation -otherwise known as the Three Men in a Boat case – a couple of days earlier, and he hoped that Frenchie had taken the opportunity to study it. Frank was waiting for his colleague at the arrivals exit area. After a few minutes delay, French emerged trailing a carry-on suitcase, and, amusingly, wearing a replica West Ham football shirt under his suit jacket.

'Are you up here looking for a fight?' Frank laughed, extending a hand in greeting. 'Although I don't think anybody in Scotland will recognise what team it is, so no need to worry about that.'

'I paid ninety quid for it in the club shop so Lily says I'd better get my bloody wear out of it,' French said laconically. 'Anyway guv, good to see you again. What's the plan for my exotic holiday?'

'The immediate plan is to grab a quick coffee here and have a chat, and then I'll take you back to New Gorbals nick where you can commandeer one of our pool cars for the duration. You'll need one when you're way out west because it's a tad remote to say the least.'

They found a seat in a concourse cafe, French waiting whilst Frank fetched their drinks. On his return, he updated the DC on their speculations on the Christie case and the fact that the priority at the moment was to establish how and when the victim had returned to the UK.

'We're still pushing ahead with the door-to-doors though I assume?' French asked.

Frank nodded. 'Yep, that starts first thing tomorrow. There's a couple of uniforms who cover nearly all of Argyllshire, but they've been allocated to the case for three days, so we should get round everybody in Strachur in that time.'

'And we're looking to find out if anyone saw the bird's body being chucked into the loch?'

'If by the *bird*, you mean our victim Alison Christie, then yes, that's the objective. Strachur's a quiet wee place but it might be the kind of village with plenty of nosey neighbours, given there's nothing much else to do. We might get lucky.'

French gave him a sceptical look. 'Half the houses are probably holiday homes so I think you might be a bit optimistic guv. But I'll have a good dig and see what turns up.' The detective hesitated then said, 'I've been looking at that dossier thing that Eleanor sent us. I had a look yesterday and I printed it out and read it again on the plane coming up.'

'And what do you make of it?' Frank asked, slightly nervously.

'Loads of stuff wasn't done by the looks of it, because everybody on the case assumed it was just a tragic accident.'

'And by everybody on the case, I suppose you mean *me*,' Frank said.

His colleague shrugged. 'I would have done just the same guv. It looked so obviously an accident.' He fumbled in the inside pocket of his jacket, removing a crumpled document and laying it flat on the table. 'There's not much in this guv. It's only four pages long. We've got the names of the three guys who were on the boat and we know which two of them died, obviously. The guy who survived goes by the name of Jack Thompson and the other guy who died was Peter Denny. We've got the name of the leader from the company who was in charge of the group. He's the geezer who was supposed to check the boat before it set sail but didn't. But that's about it.'

Frank nodded. 'I'm not sure I really want to hear this, but when you said a minute ago *loads of stuff wasn't done*, can you give me a for instance? But be gentle with me.'

French hesitated for a moment. 'Well for a start guv, nobody made a list of who was on the course. It just says there was a dozen or so participants and they were all NHS staff from the Queen Elizabeth hospital in Glasgow. But no-one took their names and I'm assuming none of them were spoken to either. It's only the guy who survived and the course leader geezer who've got a statement on the file. Oh yes, and someone talked to the landlady of the pub too. But that seems to be it.'

Frank gave a rueful sigh. Aye, someone had talked to the landlady alright, but somehow in the process had missed the fact that an unidentified man had been intent on getting the boating party pissed up before they set out on the loch. And Ronnie was right. He, the then DS Frank Stewart, hadn't talked to any other of the course participants, let alone taken a note of their names. The more he thought about it, the more he realised it had been a cock-up of quite epic proportions, and there was no-one to blame for it but himself. But now, finally, he was doing something about it.

'Okay then, what's your plan of attack?' he asked his colleague.

'I'll speak to the outward-bound geezers first and see if I can get a contact number or email for the course instructor. He's a guy by the name of Willie Armitage according to Eleanor's report. Then I'll talk to NHS Scotland and find out if the survivor guy Jack Thompson still works for them. Between Armitage and Thompson, I might then be able to make a list of who else was on the course, or at least get some of the names, so that I've got someone else to question. And then finally, I'll see what I can do about tracking down this mysterious fourth bloke that you told me about, the one who was splashing his cash in the bar.'

Frank smiled appreciatively. 'That's a fair amount of work you've given yourself Frenchie. I can see you're going to be a busy man.'

And it's work that I should have done ten years ago, he thought sorrowfully as they walked to collect his car from the car-park.

Chapter 12

There had been two developments in the Paul Davie case, each potentially of some significance, and each would have a strong influence on the agenda when Maggie and Lori met with Jack Easton, Chief Executive Officer of Torridon Systems later that morning. The first development was that DC Lexy McDonald, with the aid of the airport's powerful facial search technology, had completed her scrutiny of Heathrow's CCTV footage on the day that Davie and his girlfriend Maya Mishra had booked tickets to India. Tellingly, Lexy's work had revealed that Paul Davie *hadn't* been at the airport that day – albeit allowing for the unlikely possibility that he might not have been caught by one of the hundreds of cameras that were located in every corner of the vast terminal – whereas his girlfriend *had* been. Further research had revealed that she had boarded a flight to Delhi rather than the Bangalore-bound flight she and her lover had been originally booked on. What exactly this meant, Maggie could not say at this point, except that it suggested Mishra was involved in some form of subterfuge or conspiracy, the motive for which she could not yet discern.

The second development was that it seemed Davie had cycled to work on the two days prior to his disappearance, and whilst sorting through the pockets of his fluorescent cycling jacket, his partner Ruth had come across a USB data stick. Immediately she had passed it onto Bainbridge Associates, and now Lori and Maggie sat staring uncertainly at the device as it lay on top of a desk in their Byres Road office. 'I mean, obviously we should shove it into one of our laptops to see what's on it,' Maggie was saying, 'but with the case now being an official missing persons one, I'm just conscious of the fact that we might be compromising some important evidence if we do that.'

'I don't really see how we could be doing any harm if we're just *looking* at it,' Lori said.

'I think these data stick thingies record each time they are accessed. Meaning someone – and what I really mean is, some defence barrister – could argue that the data on it could have been tampered with.'

Lori shook her head. 'No, I don't think that's right. I'm not an expert, but I know that every file has a *last updated* stamp on it. As long as we just look but don't change anything, we should be okay.'

'Yeah, I think I understand that, it makes sense,' Maggie conceded, nodding. 'Obviously I've no evidence to back this up, but I'm wondering if this is connected in some way to Paul staying late in the office on Fridays. Maybe he was looking for something on Torridon's systems and had copied it on to this USB stick. Anyway, let's see if it tells us anything.'

She picked up the stick and inserted it into one of the USB ports of her laptop. Immediately, a dialogue box popped up. *Enter password to access file system.*

'Bugger, we should have expected that,' she said, slightly disappointed. 'Maybe we'll have to hand it over to the police after all. I can ask Frank if Eleanor can have a look at it.'

'No, let's not, not right away,' Lori interjected. 'Maybe first we can give it to Donnie at the computer shop and see if he can get into it. Remember we gave him Paul's brother's laptop, so I owe him another visit to see if he has managed to get it up and running yet.' She glanced at her watch. 'In fact, I might have time to nip up there before we head across to Torridon. And Donnie's a really nice guy, very helpful.'

Maggie raised an eyebrow and smiled. 'Nice as in...?'

Lori gave a sheepish smile. 'Aye, he's nice that way too.' She paused. 'I'm actually quite hopeful he might ask me out. But if he doesn't, I'm going to ask him instead. But not today,' she added hastily. 'Work always comes first for me.'

'Good to know,' Maggie said, laughing. 'Anyway, it's a great idea to take the stick to him, and we don't need to leave here for about forty-five minutes, so you've plenty of time.' She paused then grinned. 'You might even be able to fit in a bit of romance too if you're lucky.'

***

It was only a twenty-minute drive to Torridon Systems office on the other side of the river, but that was enough for Lori to give Maggie an update on the progress that Donnie the computer guy had made with the laptop and the USB stick.

'The good news is, he's managed to get into the laptop, and it was dead clever, what he did. You know how some laptops are protected by a four-digit PIN number? Like yours is?'

Maggie nodded. 'That's right. I use Ollie's birthday. Super-secure,' she added ruefully.

'Well, it turns out Jaz Davie's laptop is protected that way too, and because the same four numbers get punched in every time you access the computer, your fingers leave wee greasy deposits on the key pad. Donnie used an ultraviolet light to show which keys had been used the most, and because nearly everybody uses a birthday because it's easy to remember, you can easily work out how to arrange the four numbers into the right PIN. He says he got it on the second attempt.'

'Goodness, are you sure your Donnie isn't a spook in disguise?' Maggie said. 'That's nice work.'

Lori laughed. 'He's not my Donnie yet, but like I said, he's dead clever. And he told me something else that was really interesting.'

'What was that?'

'He says that lots of big companies have security software which detects if someone has inserted a USB stick into a computer anywhere on the network. Donnie says it's to protect against viruses being introduced to their systems and also to stop people stealing confidential data and stuff like that. And he says most people don't know that this cyber surveillance stuff is running. He said maybe our guy was one of them.'

'That *is* interesting,' Maggie mused, but then something struck her. 'But Paul Davie was an experienced IT guy. Surely *he* would have known about that kind of security stuff?'

'Maybe he did, but he went ahead anyway,' Lori speculated. 'Maybe whatever he was doing was so important to him that he didn't care if he was found out.'

'Yes, maybe he'd finally found what it is he was looking for and was copying it onto the data stick. And as you say, if that was the culmination of his quest, he might not have cared if he got found out.'

Lori nodded. 'Donnie thinks he'll be able to crack the stick's password no bother so hopefully we'll find out soon what's on it. That might answer the question.'

'That would be good,' Maggie said. 'Anyway, we're nearly here. And we've got plenty to talk about with Mr Easton.'

As they waited in Torridon System's reception area for the Chief Executive Officer's PA to escort them to the meeting room, she ran through in her head the questions she was going to ask the man. For a start, she thought it interesting that this important figure wanted to meet with the representatives of a small detective agency who were investigating the disappearance of a former employee of his company. Paul Davie had been a contractor, so hadn't actually been on Torridon's payroll, and he had only worked with the company for six months and in a relatively junior position too. Maggie's original intention was to have a follow-up discussion with Sarah Duncan, the company's head of operations whom they had met earlier in the investigation, and was surprised to be told that Easton would be sitting in on the meeting. She couldn't help wondering why that was. Obviously, the company, if only for PR reasons, would want to show its concern for a former member of its team by cooperating with Maggie's investigation, especially since his disappearance was now an official police matter too. But most organisations would delegate responsibility for a matter like this to their human resources department, and yet here was the CEO evidently wishing to be directly involved. That was quite odd she thought. Easton of course had been one of the last people to see Alison Christie alive, and as the then Financial Director of the company, must have known the murdered businesswoman very well. Maggie wondered what he made of the speculation circulating in the media about the body of a woman that had been found in Loch Fyne. Frank had told her the astonishing news that it was highly likely that it *was* Alison Christie, but that news had not yet been shared with the media, pending formal identification of the body. She pondered whether she should bring it up in the meeting or wait to see whether Easton himself referred to it. With the story being so prominent, it would be odd if it didn't come up, if only in passing.

After about five minutes or so, a smartly-dressed middle-aged woman appeared in reception and exchanged a few words with the receptionist, who Maggie realised was the same one who had given her the conflicting account of Paul Davie's return to the office the day after he had left the company. The woman walked over to them, introducing herself as Margaret, then handed each of them an access pass and said 'please, follow me' in a friendly tone. They swiped through the security turnstile then took the same escalator they had used on their first visit, but this time they carried on to a second escalator which took them up another level, this one rather smaller than the lower level which housed the cubicles where the technical staff spent their days. Around a central seating area decorated by giant houseplants were six or seven large glass-panelled offices, presumably for the company's senior managers. In a corner was the biggest of all, this office large enough to accommodate a boardroom table, a light oak desk and a comfortable leather-settee-equipped seating area. To Maggie's surprise, it was two men who were waiting for them, one whom she recognised as Easton from various photographs she had seen online. The pair sat side-by-side at the large table, each with blank notepads in front of them. As Maggie and Lori were ushered in, Easton stood up and beckoned them to sit opposite, extending a hand in greeting as they took their places.

'Hello, I'm Jack Easton,' he said, his voice smooth and corporate, 'and this is Bill Warren, who's our director of security and compliance. Welcome to Torridon Systems. *Again*,' he added, the smile practised and radiating a sincerity which was probably faked but still convincing. She smiled to herself. In her time as a not-very-good barrister, Maggie had met plenty of the type; always tall and always good-looking, theirs had been an effortless path from public school to Oxbridge to a lucrative career in a leading accountancy or legal firm. In this particular case, Jack Easton had then made the short leap from being a corporate advisor to Alison Christie's embryonic software firm, to become its Financial Director, no doubt bagging a fistful of lucrative share options as part of his employment package. The other man however was a different kettle of fish. Bill Warren was short, with cropped grey hair, and wearing a narrow navy tie and a white short-sleeved shirt that showed off a pair of bulging biceps. The first impression he gave was that of a night-club bouncer, but that was immediately superseded in her mind by a more likely suggestion. She would reserve judgment until she heard him speak, but she thought this man had ex-policeman written all over him.

'We were expecting to meet with Sarah Duncan,' Maggie said as she took her seat, simultaneously swinging her handbag off her shoulder and placing it on the floor. 'Isn't she joining us?'

Easton smiled. 'Sarah's the busiest person in this building, and at this moment in time, another urgent matter is demanding her attention. But she's fully briefed me on the Paul Davie situation, which is why I decided to get personally involved, and why Bill is here with me today.'

'Okay,' Maggie said, looking puzzled. 'I assume you're going to explain all?'

'Of course,' Easton said. 'But before that, perhaps Bill you could give our guests an overview of your role here at Torridon?'

'Sure Jack,' Warren said in a soft Belfast accent. 'I'm director of security and compliance for my sins, and a big part of my job is to manage the visa status of the contractors who come to work for us from overseas. My team has to make sure everyone has the correct work permits and all the paperwork that goes with it, and that we file the monthly government reporting properly.'

'But I remember Sarah told us that you get your overseas staff through a big Indian IT company,' Maggie said. 'I should have thought it was their responsibility to manage the visa paperwork?'

'Yes, partially,' Warren conceded. 'But if anything's amiss, then the buck stops with the company, and believe me, the government's Visa and Immigration squad come down on you like a ton of bricks. So, it's my and my team's job to make sure that doesn't happen. We don't like to leave anything to chance.'

'Which brings us to the Paul Davie situation,' Easton said. He hesitated for a moment before continuing. 'It's regrettable, but we now believe Paul was the unwitting victim of what we call an immigration honeytrap.'

Warren nodded. 'Sadly, that seems to have been the situation and I'm not exactly feeling good about it I must confess. We've had these situations from time to time in the past, and of course it's not something we tolerate in our company. But on this occasion, it unfortunately slipped under our radar.'

'Sorry, I don't exactly understand what you're telling us,' Maggie said, still puzzled.

'We think Paul was deliberately targeted by Maya Mishra,' Warren explained. 'I expect he showed some romantic interest in her, and she decided to seduce him. That's how the scam works you see. The aim is to marry the victim and then the perpetrator can claim automatic residence in Britain.' He paused. 'We have of course taken up the matter with

Bangalore Infotech and told them in no uncertain terms that they have to improve the vetting of their contractors.'

'But Paul Davie had a partner and a little girl. He wasn't single. So why was he targeted by this woman?'

'Yes, a partner, but not a wife,' Easton pointed out. 'Which left an open door for Miss Mishra I'm afraid.'

Maggie shook her head. 'But they weren't having an affair. We've been able to track Paul's movements over much of the time he worked here and we're pretty convinced nothing could have been going on. As far as we could see, he lived a very boring life. He got up, went to work, came home, except on a Tuesday when he played five-a-side football with some friends. And he'd never been to Maya Mishra's accommodation, not once in all that time.'

Warren smiled. 'What you mean is, he never took his *phone* to her accommodation. The fact was, we've discovered they were having sex on company time. Long lunches where they would go back to her accommodation and make love. As I hinted, it was a regrettable lapse in the part of our operation management team. It should have been detected and dealt with much earlier, and we're very unhappy about that. But it is what it is.'

So perhaps that explained why Sarah Duncan hadn't been invited to the meeting, Maggie thought. This love affair was being conducted during working hours when they should have been chained to their desks, and Duncan was taking responsibility for the supervisory lapse. It made sense, but at the same time, it shot most of their own theories down in flames.

'Can you prove that they were sneaking off?' Maggie said, her head struggling to make sense of what had been revealed to them in the last few minutes.

He shrugged. 'We have the statements of Maya's colleagues, who knew what was going on. That was enough for us.'

'And what about the raunchy text messages that she sent him, the ones that his partner discovered?' she asked. 'Did you know about them too?'

Warren nodded. 'We do, and we assume they were all part of the honeytrap operation. Many of them were faked of course, but not difficult to accomplish. Bangalore Infotech has written ninety percent of the systems that the UK's mobile phone companies use every day of the week, and we assume Maya could have got one of her colleagues to write some code for her. Probably no more than a ten-minute job for a coder with their level of expertise.'

'And you know all this for sure?' Maggie asked, becoming more and more bewildered by the speed that this thing was unfolding.

'We do,' he said again. 'As soon as Sarah made us aware of the situation, we launched a thorough investigation.'

There was a pause as Maggie desperately tried to gather her thoughts.

'But you then sacked both of them, or at least you terminated their contracts.' she said. 'Why was that?'

Easton smiled again. 'That was totally unconnected to this matter. The simple fact was we decided to curtail a couple of projects that we didn't think were going to deliver value for money. A routine business decision, nothing more than that.' He paused for a moment. 'And of course those decisions happened before Bill's compliance team knew what was going on. As I said, the events were totally unconnected.'

Now Lori spoke for the first time. 'This is all dead interesting, but it doesn't explain why Paul Davie just vanished off the face of the earth exactly one day after he'd stopped working here. And there was something very fishy going on at the time, because Sarah Duncan said he came back to the office on that day but your wee receptionist was adamant that he didn't. How do you explain that?'

There was a pause as the two men exchanged glances. Then Warren said, 'This is something we weren't aware of. But thank you for bringing it to our attention. We'll look into it right away, although I would imagine there'll be a simple enough explanation.'

'And there's another thing,' Lori continued. 'We think Paul might have copied some stuff onto a USB stick on one of the last days he worked here, and I expect your security systems would have detected him doing it.'

Warren hesitated momentarily before answering. 'That too is something I'm not aware of and in fact, I'm not even sure if our systems have the technical capability to do that sort of thing.'

Maggie gave him a sharp look. 'Just to be clear, you say you have no knowledge of someone inserting a USB stick onto your network?'

'Not personally, no,' Warren said. 'I'll obviously check with our IT team to see if they know anything about it, and we'll let you know if we find anything of course.'

'So do either of you have any thoughts about what might have happened to him?' she continued. 'Was there anything any of his or Maya's colleagues said that might have given any clues to his state of mind, or gave any insight into his plans for the future?'

Warren shrugged. 'A couple of her colleagues thought it was the real deal. That they'd fallen in love, I mean, or more like in lust perhaps.' He hesitated for a moment. 'But maybe he felt that way but she didn't, and he couldn't deal with it. The rejection I mean.'

'Wait a minute, are you suggesting he might have *killed* himself?' Lori asked.

Warren shrugged again. 'Just my speculation, and of course I didn't know the guy. But it's a possibility, isn't it?' He shot a smirk in his boss's direction. 'Or maybe his other half murdered him because he cheated on her. I don't believe that by the way,' he added hastily. 'But if you were writing a detective book, you wouldn't rule it out, would you?'

'No, I don't suppose you would,' Maggie said. 'Actually, we did consider that possibility ourselves, but we've got to know Ruth Davie quite well and we think it's highly unlikely.'

'Or I suppose he could have had some sort of accident,' Easton said. 'And he's lying dead somewhere. I know it's a horrible thought, but I suppose it's a possibility.'

'I guess so,' she said, and as she said it, it struck her that, given what she had learned during this meeting, it was in fact as a good a theory as anything they had come up with so far themselves. She paused for a moment then said, 'Well thanks to both of you. You've been very helpful, but we've probably taken it as far as we can right now.' She hesitated, then after a brief internal wrestle with her conscience said, 'You must have a lot on your plate at the moment Jack, with all this speculation in the press about the fate of Alison. I guess the media aren't giving you a minute's peace.'

Easton gave a wry smile. 'Yes, you could say that. But we've got a great press office here and they're doing a fantastic job of keeping the hounds at bay.'

'But do you think it really could be her?' Lori asked. 'Because it seems totally crazy to me.'

He nodded. 'And to me. Look, I was on that trip with her and she was the same old Alison that she always was. She was one hundred percent focussed on getting the deal done and then she was looking forward to squeezing in a couple of days skiing. I know there was stupid speculation in the press afterwards about her state of mind and about the finances of the company, but that's all it was, speculation.'

'But it must have been a great blow to you and to the company when she disappeared,' Maggie said.

'Well of course it was,' he agreed. 'From a personal point of view, we had a close working relationship and on top of that, I hadn't before experienced the death of someone I knew so well. But although it might seem a little cold for me to say this, Alison and I were just colleagues. Close colleagues admittedly, but I wouldn't say we were even friends, we didn't socialise outside work or anything like that. After her death, my focus was making sure the impact on the company was minimised, for the sake of our customers naturally, but above all, for the sake of our great team of staff, to make sure their jobs weren't threatened. It was a difficult transition, because Alison was the driving force behind the company, but we managed it. And now here we are.' He paused again. 'So, could that body be Alison's? I can't see how it possibly could be, but I was never inside Alison's mind. No-one was. She was a very singular and unusual personality.'

'Did you like her?' Lori asked.

He shrugged. 'Let's just say I admired her, I respected her and I didn't *dislike* her. As I said, she was a singular personality.'

'But what about her family? It must have hit them hard,' Maggie said.

He shrugged again. 'She'd been separated from her husband for six months or more before she went missing so to be blunt, I don't think he was too concerned. I expect it was hard on her daughter Rebecca, but I can't really say, because I hardly know her. I've met her a few times of course, but she spends much of her time in Australia where she has a house.' He paused, then smiled. 'I know this is all very interesting, but probably not too relevant to Paul Davie's situation. So if you don't mind, I need to get on with my day. I'll give Margaret a shout and she'll see you off the premises,' he added, grinning. 'And it's been very nice to meet you both.'

***

Afterwards, they sat in the car in silence, each evidently struggling to process what they had just heard. Finally, Maggie sighed then said,

'It's all one hundred percent plausible, isn't it? Every bit of it. Everything they said.'

Lori nodded. 'I agree Maggie. I actually think they might be telling the truth. No, more than that, I'm sure they are. And Jack Easton comes across as a very straightforward and honest guy. He didn't get prickly when we brought up the Alison situation, and he didn't give us any bullshit about how much he loved her or anything like that. And that honeytrap thing, I've read about it before. It definitely happens.'

'But where does that leave us?' Maggie said, thinking out loud. 'Because Paul Davie is still missing and it seems now as if we're going backwards in the investigation.'

'Yes, he's still missing, and we didn't get answers to our questions about his last days at Torridon, did we? About whether or not he was there the day after he left. And I'll tell you something else too,' Lori added. 'This thing about the

USB stick. Do you really believe that Bill Warren, who's supposedly their director of security, wouldn't know if they run that USB surveillance stuff on their network? See, when I think back, I think there was a wee pause before he answered my question about it.'

Maggie's eyes widened. 'I think you're right about that. It's going to be interesting to see what they come back with, because remember, they promised to look into both of the points we raised.'

'And until then?' Lori asked.

'Until then, the drawing board beckons,' Maggie answered morosely. 'As in, back to the flipping drawing board.'

Chapter 13

With Eleanor Campbell's facial recognition wizardry all but confirming the identity of the body dredged up from the bed of Loch Fyne, the rush was now on to complete the formal identification before the news was released to the media, at which point it was expected that all hell would be let loose. There was enough of a frenzy right now, when the identification of the body as that of Alison Christie was nothing more than rumour and speculation. Once the sensational truth finally emerged, it would be the biggest story in years, right up there with the kidnapping of Shergar and the disappearance of Lord Lucan. Frank, however, decided against sharing these comparisons, figuring correctly that the much younger DC Lexy McDonald wouldn't have a clue who or what he was talking about. They were in Frank's police BMW, steaming along the dual carriageway that skirted the north side of the Clyde estuary, on route to an anonymous warehouse near Bowling, which much to his surprise, he'd discovered housed a film studio complex owned by the streaming giant who produced *Stornoway*.

'Do you watch the show?' Frank asked his colleague as they approached the gates of the complex. 'My Maggie loves it, but you know how I feel about cop dramas. I hate all of them.'

'Actually, I think it's great,' Lexy said. 'But only because I think David Stirling is seriously good-looking. I can't wait to meet him. I might even ask for a selfie.'

'Aye, and that lassie who plays his DS sidekick is pretty good-looking too,' he responded.

She laughed. 'I thought you didn't watch it sir? Hannah Grainger is her name, the actress I mean. And she's English, although you'd never be able to tell when you see her in the show. When they do the Gaelic bits, you'd think she'd been brought up on the islands.'

'Aye, well you should know, being a native of those parts yourself.'

She nodded. 'She's got it to a tee, accent, pronunciation, everything. Oh, and by the way, she's fifteen years younger than him.'

He gave a wry grin. 'And *you're* fifteen years' younger than me. So that bit's realistic at least.'

She laughed. 'Yeah, but we've not been caught doing it in the back seat of your squad car, have we?'

'I'm not quite sure what to say to that,' he said, momentarily nonplussed, 'but no, we haven't. But I remember now. Maggie told me that was the big cliffhanger at the end of the last season. They got caught shagging in the back seat of his car on police time, and now they're waiting to find out if they're going to get the sack.'

'Maybe they have been sacked and now they're private detectives like Maggie and Jimmy,' she said, grinning. 'That would be a wicked plot twist.'

He shrugged. 'I don't suppose he'll tell us, because they keep these story-lines more secure than Fort Knox. Something we could bloody learn from,' he added ruefully, thinking how easily the Alison Christie story had leaked out of New Gorbals.

They pulled up in front of a barrier, then waited as a security guard emerged from his hut in slow-motion to check their IDs. Satisfied, he gave a few words directing them to the reception area then retreated to his sanctum to raise the barrier. A few minutes later, they were introducing themselves to a male receptionist, whose epauletted white shirt and smart navy tie suggested he too worked for the studio's security section.

'Mr Stirling is on set with Miss Grainger at the moment,' he said. He glanced at his watch then picked up a clipboard, examining the single sheet of paper that it held. 'Ah yes, he'll be out in five minutes according to the schedule. You can take a seat over there,' he said, nodding in the direction of a group of leather armchairs, 'and please, help yourself to hot drinks from the machine.'

'Can't we go in and watch?' Lexy asked hopefully.

The receptionist shook his head. 'Sorry, the soundstage is strictly off limits except to cast and crew.' He pointed over to a pair of closed double doors. 'See that light above them? It's red. That means they're filming right now.'

'But we're the police,' Frank said, tongue-in-cheek. 'The *real* police.'

'It's strictly off-limits, even to you guys,' the man repeated, firmly but politely. Then he smiled. 'If you want to find out what happens, you'll have to wait until the new series comes out, just like the rest of us. It's going straight to streaming, so you can binge-watch the whole thing in one night if you like.'

'But come on, just tell us one thing,' Lexy persisted. 'Do they get the sack? That's what the whole country is dying to find out.'

The receptionist turned back to his computer screen, making it clear that the conversation was at an end as far as he was concerned. They grabbed a couple of coffees then sat down to await the arrival of David Stirling. A few minutes later, a loud bell rang, like the kind schools used to use to herald breaktimes, and the red light above the doors turned green and simultaneously, they slid open to reveal the vast soundstage beyond. Able to only look from afar, Frank still had no trouble in identifying the fictional interior of Stornoway police station, no doubt constructed out of plywood and card but impressively realistic nonetheless. Figures now began to emerge from the doorway and a few seconds later, he recognised the leading man, alongside whom walked the leading lady. There was no doubt about it, he thought. David Stirling and Hannah Grainger were a sensationally photogenic couple. He was tall, slim and willowy and she matched his height, with a supermodel skinniness that probably wasn't fantastically healthy but looked fabulous. Stirling had evidently noted their presence, because he nodded in their direction, then squeezed her waist and kissed her on the lips before she retreated back through the doors to the soundstage.

The actor walked over to them and extended a hand. 'Hi, I'm David Stirling. Welcome to Bowling Studios, Scotland's best-kept secret. Or is it worst-kept, I'm not sure.'

The detectives stood up and each shook his hand. 'Best-kept I think, because I'd never heard of it before,' Frank said, smiling. 'I'm DCI Frank Stewart and this is my colleague DC Lexy McDonald. We spoke to one of your team the other day so I'm guessing you know what this is about.'

Stirling nodded as he flopped into one of the chairs. 'Yeah, I do. And it seems absolutely nuts to me. I mean, how can it possibly be Alison? She disappeared in Colorado five years ago and hasn't been seen since. Everyone knows that.'

'We ran a facial recognition scan and the science is telling us that it definitely is her,' Frank said gently. 'Right now, we've no theories or explanations as to how this could be, and we won't have any until we start our investigation proper. Our priority for now is purely to have the body formally identified, and believe me, I know how hard that always is for the person or persons involved.'

The actor gave a sharp intake of breath. 'Well, I can't say I'm looking forward to it, but I'll do it, of course I will.'

'That's good of you sir,' Frank said, 'We'll whizz you down to the morgue in Glasgow and the identification will only take a few seconds. Then if you're up to it, we'll bring you straight back here.' He paused for a moment. 'But it's not an easy thing to go through, so you might like to think about having a few hours to yourself before going back to work. But it's up to you of course,' he added. 'And by the way, you can bring someone with you if you want.'

Stirling shook his head. 'No, I think Hannah is tied up with filming all afternoon. I'll be fine on my own, but thank you for the offer.'

'That's great,' Frank said. 'If you don't mind, we've got a few wee general questions to ask you, but we've plenty of time to go through them on our journey, if you're okay with that.'

'Sure.' He paused and smiled. 'And I hope you've come in a marked car.'

'No, we haven't,' Lexy said, sounding puzzled at the comment.

'Pity,' Stirling said, laughing. 'Because what a picture that would have made for the paps hanging around the gate with their telephoto lenses. DI Sandy McLeod getting shoved into the back of a real cop car,' he added, referring to the name of his character in the hit show.

'You mean the paparazzi?' Frank asked. 'I'm afraid we can't do the cop-car bit, but we can slap you in cuffs if you like, then bundle you out the front door in full view of the cameras.'

***

They hoped to cover a lot of ground on the trip back to Glasgow, David Stirling occupying the front seat alongside Frank, with Lexy sat behind her boss. Fortunately, and contrary to Frank's expectations, the actor seemed willing to help, even when the questions inevitably turned to the personal.

'So can I ask you about your marriage to Alison?' Frank said. 'I believe you were separated at the time of her disappearance, is that right? You had started a relationship with an actress I think?'

Stirling nodded. 'Yeah, that's right. I'd met Natalie on a film and well, you know what can happen.' The actor continued before Frank had a chance to say *actually, I don't*. 'I wasn't cheating on Alison, despite what the press said at the time. I'd already moved out of the family home. and bought my own place in the West End by then. I'd long known that our marriage was over,' he added.

'In your eyes?' Lexy asked.

He shook his head. 'No, it was over for both of us, and more for her than for me if I'm being honest.' He paused for a moment. 'The thing is, I discovered early on in our marriage that Alison really only had room in her life for one person and that was herself. And her bloody company too of course,' he added, with obvious bitterness.

'This would have been at the time she was pursuing the merger with the American company, is that right?' Frank asked.

He nodded again. 'Yeah, Alison Christie and her plans for world domination.' He paused. 'That was what it was all about for her, you know. It wasn't the money that drove her, it was the fame and the recognition.' He gave a short laugh. 'As you can imagine, there's no shortage of narcissists in my game, present company included. But in comparison, my darling Alison was off the bloody scale. Looking back, I often wondered if that was why she wanted to marry me. You know, so that she could turn up looking stunning and slinky at all these glossy award ceremonies that I get invited to.'

'And why did you want to marry *her*?' Lexy asked.

He gave a rueful smile. 'You've seen her pictures, haven't you? She looked amazing and she was interesting and for a while I was consumed with lust. It wore off pretty quickly when I got to know the real Alison, but I'm over it now.'

'And you're not with Natalie Scott any more I'm guessing?' Lexy said cautiously. 'Sorry David, but I saw you kissing Hannah Grainger back at the studio and it looked very romantic.'

'No. The thing with Natalie was just a fling. We had fun together for a few months and then we agreed to go our separate ways. We're still great friends. But as I said, that had nothing to do with the breakup of my marriage to Alison. It was already over by then.'

'But you were still married at the time of her death, weren't you? I guess that means you would have been a beneficiary of her estate?' Frank said. 'How did all that work out?'

He laughed. 'I didn't want or need her money, which is just as well, because I didn't get anything. Sly little Alison had changed her will a few months earlier to exclude me completely. I think that perhaps confirms what she thought of our marriage at that time.'

'So where *did* her money go, do you know?'

'Well, it didn't go anywhere for nearly a year, because there was no body to confirm her death. But we found out there's something in law called Specific Peril, which makes it easier to officially declare a death if the missing person has been engaged in something that's obviously dangerous, exactly like skiing or mountain-climbing or something like that.'

'When you say *we*, who exactly are you talking about?' Frank asked.

'Oh, myself and Rebecca, her daughter. Obviously, we were both anxious to have some closure on the tragedy, and we had a lot of help from the authorities in Colorado, because sad to say, it's not an unusual occurrence for people to disappear without trace in those mountains. And I know it sounds rather cold to say we wanted to get it all tidied up, but it's agony not knowing what's happened to someone you're close to. We wanted to have a proper funeral and to properly celebrate Alison's remarkable life.'

Frank nodded. 'That's perfectly understandable. So when were you able to achieve that, assuming you did?'

'The Specific Peril paperwork came through from the States about nine months after her disappearance and we had a ceremony in Glasgow shortly afterwards. Rebecca asked for just a few people to attend because she didn't want a big media shindig, so that's what we did. Alison would have wanted a big glitzy do of course, so we held a media reception afterwards as a kind of compromise, where we served champagne and canapés and reminded the world how brilliant she had been,' he added, laughing.

'And the money?' Frank asked. 'Where did it all go?'

The actor laughed again. 'Yes, the *money*.' He hesitated. 'There wasn't as much as you might think. Torridon had done well enough, but Alison had always re-invested most of the profits back into the business. She had a couple of properties including the house that we had shared, but they both had big mortgages on them. They went to Rebecca, but she immediately sold our marital home to clear the debt. She still owns the other one I think, but I'm not sure.'

'This might seem an odd question,' Frank said, 'but how well do you know Rebecca? Because I guess at one point, she would have been your step-daughter.'

He shrugged. 'Not well, to tell the truth. Her and her mother weren't particularly close and Rebecca kind of ploughed her own furrow, so she didn't come round our house very often. There wasn't any real antagonism, it's just that they didn't seem that bothered about having any sort of relationship with each other. And to be honest, Alison wasn't what you would call motherly in any way. If I'm being brutal, I don't think she gave her daughter much thought. She looked after her financially, but that was about it.'

'You say Rebecca ploughs her own furrow,' Lexy said. 'What furrow would that be?'

The actor smiled. 'She's a painter, landscapes mainly. She's quite good and I think she's got a bit of a following too. I doubt if she makes much money but that doesn't seem to concern her. She spends most of the year in Australia and I never hear from her. I don't even have her address or an email or anything. But if you're looking for her, her gallery has probably got a website.'

'That's a handy tip, thanks,' Frank said. 'And what about the company itself? Because Alison owned most of it herself, didn't she? That must have been very valuable surely?'

He shrugged. 'It's not really my area of expertise, but there were just two other shareholders, I think. Jack Easton, who's the current boss, had about twenty percent and a guy called Richie Whitmore, who was Alison's original business partner and who wrote the first iteration of the Nurses Direct app. He had a couple of percent I think, although I'm not sure about that.'

'That means Alison owned more than seventy-five percent of the shares by my calculation,' Lexy said. 'What happened to them?'

Stirling laughed again. 'Those were the shares earmarked for the deal with the US guys, but after her death, that deal fell apart, and they went into a kind of limbo for a while. I think they became owned by the company itself under some sort of complicated trust arrangement, if that makes sense. But please, don't take my word for it because I haven't got a clue about that sort of stuff.'

'Does that mean that nobody directly benefited from them?' Frank said. 'Not her daughter, nor these two other shareholders you mentioned?'

He shook his head. 'Nope, not as far as I'm aware. They had a floatation a couple of years after her disappearance and the money went back into company funds, I think. It's those new shareholders who own the company now I guess, and in fact a lot of them are the employees, who got forty-percent of the shares in the sell-off. But as I said, it's not my area of expertise. I find all this stuff bamboozling quite frankly, and it's not something I'm interested in either.'

Frank laughed. 'Aye, you and me both David, but thanks, all of this has been terribly helpful. Anyway, we're nearly at the morgue, so we'll get parked up and then we can take a moment for you to prepare yourself. Lexy's happy to come in with you if you need some support.'

***

The identification had taken no more than thirty seconds, David Stirling giving an almost imperceptible nod of acknowledgement as he stared sad-eyed at the lifeless body of his wife, before shedding real tears. Afterwards, Lexy tried to comfort him with an arm around his shoulder and some sympathetic words, which seemed to have a positive effect.

'I'm fine now, but it was a shock,' he said quietly. 'Alison looked exactly like the day I last saw her, perfectly preserved. I did love her you know, despite everything.'

'I can see that,' Lexy said in a kindly tone. 'And thank you for doing this. We'll get a driver to take you back to the studio if you're up to it, otherwise we can take you home. Though before you go, there's just one more question we need to ask you.' She paused momentarily. 'And it's were you in or around Loch Fyne between the fifth and the fourteenth of November this year?'

He looked at her in surprise. 'What, are you thinking I might be a *suspect*? Because that's just crazy.'

'It's just routine David,' Lexy said. 'It's a question we have to ask everyone.' She paused and smiled. 'Your character in Stornoway must have asked it a dozen times at least.'

'Yeah, you're right,' he said, breaking into a smile. 'And the answer to your question is, I was on Lewis until about the tenth and then we came back here to start on the studio shots. And there's about a couple of hundred cast and crew who can vouch for me.'

Lexy smiled. 'That's fine, thank you for that. So can we take you home, or do you want to go back to the studio? We've got a driver standing by.'

'Studio please,' he said. 'I need to get back to work and I need to be with Hannah.' He stood up and shook her hand. 'Anything else I can help you with, just let me know.'

She took him to the entrance area, where a uniformed officer was waiting to take him back to Bowling, then returned to a small meeting room where Frank had been waiting during the identification.

'Nice to get that out of the way,' he said with a sigh. 'Now we can get on with the investigation proper.'

'And David Stirling was, or is, our first suspect I suppose?' Lexy asked. 'That's why we were asking him these questions on the way here, wasn't it?'

He nodded. 'Aye, and in my opinion, he didn't do himself any harm in that regard, because as far as I can see, he didn't have the slightest motive to kill her. *He loved her for a while and then he didn't* just about sums it up.'

'And he didn't inherit a penny from her either. And even before she disappeared, he knew he wasn't going to.'

'He *says* he didn't,' Frank corrected. 'And remember, this murder only happened a few weeks ago. We can't rule out the possibility that the marriage breakup was the reason for her crazy mental breakdown and then after lying low somewhere for five years, she decided to come back to Scotland and confront him. To take some revenge maybe,' he added.

She gave him a sceptical look. *'Really* sir? I don't think so.'

He laughed. 'No, neither do I. Anyway, what news of her return to Blighty? Have you heard from the Border Force guys yet?'

'They've promised me an answer this afternoon,' she said, then glanced at her watch. 'Should be pinging its way into my inbox sometime soon.'

'Good to know. So what about the daughter Rebecca? Any progress in tracking her down?'

'Yes, some progress sir. The house that David was talking about, the one that she kept, is up in the Highlands, near Coylumbridge. And the Australian visa and immigration office has got an address for her in Sydney. They're arranging for a police officer to go round there in the morning. That's *their* morning of course, which is eleven hours ahead of us. And they know to send a family liaison specialist, given the delicate circumstances.'

Frank frowned as he tried to get his head around the time difference. Finally working it out, he said, 'Ah, that means we should wake up to the news of how they got on then. Because our eight o'clock in the morning will be their seven o'clock at night. I *think*,' he added, uncertainly. 'Right, I just need to knock out a wee press statement and my day is done. It'll be a case of light the blue touch paper and retire fast.'

As he spoke, he heard a ping on Lexy's phone. Keenly he watched her as she read the incoming text, his colleague becoming more and more wide-eyed in the process. After a few seconds she said, 'You'll never guess what sir. This is from the Border Force and it's telling me that Alison Christie flew into Oban Airport on a private jet from Westchester County Airport just three days before her body was found.'

'Bloody hell,' he said, stunned. 'And Oban? I didn't know Oban had an airport. And where the heck is Westchester County when it's at home?'

'In answer to your first question sir, yes, Oban has a small airport with a few commercial flights every day, mainly to the islands. Westchester County, I don't know exactly where it is, but I guess it's in the US somewhere.' Pausing, she punched a few lines of text into her phone. 'Yep, Google tells me it's in New York State.'

'This is just nuts,' he said, shaking his head in disbelief. 'Does this mean that after hiding out in America for five years, suddenly out of the blue Alison Christie decides to take a wee trip back home? On a flipping private jet?'

Lexy shrugged. 'Seems like it sir.'

'But how the hell did she get in to the country?' he protested, thinking out loud. 'She was officially dead, so her passport must have been cancelled. Don't they do passport checks at Oban?'

She shrugged again. 'I don't know the answer to that question sir, but the Border Force has sent me the official entry record with her passport number on it, so *someone* must have examined it. So that probably means it wasn't cancelled. To be honest, I don't know how any of that official stuff works, but I'm sure I can find out. Leave it with me sir.'

He gave her an appreciative smile. 'Okay, I will, and thanks Lexy. Anyway, let's head back to New Gorbals and equip ourselves with the strongest coffee they serve. Because I don't know about you, but my brain desperately needs some serious turbo-charging.' But then he had a *much* better thought.

'Or, we could just go straight to the pub and recharge there instead.'

Chapter 14

Overnight, an email had arrived from an Officer Demetriou of the New South Wales Police family liaison division, stating she had been to Rebecca Christie's home in Manly with a colleague and had broken the sad news to the woman about her mother. At least with David Stirling having agreed to do the formal identification of the body, the officers had been spared the need to ask the woman to take a mouth swab to obtain a DNA sample, which would have no doubt caused her further and unnecessary stress and dismay. The officer's message, short and businesslike, gave no hint as to how the news was received, simply that Rebecca would attempt to call them on the number that Frank had given them at 10am UK time. Now, with a good hour before that call came in, he could briefly turn his attention to the matter that had been eating away at him this last three weeks. Ronnie French was now resident in a super-comfortable bed-and-breakfast in the pretty village of Strachur, and it being almost nine o'clock, Frank knew exactly where the leisure-loving ex-Detective Constable would be. He picked up his phone and swiped down to his favourites.

'*Morning guv,*' French answered, his voice perky as usual. '*Just grabbing a bit of breakfast and taking a read at the paper before I get started on the day's work. Where are you?*'

'I'm in my office, but I'm glad you're being looked after up there. Scottish hospitality is justifiably famous. Or is it infamous, I can't remember which.'

'Yeah, this Mrs Gilmour's an absolute genius with a frying-pan, and make no mistake. And there's haggis every morning. I didn't think I'd like the stuff but it's bloody marvellous.'

'I'm sure she catches the wee buggers fresh off the hills,' Frank said, laughing. 'Anyway, it's good to hear you're settling in. I'm just calling for a quick update on the two matters you're working on. Assuming you've managed to drag yourself away from Mrs Gilmour's table for an hour or so.'

'Yeah, we've done reasonably okay on the door-to-doors guv. I've got two PCs from Inveraray helping me and we're probably two-thirds through.'

'But I'm guessing no-one has reported seeing anything so far?'

'Nah, not yet,' French admitted. *'And there's a lot of holiday homes up here and so a lot of the places are shut up for the winter. But there's a bunch of really fancy houses dotted along the road that heads south out of here, and they're right on the loch, so if anyone saw that body being dumped, they're the most likely candidates. We're doing them this morning, and after a couple more coffees I'll be out there, door-knocking.'*

'Aye, well don't wear yourself out Ronnie. So what about my three men in a boat case? Got anything to report on that?'

He heard French take a slurp of coffee before he answered. *'Yeah, some good progress on that one too guv. First, I managed to get in touch with the outward-bound company that organised the course, and they told me that after what happened, the instructor guy who should have checked the boat left the company. That's the Willie Armitage geezer.'*

'Was he sacked?' Frank asked.

'Left by mutual consent is how they put it. The last they heard of him, he had moved to Braemar and was working as a mountain guide. That was a while ago of course.'

'Braemar? That's where my brother Jimmy lives now,' Frank said, surprised. 'And he's in the outdoor game too, maybe he knows this Armitage guy. I'll check afterwards.'

'The other thing is, they think they might still have the list of course attendees from back then. They're going to dig through their archives and let me know.'

'That *is* good,' Frank said. 'And what about the third man in the boat, the guy who survived?'

'Yep, some progress on that one too guv,' French said laconically. *'I called the NHS Trust in Glasgow and it turns out Jack Thompson still works at the same hospital, in the accounts department. Once I'm done with the door-knocking I'm planning to go and see him. Unless you've anyone else to spare of course.'*

Frank shook his head. 'No, the Christie murder is the priority and the DCS would string me up if I diverted anybody else onto the boat case, so you'll have to do that one yourself I'm afraid.' He paused. 'But finally, what about our mysterious fourth man in the pub? Anything on that?'

'Nah guv, I think that'll have to wait until I talk to Jack Thompson. I expect he'll know who he was, given the amount of drink he took off the geezer. A mate I expect.'

'Well obviously that's something we need to find out,' Frank said. 'Anyway, I won't hold you up any longer. You'd better get some door-knocking in so you don't miss your mid-morning coffee break.'

***

DC McDonald had joined Frank in his office as they awaited Rebecca Christie's call from Australia. Given the extraordinary and disturbing news that the woman had just been given, they'd decided to play it rather as they had done with David Stirling, that is to say, sensitively yet purposefully too. Because as Lexy had pointed out, the woman had to be considered a suspect for the murder of her mother, however unlikely that might be. They were just chewing this over when Frank's phone rang, precisely on schedule.

'Hi, I'm Miss Rebecca Christie, is this DCI Stewart?' Her tone was subdued and hesitant, but unmistakably Scottish, the accent of the soft and sparkly variety that was much sought-after by news broadcasters.

'Yes, I'm DCI Stewart and I'm here in my office in Glasgow with my colleague Detective Constable Lexy McDonald. We've got you on speaker-phone, just so you know.'

'Good morning Rebecca, or should I say good evening,' Lexy said, leaning over towards the phone. 'Nice to speak to you, although not in the best of circumstances of course.'

Frank nodded. 'Yes, and thanks very much for finding the time to call us. Because you must have been through the ringer in the last twenty-four hours, and we're sorry we had to break the news the way we did.'

'Yes, it was a terrible shock,' Rebecca said. *'But it can't be true. I just don't see how it possibly could be. It isn't logical.'*

'I'm afraid it is true,' Lexy said gently. 'Mr Stirling identified the body yesterday and he was a hundred percent certain it was your mother.'

'I'm sorry, but I'm afraid it is true,' Frank confirmed. 'But Rebecca, if you are in any way doubtful about it, we'd be more than happy to do a family DNA match, if you were able to take a swab. It'll be no trouble, and perhaps that would give you some peace of mind. And I can understand why you might want to do that, so as I said, it'll be no trouble.'

'I'd like that,' the woman said quietly. She was silent for a moment then said, *'The policewoman who came to see me couldn't really tell me very much about what happened. All I know is a boat dragged up my mum's body, but that she didn't die from drowning. That didn't make logical sense to me.'*

'No, it is correct,' Frank said. 'I'm afraid your mother was strangled, and then her body was wrapped in polythene and then it was dropped into the loch after that. We're not exactly certain of this, but we believe that happened not far off the shore near the village of Strachur. That's on the eastern side of Loch Fyne, if you know the area at all.'

'I don't Inspector, I live in Australia,' she said. There was a pause and then she said. *'Can I ask what is going to happen now? With my mum I mean?'*

'We're waiting for the Crown Office pathologists to sign off that they have completed their examinations of your mum's body, and then it will be released to the family.' Frank paused for a moment before continuing. 'I guess you haven't thought about this, but you'll probably want to have a funeral. I know that will be difficult.'

There was a sigh at the other end of the line. *'Yes, we will, I think. I'll need to track down David and see what he thinks I suppose.'* She paused again. *'But I expect my mother will be pleased if she's looking down on us from above. It will give her one final chance to be in the limelight. I think she would like that.'* It was an odd thing to say, but Frank considered it was said affectionately, not maliciously.

'One thing we discovered was that your mother flew back to the UK from the US just three days before the date on which we think she was murdered,' Lexy said.

'That's illogical,' Rebecca said. *'My mother died on that mountain, five years ago.'* She paused abruptly, then said. *'But of course, it seems now that she couldn't have. So where has she been all this time? Yes, where has she been?'* she repeated. *'It's very disturbing and it's making me very sad.'*

'Is there anyone who can be with you Rebecca?' Lexy asked, alarmed. 'I know it's been a lot to take in and you're almost certainly in shock.'

'I don't need any friends thank you, I'm happy with my work. But thank you for asking.' Her answer surprised the detective, causing her to look at Frank with a raised-eyebrow expression.

'That will be good,' Frank said, returning his colleague's look. He hesitated for a moment then said, 'Rebecca, would it be okay if we asked you one or two questions, just so we can get a little bit of background? Five minutes is all it'll take, then we'll let you get on.'

'Yes, of course,' she said.

'Thanks. So can I just ask how you got on with your mother? Because I know she had you when she was just sixteen and brought you up as a single mum. That must have been tough.'

'That's a difficult question to answer,' Rebecca said. *'I was perfectly happy, but she was detached I suppose, that's the best way of putting it. I often feel I was processed rather than nurtured, if that make sense to you?'*

'I'm not sure it does,' he admitted.

It seemed she was prepared to elaborate. *'Mum was driven, always driven,'* she said. *'When I was a baby, she was training to become a nurse, and then later, she had this big business idea and became obsessed with getting her company off the ground. That's the bit I probably remember the most, when I was twelve or thirteen or something like that. She was always on her laptop or on the phone or doing things with Richie and she didn't have much time for me. But I didn't really mind. That's when I started drawing, I suppose. I spent hours with a pad and my colouring pencils. But we never argued or anything like that. I was just a quiet little mouse who sat in the corner. But I wasn't unhappy, and I was fine at school. I didn't have many friends but I was perfectly happy on my own.'*

'Can I ask you how you got on with David Stirling, your stepfather?' Lexy asked.

'David? I didn't really know him that well. I was at art college when mum and David started going out and I was nearly twenty-one when they got married. They had an amazing wedding with loads of famous people there, politicians and actors mainly, and I went with my college friend and it was a huge party. And then after college, I threw myself into my painting career, so I hardly ever saw them. Once or twice a year, if that.'

'But I guess you found out at some point that the marriage was in difficulties?' Lexy asked.

'That just sort of emerged I suppose. To be honest, I've no idea why she married him, and I don't mean any disrespect to David, because he was nice. And rather good-looking too,' she added, sounding a little sheepish. *'But mum was only interested in mum. I don't know why she married anyone to be honest. She was like me, she really only needed herself, deep down.'*

Frank paused. 'You mentioned a Richie a minute ago.' He turned briefly to Lexy. 'David mentioned someone by that name, didn't he?'

'That's right sir,' Lexy confirmed. 'Richie Whitmore. He was the guy who wrote the original Nurses Direct software.'

'Yes, that's right,' Rebecca said. *'I remember he was always around the house when I was younger. Right through my childhood in fact.'*

'Was he in a relationship with your mother, do you think?' Lexy asked.

'I don't know,' the woman said. *'I don't remember him staying with us and we didn't go out together as a family very much, so probably not.'* There was a silence and then she said, *'Goodness, I haven't thought about this for fifteen years or more, but I remember thinking at the time he was like her little puppy, always eager to please and hanging on her every word. So maybe he wanted more from the relationship than she did, I don't know. But he was nice. Quiet, but nice.'*

It had begun to occur to Frank that somewhere out there, Rebecca Christie had a father, although he remembered from Yash Patel's articles that her mother Alison had always refused to say who that man was. There had been media speculation that it had been one of the staff at the children's home where Alison had stayed between the ages of fourteen and sixteen, but Frank considered that unlikely. Had the businesswoman been the victim of such exploitation, she would definitely have said. It was more likely that it had been one of the other teenage residents and that she had decided that she didn't need or want that person in her life or that of her child. He wondered if Rebecca had made any attempt to trace her father, or had her mother shared the secret of his identity with her before her disappearance? Whatever the case, he decided that today probably wasn't the day to bring up this sensitive matter. But before he brought the meeting to a close, there was another matter he decided he had to raise.

'I know this might be a difficult question,' he said hesitantly, 'but did you ever have any suspicion that your mum might not have died on her skiing trip?' He paused, wondering whether it was wise to continue with this line of questioning. 'Because I recall there was some speculation at the time about the true state of the business and also about her state of mind. Did it ever occur to you she might simply have wished to disappear?'

There was a silence and then she said quietly, *'I prayed that's what had happened, over and over again. I dreamed that she'd had some sort of mental breakdown and she was living a quiet life in a log cabin somewhere. But of course, I knew it couldn't be true.'* She hesitated. *'But now it seems it was true, doesn't it?'*

'And she never tried to contact you during those years?' Lexy said.

'No,' the woman said, *'never.'* But then she hesitated again. *'Except there were phone calls. Every year, around the time of my birthday.'*

'Sorry, phone calls?' Lexy said, surprised. 'What phone calls?'

'Calls from an unknown number,' Rebecca said. *'But when I answered, there was no-one there.'* She paused. *'I thought it*

was someone playing a cruel trick on me. And I know this isn't logical, but I even thought it might have been the ghost of my mum.'

'But who would want to play such a trick on you?' Lexy asked.

The woman gave a short laugh. *'No-one, obviously. But that's just the way my mind works. I miss my mum so much, and your mind just plays these horrible tricks on you. It's only in the last twelve months I've began to feel better, and now this has happened. Now I just don't know how I'm going to go on.'*

'Look, I'm sure we can get a family liaison officer to come and see you and I'm sure they can point you in the direction of local services that can support you at this very difficult time,' Frank said, knowing only too well that he was winging it. He paused. 'Rebecca, you've been very helpful but I think that's enough for today. It's a very perplexing situation and we think it's going to change a lot as it develops and we find out more. We'll probably have plenty more questions for you over the coming days and weeks, but for now, we'll leave you in peace.'

'Yes, thank you,' Lexy added, then said gently, 'Will you be coming back to Scotland for the funeral? I expect you will be.'

'I don't know, I expect so,' she said. *'I need to talk to David I suppose. But it's all very raw and unreal at the moment. I'll need a few days to work it all through before I can make any plans. But I don't really like to leave my house,'* she added.

'I'm happy here with my painting. That's all I really want to do. It's what keeps me alive.'

'I can understand that,' Frank said, not sure that he did. 'Anyway, Rebecca, I think we're about done now. We'll arrange for the local police to come round and take a saliva sample from you and then we'll do the DNA check and let you know the result right away. Will that be okay?'

'Yes, that would be very good,' she said firmly. *'I would very much like to know for certain please.'*

'That's great, we'll get that organised as soon as possible,' Frank said in a kindly tone. 'So as I said, I think that's enough for today. Although we've just got one last routine question if I may?'

'Sure,' she said. *'Go ahead.'*

'Can you confirm you weren't back in the UK and in the vicinity of Loch Fyne between the fifth and the fifteenth of November? Just routine as I said.'

Her answer came instantly. *'No I wasn't. I rarely leave Australia and I don't leave my house very often.'*

'Okay, thanks for that Rebecca,' Frank said, 'and thank you again for your time, and goodbye.'

After the call, they were silent for a good thirty seconds or more, then Lexy said, 'Poor woman, her head must be all over the place. It's like she is having to get over the death of her mother all over again, isn't it?'

He nodded. 'Aye, it's horrible for her, no doubting that. And I don't know if you agree, but she seemed a bit of a cold fish, didn't you think? A little bit odd too perhaps?'

Lexy nodded. 'Yes, perhaps. But maybe that was just her way of coping with the situation.'

'She certainly seems quite a solitary woman, but then again, I think a lot of artists are like that. But what about those phone calls she talked about? That's bloody weird, isn't it?'

'Spooky,' Lexy said. 'But whoever it was, it wasn't the ghost of her mother. I don't think there's such a thing as ghosts.'

'It might have been her real mother,' Frank said. 'But even that sounds ridiculously far-fetched.'

'Are you putting Rebecca down as a possible suspect sir?'

He shrugged. 'We can't completely scratch her off our list I suppose. Although to be fair, I think she would come pretty near the bottom of mine, based on opportunity if nothing else. Because it's hard to chuck someone in a loch when you're ten thousand miles away.'

'I suppose we need to check that though, don't we?' Lexy said. 'That she actually *was* in Australia at the time the body was disposed of? Because it only takes twenty-four hours to get here, even if it is a long way away.'

He nodded again. 'You're right Lexy. Anyway, that's us done the initial formalities I suppose. Now we need to round up Andy McColl and get this investigation really cooking with gas.'

Chapter 15

When they had all worked in London, the Thursday evening after-work get-together at the Old King's Head had been an immovable ritual, but since the move to Scotland, with she and Frank having little Isobel and Jimmy now living in Braemar, the event had fallen by the wayside, though more through lack of opportunity than by any grand design. The fact was, Maggie really missed these get-togethers, but now a one-off opportunity had arisen to get the band back together again, to employ the over-used cliché. Ronnie French was back in Glasgow to interview an administrator at the big Queen Elizabeth hospital, and Jimmy had popped down to the city with his business partner Stew Edwards for a meeting with a potential client. Accordingly, they had gathered – Stew excepted - at the Horseshoe Bar on Great Western Road for a quick drink before she had to rush back home to relieve the nanny and get Isobel ready for her bath.

'Hey Ronnie, you can get them in,' Frank was bellowing above the noisy chatter in the bar. 'You've got a wee daily allowance to spend on your trip, so you might as well spend it on your best pals.'

'Right you are guv,' French laughed. 'But remember, I only get twenty-five quid a day.'

'Maybe I should get my own,' Jimmy said. 'I wouldn't want to be a burden on the public purse, and I don't want my own brother getting done for corruption either.'

'No worries on that score, you can get the next round,' his brother said.

As she waited for her drink, Maggie did a quick headcount. Excluding herself, present were Frank, Jimmy, Lori Logan, DC Lexy McDonald, and DC Ronnie French – five in all. And the astonishing fact was that four years earlier, she hadn't known a single one of these people, and now they numbered an adored husband, a much-loved brother-in-law and three brilliant friends. Someone had once written *from the depths of despair, hope can rise like a phoenix,* and here in this cosy Glasgow pub was surely the living proof. As ever, the conversation was lively, and as ever, it soon strayed into work.

'We've got a person of interest up in Braemar,' she heard Frank tell his brother. 'A guy by the name of Willie Armitage. You don't happen to know the fella, do you?'

Jimmy nodded. 'Aye, I do actually. He's an older guy, quiet chap in his fifties I'd say. He's set himself up as a mountain guide, takes wee groups of walkers along the Lairig Ghru. You can usually find him propping up the bar at Ferguson's place when he's not up on the mountain.'

'Have you spoken to him before?' Frank asked.

'Exchanged a few words in the pub, that's all. Why?'

'I'm guessing then that he won't have told you about the tragedy he was involved in? Ten years ago it was. On Loch Fyne. Where we all were two weeks ago on our wee holiday.'

'No way,' Jimmy said, open-mouthed. 'Willie's your boat guy, is he?'

Frank nodded. 'He is, would you believe.' He paused for a moment. 'The thing is, my cold case isn't really totally official, at least not yet. So I was wondering if you might be able to have a quiet wee word with Mr Armitage about what happened back then? What me and Ronnie are really interested in is why he wasn't there to check out the dinghy before it set out on the loch with these three guys on board. The *real* reason I mean, not the bullshit he gave my original investigation.'

Jimmy raised a quizzical eyebrow and looked at Maggie. 'What do you think boss? Can we do a bit of freelancing for this very senior police officer? In the public interest and all that?'

She laughed. 'It depends if my darling DCI Stewart is able to make his very senior forensic genius available to us for a few hours in return.'

Frank grinned. 'Might be able to do that, but you know what Eleanor's like, she's a law unto herself. On paper, she works for me but it still feels as if I have to go down on bended knees if I want her to do something for me.'

'She just enjoys winding you up,' Maggie said, laughing. 'She's a pussy-cat in *my* hands. And Lori and I only want to ask her one question, and then, depending on the answer, we might need her for an hour or two at the most, no more than that. That's right Lori, isn't it?'

Her assistant, who had been leaning against the bar and chatting amiably with Lexy, looked over. 'Aye, that's right boss. We just need to know exactly what Paul Davie was doing on those last two days.'

The need for Eleanor Campbell's services had emerged as a result of a brainstorm Maggie and Lori had conducted following their astonishing meeting with Jack Easton and Bill Warren at Torridon Systems. The revelation that Paul Davie might have been the victim of a honeytrap scam, organised by his alleged lover Maya Mishra, had upset all their previous theories, but it hadn't altered the fact that Davie's last movements were a subject of huge uncertainty. That his phone had been at Torridon on both the final day of his employment and the day after that was not open to dispute. But what they had noticed from their Google location searches was that the phone had seemingly not moved for nearly twenty-four hours of the crucial period. Further research had revealed that this might have been a limitation of that search technology, its precision apparently being no more than fifty metres or so in all directions. The question that Lori had raised in their brainstorm was, could the phone's movements be tracked in any finer detail? Specifically, what they wanted to know was, had Davie been sitting at his cubicle on both the day he left *and* the day afterwards? Was what he'd been looking for so important that he had somehow felt compelled to sneak back into the office the day after he was supposed to have left?

Frank gave a nod that signified his agreement to the proposal. 'I suppose we could do a wee swap. I get a few hours of Jimmy so that me and Ronnie don't have to go trekking up to Braemar, and you get a few hours of Eleanor in return. And if it's to do with the Paul Davie affair, well that's an official missing persons enquiry, so it's all good.'

'It's a deal then,' Maggie said. 'We'll give her a call first thing in the morning. Oh, and maybe I should do the talking?' she added, giving a wry grin.

***

Since having her little baby Lulu, Eleanor had been easing herself back to work, attending the Maida Vale labs of the Met's forensic services department on two days of the week and working a third from home. It turned out that today was one of those working-from-home days, which Maggie hoped would find the forensic officer in a more amiable mood, given her day would not have started with a long and frustrating commute to West London. Mind you, as Frank took delight in pointing out, with Eleanor, amiable was a strictly relative term.

'Hi Maggie,' Eleanor said, picking up on the second ring. *'Is Frank with you?'* she added, the tone not noticeably souring on the mention of his name, which was a good thing, if unusual.

'No no, he's not,' Maggie replied cheerfully. 'Well, at least not in the room with me. I'm at home and he's just pottering around somewhere, getting ready to head to the police station.' She paused. 'What it is Eleanor, Bainbridge Associates is working on the Paul Davie missing person case on behalf of his partner Ruth, and we – that's me and Lori by the way – we wanted to ask you if there was a way of more accurately pinpointing the location of a mobile phone in a building? We've used Google location tracking but I've read it isn't hugely accurate.'

'Do you want to track in like real-time or historically?' the forensic officer asked.

'Sorry, I'm not sure I understand the question,' Maggie said.

'What I mean is, do you want to know where the phone is, or where it was?' Eleanor clarified.

'Ah, I see. We want to know where it *was,* and this would be about eight or nine weeks ago.'

'That's a pity,' Eleanor said. *'Because locating where it is can be more accurate because you can use wi-fi, assuming it is connected to a wi-fi router, which it would be in an office. Locating where it was uses mobile phone mast cell triangulation, and that's not so accurate. That's only accurate to about twenty or thirty metres.'*

Maggie thought she knew the answer to her next question but she decided to ask it anyway. 'So would that cell triangulation thingy be accurate enough to locate a phone at a particular desk in an office building?'

'No way,' Eleanor replied firmly. There was a silence on the line, then she asked. *'How important is this case? Is it like a murder or terrorism or something?'*

Maggie hesitated. 'Not terrorism, but it *could* be a murder case, although we can't be sure at this stage. Why do you ask?'

'Because you can get way better accuracy if you use a fourth location point. That would probably be enough to locate someone at a desk or at least very close by.'

'And can you do that? What I mean is, can it be done?'

'Yeah,' Eleanor said. *'It can be done.'*

Maggie didn't immediately respond, expecting the forensic officer to elaborate. When it became clear that she wasn't going to, she asked, 'And Eleanor, how can that be done exactly? Is it something you personally can do, or is there some other clever technology involved?'

'Satellite tracking,' Eleanor replied. *'That's where the fourth location point comes from, from space. And the satellite's owned by GCHQ and they only release the data to the police when it's a matter of national security.'*

'Ah, I see,' Maggie said, disappointed. 'Paul Davie's disappearance certainly isn't a matter of national security.' She sighed. 'It's a shame. But thank you for giving it your consideration anyway.'

Out of the blue, Eleanor said, *'There might be another way. Some big-scale wi-fi systems keep a log file. For several months.'*

Maggie frowned. 'Sorry Eleanor, but it won't surprise you to hear that I don't understand. How would this help?'

'It's like mega-complicated,' Eleanor explained. *'In a big office you need like dozens of wi-fi boosters. And with that, triangulation is super-accurate and if the organisation keeps the log, you can track the location of each device connected to the network going back in time. And it works in 3-D too, if they have boosters on different levels. Which they will have, in a multi-storey building,'* she added confidently.

Maggie frowned. 'I'm still not sure I *totally* understand. How does 3=D help?'

'You can tell which floor a device is on. Which you need to be able to do, obviously.'

'That sounds amazing. So do we just ask the organisation if they can give us the log file, and you can do the rest from there?'

'It's like way more complicated than that,' Eleanor said. *'We would need a 3-D plan of their building and we would need to know the identity and location of each wi-fi booster. But yeah, if we have that and the logfile, we can like pinpoint the location of the phone you're interested in.'*

'That's brilliant Eleanor. And this is something you could do for us?'

'Yeah, I could. But it's not one hundred percent guaranteed, like if there are a lot of brick walls in the building for example you can still get blind spots.'

'I'm no architectural expert,' Maggie said. 'But it's a modern building and the layout is really airy and open-plan. I don't think I saw many walls at all when I visited it.'

'*That's good,*' the forensic officer said. *'But there is one more thing, The logs are normally only kept for a few weeks' maximum. You don't normally need to keep them longer than that.'*

Maggie nodded. 'Which means we need to act fast.'

Especially, she reflected, if these logs might reveal something that the management of Torridon Systems would rather keep to themselves.

Chapter 16

With the identity of the woman in the loch now formally confirmed as Alison Christie, and with the first interviews with her closest living relatives now completed, it was time to spread the wings of the investigation. The first step was to suck in as much new information as they could from as many sources as they could identify. Accordingly, DI Andy McColl was standing in front of the white board, pen in hand, poised to scribble any nuggets of inspiration his colleagues threw in his direction. At the top of the board a photograph of the victim had been attached, with her name and age written above in marker pen. Beneath that, two additional names had been written. Other than that, the board was blank.

'Right then Andy,' Frank said. 'So, we've got David Stirling and Rebecca Christie up there as our first possible, if unlikely, persons of interest, and we've had a wee chat with both of them.'

'We've got a photograph of Stirling, but we've not got one of Rebecca yet,' Lexy pointed out.

'You're right,' he said. 'I think I remember someone saying she's got a website for her landscape painting business, so there's bound to be a mugshot on that. Put that on your to-do list, will you Lexy?'

'Will do sir.'

'Good. So, let's see if we can come up with a few more names we can talk to. Andy, you were going to email the local Colorado police to see what they could share with us about Alison's original disappearance? Any luck with that?'

'Yes sir,' the DI nodded. 'They've sent me their incident report and I had a quick skim through it before this session. It identifies the last recorded person to see her, that's a Julia Gomez who was a ski-lift attendant the day Alison disappeared. I've got an email address for Julia, so I'll drop her a message once we're done here, see what she remembers, if anything.'

'Okay, makes sense,' Frank said. 'You'd better scribble her name up on the board, just for completeness.' He paused. 'Now, the last person to see her alive and who actually knew her was her colleague at Torridon Systems, wasn't it? That would have been at that meeting with the US company in New York somewhere.'

'That's right, his name's Jack Easton,' Lexy said. 'Although I guess the people from the American company would have been there as well. Hudson Medical Staffing, that was their name.'

Frank nodded. 'Funnily enough, that missing person guy we've got on the books worked at Torridon Systems and my wife's detective agency has already interviewed Easton in connection with that matter. Anyway Andy, we'd better get his name on the board. Scribble Jack Easton on it, will you?'

Andy held the pen aloft and smiled at his boss. 'On it sir.'

'And Lexy, you'll follow up with these Hudson folks in the States?'

She gave him a wry look. 'Yep sir, on my ever-growing list.'

Frank laughed. 'You're beginning to sound like Ronnie, perish the thought. Actually, leave that one with Andy, because you're down to chase up the Border Force guys, aren't you?'

She nodded. 'I've actually already spoken to them, yesterday afternoon. I was going to bring it up at the end of this meeting. Once we'd got all our persons of interest on the board.'

'You might as well tell us now,' he said.

'Sure. So, I talked to the manager of Oban airport and she told me the procedure when they have arrivals from abroad, which by the way, they only have a couple of times a month, if that. First of all, the flight-plan has to be filed with them forty-eight hours in advance, so that they can make sure they have a landing slot available. At the same time, they contact Revenue & Customs and the Border Force so they can send representatives to the airport to process the flight when it lands.'

'And this all happened for Alison Christie's flight?' Frank asked.

Lexy nodded. 'Yes, pretty much. They didn't send a Revenue & Customs agent, which apparently is often the case because they only do random spot checks, just like they do at the big airports. But they did send a Border Force agent, who checked Alison's passport, then afterwards updated the immigration database to record her arrival into the country.'

'And you spoke to this Border Force guy, did you? Because we wondered why Alison's passport hadn't been cancelled. Is this something these mobile border officials can do? Check if it's still valid I mean?'

'Yep, I did speak to him, and yes, apparently, they can. They have an app on their phones where they can look up the passport number and yes, they can check if it's still valid. And it was.'

'But she'd been declared dead,' Frank said, puzzled.

'But remember, that was in America, under that specific peril law of theirs,' Lexy said. 'And there's no automatic link between their systems and ours. Apparently, it's up to the relatives to have a passport cancelled and it seems that neither David Stirling nor her daughter did that.'

'That's a big loophole in the system,' Andy McColl observed.

'I suppose,' Lexy said, 'although I guess there are thousands of passports stuck in drawers all over the country that won't be getting used again because their owner is dead and the relatives hadn't sent it back. Most people wouldn't know you have to do that.'

'True,' Frank said. 'Well at least we know she was let into the country properly. So where did she go after she arrived, that's the question? We know that somehow, she got to the Loch Fyne area, which is what, an hour or two's drive from Oban? The question is, how did she get there, and where was she staying, and who was she staying with? Or did she stay in Oban for a while? We need to find that out, as a priority.'

Lexy laughed. 'On my list sir.' Then she paused, obviously thinking about something. 'She's got a house still, hasn't she? Or at least her daughter has, the one in the Highlands that Rebecca inherited from her mum. She could have gone there I suppose. Although it must be at least a hundred miles away I guess.'

'Everywhere's a hundred miles away from Oban,' Frank said. 'But that's a good shout. Maybe I'll get Jimmy to check it out for us, see if there's been any sign of recent visitors. Good. Anyway, let's push on.' He paused then said, 'Who was the guy that the daughter mentioned, the software guy who may or may not have been in a relationship with Alison at one time?'

'That was Richie Whitmore,' Lexy supplied. 'He wrote the original Nurses Direct software, according to Rebecca. And he was a minor shareholder in Torridon Systems too.'

Frank nodded. 'Aye, wasn't he the guy who has the mental health problems and now lives in a care home somewhere? Stick his name on the board Andy, and speak to Patel to see if he knows where this home is.'

'I think it's in Helensburgh sir,' Lexy said. 'And he was sectioned, remember, so I suspect it might be a secure home and he might only be allowed out under supervision, if at all.'

'Fair point Lexy,' he conceded, 'but we'd better have him on the board anyway. Anybody else we should be looking at?'

'Rebecca must have a father,' Lexy said. 'And I think Patel's article suggested that in the past, a couple of men had come forward claiming to be that person. I guess we need to follow up on them.' She smiled at Frank as she said it. 'And before you ask sir...'

'Excellent DC McDonald, it's on your list,' Frank grinned.

Lexy frowned. 'What I was going to say was, I'm not sure I've got the capacity to add that one to my list. And I'm not sure if it's likely to be relevant to our case anyway. Rebecca Christie is what, twenty-five or twenty-six? She was born quite a long time ago, that's what I'm saying, and the dad would probably have been another one of the kids that was in care with her mother. He might not even have known that Alison had got pregnant.'

'All of that is true,' Frank conceded. 'But you know what they say about revenge being a dish served cold. Maybe this guy has harboured resentment for all these years.' He hesitated. 'But aye, I admit it's probably one of our least likely scenarios, so maybe I'll ask Bainbridge Associates if they can spend a few hours looking into this for us. We've got a few quid in the sub-contract budget so we can afford it.'

'That would be good sir,' Lexy said, sounding grateful.

Frank smiled. 'No problem. So Andy, you'd better draw a wee blank square on our board and write *unknown father* underneath it.' He took a step back and admired the rapidly-filling-up board. 'Pretty good work you two, and more to the point, we've now got something to show Charlie Maxwell the next time he swings by. It'll mean when the Super's being grilled on the evening news, he can say we're pursuing a number of lines of enquiry without having to lie through his teeth. So now, I just need Frenchie's updates from yesterday's hospital visit and from the beautiful shores of Loch Fyne and we'll be ready to rock and roll.'

***

It was evident that French was outside and that the wind was gusting strongly, making Frank's call with the former detective constable something of a challenge.

'I'm only getting every second word Ronnie,' he said, covering one ear and shouting into his phone, as if that would make the conversation easier.

'Yeah, sorry guv,' his colleague shouted back. *'It's blowing a bleeding gale over here today. It's just as well I've still got me own hair or my wig would be half-way to Inveraray by now. But hang on, I've just spotted a bus-shelter across the road. Just give us a second and I'll take cover in there.'* Half a minute later, French was back on the line. *'Ah, that's better guv,'* he said. *'Listen, something interesting's turned up. Well, it might be interesting, put it that way.'*

'Oh aye, what's that?'

'What it is, there's a little development of luxury properties on the road south out of the village, right on the lochside, and I knocked on their doors earlier. I only found one resident in, and that was a lady called Mrs McKenzie, Meg she said her name was. There are four houses in the development but Meg said they're the only ones who live there all year round, the rest are all holiday homes. Anyway, to cut a long story short, she said that six or seven weeks ago her husband casually

mentioned he'd seen a couple of guys in a van on their shared driveway, and she said he had words with the guys to see what they were up to, because apparently no–one ever goes to this house next door other than the cleaners, who give it a quick dust once a month. She told me her husband had been quite exercised about the whole thing, but she said she wasn't really listening to him because all he ever talks about is golf. But she remembered he told her he'd noted the van's number plate.'

'Interesting right enough,' Frank said. 'And you got this number I'm assuming?'

'Afraid not guv. She said her husband didn't tell her what it was and she doesn't know where or if he wrote it down.'

Frank laughed. 'Brilliant. And what about *Mister* McKenzie. Is he not able to speak for himself or does Meg do all the talking for him?'

'He's away in Portugal on a golfing trip guv,' French said. *'But I told the woman to get in touch with her old man and for him to phone me as soon as he can. He's due back in a couple of days so I'll chase him up if he doesn't call me before then.'*

'Okay Ronnie, let me know as soon as you hear anything. So what about your meeting with the guy at the hospital. How did that go?'

'That was interesting too guv. The geezer's name is Jack Thompson, though you probably remembered that yourself.'

'I didn't, so thanks for that.'

'Nice guy,' French continued, *'but he says he still gets nightmares about what happened back then.'*

Frank nodded. 'You would do if you'd seen two mates drowning right in front of you and you couldn't do anything to save them.'

'Yeah guv, he obviously still feels really sore about that. They'd all been messing about and it just happened in a second. He says they just disappeared over the side and when he looked for them, they'd already gone under. He said he knows he should have gone in after them but he bottled it. Besides which, he said he was pissed out of his mind. They all were, that's what he says. That's why it took him so long to ring for help, or so he says.'

'He'd have been in shock, and he probably couldn't have done anything anyway. That water's always bloody freezing and you wouldn't last five minutes in it.'

'You're probably right guv,' French said. *'Anyway, obviously I asked him about the events leading up to the incident and particularly about the big piss-up in the bar before they set off.'*

'One of their mates turned up and it was this mate's birthday, and he was buying all the drinks. That's the gist of it, isn't it?'

'Correct guv. The guy was apparently a mate of Jaz Davie, someone who worked in the same IT department as him at the hospital. A bit of a weird guy too, according to Thompson.'

'Weird? What does that mean when it's at home?'

'Don't know guv. Thompson just said the guy was a bit short of conversation.'

'But it evidently didn't stop them taking drinks off the guy,' Frank said acerbically. 'So did your Jack Thompson not know this weird guy too? Because they all worked at the same hospital, didn't they?'

'Only by sight. He says he'd seen him around the place but he didn't know him to talk to. Remember, the hospital is bloody huge so you can well understand that. Anyway, the guy had arranged to meet his pal Jaz at the bar and he turned up as scheduled and started buying them all drinks. His story was he'd come down to do a bit of fishing, but knowing that Jaz was on a course in the same vicinity, he decided to have a few beers with his mate first.'

'Okay,' Frank said. 'This guy looks up his pal Jaz and proceeds to get him and his two boat-mates drunk out of their heads. That's what happened, was it?'

'That's about the gist of it. Thompson says he knew they probably shouldn't have been drinking so much before they took the boat out, but they were just young lads having a laugh. Stupid, but that's what you do at that age, isn't it? Especially when someone's supplying you with drinks for free.'

'You're right,' Frank conceded. 'But can we cut to the chase now? Because what I want to know is if you've got a name for Jaz Davie's super-generous drinking buddy?'

French hesitated for a moment. *'Didn't I say guv? Unfortunately, Thompson couldn't remember the guy's name.'*

'What?' Frank said incredulously. 'He was drinking on this guy's tab all day and yet he can't remember his bloody name?'

'That's what he says and I believe him. Remember, the geezer was Jaz Davie's mate, not Thompson's, and it was ten years ago.' There was a pause, then French continued, *'But listen guv, not all is lost. At least we know the mysterious fourth guy used to work in the same IT department as Jaz, at the hospital. I'll get on to their HR department and get some names. And you never know, he might still work there.'*

'Aye, you're right,' Frank conceded. 'Get onto that bloody hospital as soon as you can because this case is going nowhere until we identify our missing man.'

It wasn't the answer he'd been hoping for, but at least it was progress.

Chapter 17

Bainbridge Associates' Paul Davie case had slipped into somewhat of a holding pattern, whilst they awaited the outcome of the investigation into his last known movements, that probe itself being dependent on two separate strands of activity. Firstly, it had to be established whether Torridon Systems retained the logs from their office-wide wi-fi network, and if they did, whether they would be willing to hand them over to the police and also to allow them to map the layout of the building too. Secondly, Eleanor Campbell had to deploy her technical wizardry on that data and as she had made plain, a positive outcome from that exercise was by no means a foregone conclusion. With regard to the first point, it was going to be interesting to see how Torridon reacted to the request for the logs, a request that was going to be made by Frank when he shortly interviewed Jack Easton in connection with the Alison Christie murder. Despite the plausibility of the honeytrap theory propounded by the company's management, there was something in Maggie's gut that caused her not to trust that explanation. She had become convinced that Davie had been looking for something, something that Torridon would very much prefer not to be found, and if they were resistant to the police requests, then that would provide evidence that her hunch was correct, even if that evidence was purely circumstantial. Whatever the case, there was nothing that could be done about it for the present. But that didn't leave them at a complete loss, because earlier that day, Donnie from the Byres Road computer shop had texted Lori to say he'd managed to crack the password of the USB data stick that

Ruth Davie had found in the pocket of her partner's cycling jacket. Accordingly, Maggie and Lori were making their way up the road to his premises, the pavement busy as usual with students and shoppers.

'I'm really looking forward to meeting him,' Maggie said, grinning at her friend and colleague. 'And please don't say anything, because I've got a picture of Donnie in my mind and I want to see how wrong I am when I meet him face-to-face.'

'Okay, so tell me what you imagine,' Lori said. 'And I promise, I won't tell you whether you're warm or cold.'

She nodded. 'Okay. So, I think he's rather good-looking and quite young, maybe thirty or thereabouts. And he's got a mop of blonde hair which is pretty unruly, and he's got a beard, a gingery full beard. A hipster beard, I think that's what they call it. And he's quite tall, about five-foot ten, and skinny too. And he'll be wearing a black T-shirt with the name of a band that I've never heard of on it.' She paused. 'How am I'm doing so far?'

Lori's face adopted an inscrutable expression. 'I'm not saying. You'll have to wait until you get there.'

'Okay. And initially I thought he might be a bit grumpy and quirky like Eleanor, you know, because I imagine all computer geeks are like that. But then I changed my mind, because I didn't think you would like him as much as you do if he was like that. Now I think that he's probably quite funny and very easy-going.'

'Who says I like him so much?' Lori protested.

Maggie laughed. 'Your face does. Every time you mention his name.'

'Is it that obvious?' her colleague asked wistfully. 'But yeah, he is dead nice. And dead clever too.'

'Which is a winning combination. Anyway, we're here. Lead the way, please.'

Lori pushed open the door and they walked into the shop. Behind a broad counter, a man wearing a head-mounted magnifier was hovering a soldering iron over a large printed circuit board. Detecting their arrival, he carefully replaced the iron on its stand and pushed the magnifier up onto his forehead.

'Lori,' he said, beaming a huge smile. 'Great to see you again. And you must be Maggie. Forgive me if we don't shake hands but I'm totally covered in that smelly contact cleaner stuff. Acetate, I think it is. I know I should wear gloves but it's not easy to aim the soldering iron with them on. Not enough precision.'

'It looks fiendishly complicated to me,' she said, nodding in the direction of the circuit board.

'It is, believe me,' Donnie said with a wry smile. 'One slip and the whole shebang goes boom. I sometimes feel I'm a bit like a dentist, except I'm working inside computers instead of mouths.'

Maggie grinned. 'I hope you don't charge as much. My last visit to the dentist nearly melted my credit card.'

He laughed. 'I don't, you'll be pleased to hear. Anyway, let me wipe my hands and I'll bring you up to speed with what I've found out.'

As he reached for a cloth, Maggie took a discreet opportunity to compare the real live Donnie with how she had imagined him. He was definitely good-looking and around thirty, as she had suspected, but he was dark rather than fair, and of medium height and broad-shouldered rather than tall and thin. He did have a beard, but this was a neatly-trimmed goatee rather than the hillbilly-style one she had imagined. Instead of a scruffy T-shirt, he wore a light blue short-sleeved shirt with a buttoned-down collar, with the initials DCS embroidered on a breast pocket, presumably for Donnie's Computer Services. But all things considered, she thought, her pre-assessment hadn't been totally wide of the mark, perhaps a six or even a seven out of ten if she was being generous to herself.

Donnie reached over to a row of shelves behind him and retrieved a laptop, which he placed on the counter then proceeded to boot up. 'Remember I worked out the PIN code for this from the wear and tear on the keypad?' he said. 'That PIN code was 121253, which made me think it might have been Jaz Davie's mother's birthday, because she would have been born around that time, I think. So I figured that might be the kind of password format that the Davie brothers might have favoured. Family birthdays I mean. Lots of people do that, because it's easy to remember.'

'You're not saying the USB stick had the same password, are you?' Maggie asked.

Donnie shook his head. 'Not quite. But it was a variation on that theme. A simple variation, as it happens. Here, let me show you.' He took the USB stick from his pocket and inserted it into the computer. Immediately, a dialogue box popped up, the same one they had seen earlier, when they had attempted to interrogate the stick themselves. *Enter password to access file system.*

'It's 352121,' he said, grinning as he punched the number on the keyboard. 'The same code, but backwards. Not exactly hard to crack I'm afraid. Thankfully,' he added.

'But that's fantastic,' Maggie beamed. 'So that's us into the laptop *and* the USB stick too?'

'It is,' he nodded.

'But what's it telling us?' Lori asked. 'Have you had a chance to take a look?'

'I took a look, yes. The first thing to say is that the laptop is set up as a software development environment. It's not a personal computer, because there's no photos or games or anything like that on it. I know this because it's got a web server installed and a scripting language interpreter and a JavaScript debugger. And the only files I can find are program files. Computer code in other words. This computer's set up to write software.'

Maggie laughed. 'You're beginning to sound like a certain forensic officer Lori and I both know. That's a complement by the way.' *Sort of*, she thought, but didn't say it. 'And what about the USB stick? What's on that?'

Donnie shrugged. 'Same kind of stuff. Computer code mainly. There's a couple of dozen code files that have obviously been cut and pasted from somewhere. And there are some interesting things in those files.'

'It's *all* amazingly interesting,' Maggie said. 'Tell us more Donnie, please.'

'Okay, so when I was looking at some of these code files, I saw a lot of similarities between the stuff on the laptop and some of the code on the USB stick. There's some very clever SQL code on the laptop, with some hugely complicated data joins and filters.' He paused and grinned. 'Apologies, I know this is all gobbledygook for the lay person. Let me just say I learned some of this stuff when I was at college and it was so frighteningly complicated, I decided I didn't want to go near it ever again.' He paused. 'Whoever wrote this code is a genius. It's brilliant, it really is.'

'Jaz Davie, do you think?' Maggie asked.

Donnie nodded. 'Must have been. And there's something else too.' He paused again. 'I ran a file comparison between some of the files on the laptop and those on the USB stick, and there's big swathes of code that are absolutely identical.' And then he laughed. 'Look, let me show you this.' He clicked on the mouse and opened a file. 'This is all back-end server and JavaScript code,' he said, pointing at the screen, 'and no, you don't need to understand what it is or what it's doing. But do you see this?' He placed his finger on an area of text encapsulated in a bold-type box, then laughed again. 'Can you read what it says? Because it's very much in English, not in code.'

Maggie studied the line of text then burst out laughing. *'WHATEVER YOU DO, DON'T F*CKING TOUCH A F*CKING LINE OF THIS CODE!'* she read out loud, barely able to contain her mirth.

'You often get that with long–established systems,' Donnie explained. 'Some developer has written some program logic years in the past, and nobody today has a clue what it does or how it does it. All the present custodians of the system know is that it works, so it's a case of *if it's not broke, don't try to fix it*. Some wag has inserted that comment to reinforce the point, big time.'

'That was the work that Paul Davie was doing,' Lori said suddenly, looking at Maggie. 'Do you remember Sarah at Torridon told us about it? About what they called their legacy project?'

'I do,' Maggie said. 'Paul was working on a project to replace some old code in the Nurses Direct system but then they decided to can the project because the old code was working okay and it wasn't a priority any more. That was almost Sarah's exact words I think.' She paused for a moment, then said. 'Donnie, I don't know if this is even a sensible question, but do you have any idea what this program actually *does*?'

He shrugged. 'Not exactly, not from reading the raw code. But if I dug out some of my old text books, I might be able to figure out how to get it up and running on Jaz's machine. I think everything's already installed to do that, although it'll probably take a lot of cocking about, if you'll forgive me talking technical.'

Maggie laughed. 'No, we absolutely love technical talk.' She paused. 'Listen Donnie, I've just had an idea. Why don't we treat you to lunch at the Bikini Barista down the road, and then maybe you could spend the afternoon cocking about on our behalf, which of course you can add to our account.' She gave her associate a conspiratorial look then added, 'And just so you know, I might have to slip out halfway through, but I'm sure you'll be fine with Lori.'

Chapter 18

It had been a while since Jimmy had been in Ferguson's Bar, such were the demands of having a new baby in the family, not that spending time with little Viggo was anything but the greatest of pleasures. Earlier that night, he and Frida had bathed the little boy as per their usual routine, a ritual which was becoming even more delightful now that their baby son was just about able to sit up on his own. He loved to splash, arms flaying into the water and sending up a torrent of spray that drenched his head, causing him first to giggle uncontrollably, then to hiccup for at least a minute or more. He loved his bath so much that he cried when his mummy lifted him out of the rapidly-cooling water and wrapped him in one of the huge fluffy towels reserved for the purpose. The tears were half-hearted though, almost instantly replaced by a gurgling smile as the baby caught his mother's eye. With a hint of sadness, Jimmy had begun to realise that these moments would soon be in the past, as their son became a toddler. But he consoled himself with the fact that he and Frida must have taken about a half-a-million photographs, recording seemingly every second of the little boy's life since the day he was born.

It was a Thursday, the place fairly quiet with no more than a dozen or so patrons seated at tables around the large lounge area, and a couple of men propping up the bar, nursing pints. One of whom he immediately recognised.

'Hey Willie, long time no see,' Jimmy said, sidling up to the bar and taking the stool alongside the man. 'Remember me, Jimmy Stewart? Me and Stew Edwards run the Lairig Ghru outward-bound school, and my girlfriend Frida's got the wee tearoom down the road. We've seen you in there a few times.'

'Aye, nice wee place,' Willie Armitage said, his eyes avoiding Jimmy's gaze. 'They do a lovely cheese scone.'

Jimmy grinned. 'Yeah, Frida bakes them herself and they're fantastic. Anyway, can I get you a drink? Yours looks as if it's nearly done and I was just going to grab a pint myself.'

'I'll join you in a pint of heavy,' the man said, his voice betraying suspicion. 'But I'll just be having the one, mind.'

'That's what we all say,' Jimmy quipped. 'Funny how the willpower soon gives way once you've got a taste for it.' He raised a finger to attract the attention of the barman, then ordered two pints.

'How's business Willie?' he asked. 'Me and Stew are doing pretty well with the corporate stuff, but I think you work mainly as a personal mountain guide, is that right?'

'Aye, that's right,' Armitage said guardedly. 'Most folks know how dangerous it is on these hills if you don't know your way about. That's why they want a guide. But business is okay, aye.'

'That's good to know,' Jimmy said, taking a sip from his pint. 'And at least your clients *want* to be up on the mountain. Most of our guys are on their organisation's team-building and leadership programs and they've been more or less given a three-line whip to take part. They'd rather still be tucked up in their cosy offices than freezing their balls off on

Cairngorm.' He hesitated and took another sip of his drink. 'Mind you, I heard you used to do a bit of the corporate stuff yourself Willie, is that right? Back in the day?'

He could see the man tense up. 'What have you heard?' Armitage said, suddenly aggressive. 'Because whatever it is, it's all bollocks, all of it. Total shite, every single word.'

Jimmy gave him a questioning look, then said quietly, 'Everybody here knows all about it Willie. Two young lads died on that loch that day and you were supposed to have been in charge. A terrible tragedy right enough, but people talk, don't they? You can't stop them doing that. It must be a hard thing to live with.'

Armitage spat out his response. 'They were pissed out of their bloody heads, these lads. What was I supposed to do about that? How was that my fault, I ask you? If they were bloody stupid enough to take that boat out on the loch, in the state they were in?'

It was your fault because you were supposed to have been in charge of safety was the obvious answer, but Jimmy was savvy enough to know that it wouldn't exactly get Armitage on his side if he was to say it. Instead, he said, 'Aye, bloody stupid, weren't they? But I say again, two lads died as a result of that stupidity.'

'The fiscal's enquiry ruled it was an accident,' Armitage said. 'And it was ten years ago, for God's sake. It's ancient history now.'

Jimmy nodded. 'You're right. Except for the fact that some new information has emerged in the last few weeks. Information that's now in the hands of the police. So there's going to be a new investigation.'

He could see the colour drain from the man's face. 'They can't do that, can they? Not when it was all done and dusted all those years ago.'

'They can, I'm afraid,' Jimmy sighed. 'The thing is, the cop who was in charge of the investigation back then has always regretted he didn't do a more thorough job, and now they've put him back on the re-opened case. And he's a determined bugger when he gets his teeth into something. I know him well you see, and I know he's determined to get to the truth this time.'

'What truth?' Armitage said bitterly. 'We already know the truth, that was what the bloody enquiry was all about. And what the hell's it got to do with you anyway?' he added.

'Didn't I say? I work part-time for a detective agency and the police have asked us to help out on the case. And because I live up here in Braemar it made sense for me to do the interview with you.'

'What do you mean, interview? You're not allowed to just spring that on me. You've got me talking under false pretences.'

Jimmy gave an apologetic smile. 'Yeah, you're right Willie, a bad choice of word on my part. It's not an interview. We're just having a wee friendly chat, off the record. That's all it is.'

'So you say,' the man said, then took a gulp from his pint. 'You know what, I want a lawyer before I say anything else,'

'What, in Ferguson's bar?' Jimmy said, laughing. 'Where are you going to get one of them in here on a Thursday night? Look, we're just trying to find out what really happened back then. Because of the new information we've got. You'd want that too, wouldn't you? For the sake of the families if nothing else.'

Armitage gave him a sharp look, ignoring the question. 'So what new information is this?' he said guardedly.

'Turns out there was a guy in that bar in Loch Fyne, getting these three boys blind drunk. *Deliberately* getting them drunk we think. Did you know about that Willie?'

The man shrugged. 'No, why should I?'

'The reason I asked is that the police are working on a theory that this mystery guy deliberately got these lads drunk so they would be a dangerous liability if they took a boat onto the loch, whilst at the same time it was arranged for you to be absent without leave when you should have been making sure they were safe.' Jimmy paused for a moment to let his words sink in then said, 'From the police point of view, it looks very much like there might have been a conspiracy at work. You can see that, can't you? And I wouldn't even like to guess what the charges might be. Conspiracy, manslaughter? In fact, I wouldn't even rule out murder.'

'I just forgot about it,' Armitage blurted out. 'I'd been on the piss the night before and I slept in and then I got caught in traffic.'

Jimmy laughed. 'Traffic? On Loch Fyne? They only get about a couple of dozen cars a day up there. If there's a traffic jam it makes the national news for a week.' He paused for a moment then said. 'What were you really doing that day Willie? It must have been something bloody important. Or did someone pay you to be late? Is that what happened?'

'No.' The man spat out the word. 'No-one paid me and I didn't know this was going to happen, honest I didn't.'

'So where were you?' Jimmy persisted. 'What were you doing when you should have been at that wee jetty?'

Armitage stared at the floor silently. Then eventually he said, 'I was with a bird.'

Jimmy gave him a questioning look. 'What, as in, shagging a bird? When you should have been doing your job?'

Armitage bridled. 'Aye, it's all right for guys like you to laugh, but look at me. I'm not bloody Brad Pitt, am I? And she was bloody gorgeous, and it's not every day you get a chance like that, is it? At least, not for me it isn't. You'd have done the same, believe me.'

'You think so?' Jimmy said sceptically. 'And who was this temptress? Someone you just picked up in a bar when you were on the piss the night before?'

He nodded. 'Aye, that's what happened, more or less.'

'And this *bird*,' Jimmy continued, his tone making his distaste of the word plain. 'Did she have a name.'

'Anne. Her name was Anne.'

'Anne what?'

'Just Anne. I didn't ask any questions. And I was just Willie to her.'

Jimmy gave a wry smile. 'A proper wee romance then. And you didn't know who this woman was, before you struck lucky in the bar? She was just some random girl who happened to be out for a drink that night and took an unaccountable fancy to you?'

Armitage shuffled uncomfortably. 'She was on the course. One of the participants.'

'Oh dear, that's not a good look for you, is it Willie? So, did she sleep with you just so she could get a better mark in her assessment? Because forgive me, but that sounds highly improbable.'

The man stared at the floor in silence, his face a mask of misery. Finally, he took a swig of his drink then said. 'Look, I need to talk to a lawyer, and I'm not saying another bloody word until I do.' He paused again. 'But I swear to you, I didn't know anything about the other guy in the bar or that he was trying to get those lads pissed. I swear, I didn't know. Honest.'

Jimmy gave him an appraising look, then said, 'You know what Willie, I think I might just believe you. So yes, you go and get that legal advice, and then you come back to me with the complete truth of what happened that day, not this half-arsed bollocks you're spinning me. Okay?' He leant over so that his face was no more than twelve inches from Armitage's. 'Because you know what I think? I think you were just really stupid rather than criminal that day. In fact, I think you might have been a victim too, in which case you've got nothing to fear from this investigation. But that depends entirely on you telling the truth, the whole truth, and nothing but the truth.' He paused and smiled. 'And as soon as you're ready to tell that truth, well, you know where to find me.' He picked up his beer, drained it then stood up. 'Right Willie, I'm away now. And don't forget, I'll be expecting to hear from you in the next couple of days. Make sure you don't leave it any longer or we'll be having another wee chat.'

At that, he slammed his glass down on the bar and headed for the exit.

Chapter 19

It was obvious that Jack Easton should be their next formal interview in the Alison Christie case, since he had been for many years her closest work colleague and also the last person from the company to see the businesswoman alive. Frank had already been appraised of the outcome of the meeting that Maggie and Lori had had with Easton a few days earlier in conjunction with the disappearance of Paul Davie, which had been useful preparation for this morning's interview. At that earlier meeting, Easton had claimed that his relationship with Christie had been purely professional, and that they hadn't even been friends. The veracity of that claim was something Frank would be exploring in the upcoming interview, which he would be conducting in the company of the excellent DC Lexy McDonald. But earlier that morning, there had been a significant development, one which the pair were discussing as they sat in Torridon Systems' reception area waiting to be escorted to the meeting room.

'It turns out Alison was caught on CCTV a couple of times at Oban airport,' Lexy was explaining, 'and the good news is, we got a capture of the car that picked her up outside.'

'She got picked up, did she?' Frank said. 'And did we get a registration number?'

She nodded. 'Yep, we did. It was a black Audi A6, registration number AN72 URO. I'll look it up on the DVLA database when we're finished here and find out who owns it.'

'Great stuff. And what about the number plate recognition cameras? Has it turned up on any of them? Because there's a ton of them, all the way back to Glasgow.'

'That's the interesting thing sir. I did a quick search of the APNR system and it never turned up anywhere. Which makes me think she must have stayed in Oban or surroundings. Which is perfectly plausible of course.'

He nodded. 'I suppose we can get the local cops to check out the hotels and bed-and-breakfasts to see if she stayed in any of them.'

Lexy laughed. 'I don't think Alison Christie was a bed-and-breakfast sort of woman. I'd say we start at the five-star end of the market.'

'Is there such a place in Oban?' he grinned. 'Anyway, maybe I'll ask Ronnie to scoot over there and check them out. He'll be delighted.'

Their conversation was curtailed by the appearance of Jack Easton's PA in the reception area. She smiled warmly and said, 'Hello I'm Margaret. We'll just get your passes and then we'll be all set. Follow me please.'

Jack Easton was sitting at the large table that filled most of his spacious office. He stood up and held out a hand in greeting.

'Welcome to Torridon Systems,' he said, smiling. 'Please take a seat. Margaret will get us some coffee, or tea if you would prefer.'

'Coffee would be great, and thanks for seeing us Mr Easton,' Frank said. 'I'm DCI Frank Stewart and this is DC Lexy McDonald. As we said on the phone, we're here principally to talk about the murder of Alison Christie, but we also want to have a quick word about a missing persons enquiry we're working on.' He paused for a second. 'That's the Paul Davie matter. And I should just say that I know you had a visit from Bainbridge Associates recently in connection with his disappearance.'

Easton nodded. 'Yes, we had Miss Bainbridge herself here, with an assistant. We tried to help her as much as we could, obviously. And we are of course very concerned about him.'

'Aye, Miss Bainbridge told me,' Frank said. 'She's my wife by the way, just so you know.'

He arched an eyebrow. 'So detecting is a family business then? Very amusing. Anyway, I assume you'll want to start with Alison's case. Which, I should say, is just completely unbelievable in every possible way.'

'It is unbelievable,' Frank agreed. 'But the stark fact is, Alison's body was found in Loch Fyne just a couple of weeks ago and she'd been strangled before someone threw her in, hoping to make the body disappear, no doubt. Now it's our job to find out who did it and why.'

Easton nodded again. 'Of course. And I can assure you that myself and everyone in our company will support you in every way we can.'

'Good to know,' Frank said. 'Can I start by asking if you ever had any inkling of any of this? I mean, did you have an idea that Alison was planning a disappearing act and that she was going to fake her death?'

He shook his head. 'No, that never entered my mind for a moment. Why would anyone consider that? The whole idea is just plain nuts.'

'I suppose you probably knew her as well as anyone,' Frank continued. 'So I'm guessing you would have had some insight into her state of mind around the time she disappeared. How was she, would you say?'

He laughed. 'How was she? Driven, as usual. Or even more than usual, if that's possible. Positively off the scale.'

'This was to do with the takeover you were working on?' Lexy asked. 'She was excited about that?'

He nodded. 'That's right. Alison's grand design to take over the world.'

Frank gave him a sharp look. 'That sounds as if you didn't approve of this grand design, as you describe it.'

Easton shook his head. 'No no, that couldn't be further from the case. Alison had a wonderful vision for the company and she had the drive and ability and charisma to pull it off. I was simply the bean-counter. My job was just to keep score, if you will.'

'But after she died, there were reports that the company hadn't been doing as well as all the hype had suggested,'

Lexy said. 'Is that true, and if it was, how could it afford to take over the American company, which I think was much bigger than Torridon at the time?'

'The company was doing perfectly well,' Easton said. 'And the takeover was being backed by a consortium of banks, each of whom had great faith in Alison, and with good reason. She was a brilliant businesswoman.'

'But at the time, didn't the financial press report that it was going to load the company with debt and so it would be very risky?' Lexy asked. 'And that it would put massive strains on cash-flow?'

'That's the way business works,' Easton said, with just a hint of condescension. 'Yes, there would have been some pressures on the company's cash flow, but that's how those deals are structured. You take a measured risk in the expectation of great reward. And as I said, the banks had great faith in Alison's abilities.'

'And coming back to her state of mind, specifically on your trip to the States,' Frank said. 'How was she at that point in time?'

'Buzzing, absolutely buzzing,' he said. 'Hudson had arranged a private jet to fly us straight into Westchester, and we had a couple of glasses of champagne on route and she was fantastically enthusiastic about the deal. She never stopped talking about it the whole way.'

'And how did the meeting go?' Frank asked.

'Very well indeed. It was the first time we'd met face-to-face with their senior management and we got on very well. A price was set after a bit of haggling and it was agreed that the headquarters of the new combined firm would be in the US and that Alison would move there to head it up.'

'Hang on a minute,' Frank said, surprised. 'Are you saying that this was the first time you had actually met these guys?'

'Face to face, yes,' Easton said. 'We'd had plenty of phone calls of course, but in reality, most of the legwork in this sort of deal is done by the lawyers and accountants who work for the advising firms. Once the principle of the deal is agreed, then there's a ton of legal paperwork to be prepared, and that makes a ton of work for the advisors of both parties.'

'And a ton of fees as well I suppose,' Frank said.

Easton laughed. 'Yes, these guys don't come cheap and I should know, because I used to be one of those advisors myself, when I worked for Carter, Laidlaw and Fenimore. They're one of the so-called big six accounting practices, and their guys won't get out of bed for less than two grand a day.'

'You advised Alison when she was trying to raise the funding to set up Torridon Systems, didn't you?' Lexy said. 'And then you joined them,' she added. 'As the Chief Financial Officer.'

He nodded. 'That's right, I did. It's very common for the lead advisor to jump ship in this way, and in fact the lending banks encourage it. It's as if they have a voice on the inside, to keep a steady hand on the tiller and to keep an eye on their investment, but without constraining the entrepreneurial instincts of the founder too much.'

'And did you manage that?' Frank asked. 'To keep a steady hand on the tiller?'

'Pretty much. We always managed to meet our financial commitments, even as the company was growing.' He paused. 'Anyway, as to the deal with Hudson Staffing, it was all done and dusted after a long day. We all shook hands on the deal, we signed all the paperwork, and then Alison flew off to Colorado for her skiing and I flew back to Glasgow.'

'On the private jet?' Lexy asked.

He smiled. 'No, that was strictly one-way, and only because Hudson were very keen to make sure we made the trip. I actually flew economy on the return leg. It somehow felt right after the extravagance of the outward journey.'

'Okay,' Frank said. 'So let's fast-forward five years if we may. Out of nowhere, Alison suddenly turns up at Oban airport, on another private jet by the way, and not long afterwards, her body is fished out of Loch Fyne. The question I need to ask you Jack is, did she contact you before she turned up, to tell you of her plans, or did she get in touch after she arrived? An email or a phone call maybe?'

He shook his head vigorously. 'Absolutely not. I was as gob-smacked as anyone when I heard that it was her body in the loch. It was crazy and surreal at the same time. Totally unbelievable, in every way.' He paused for a second.

'Actually, are you absolutely *sure* it's her? Because it still seems impossible to me.'

'We're sure,' Frank said. 'So, as to your whereabouts between when Alison arrived in Oban and when she disappeared. We'll need you to account for that whole period if you would. That would be between the fifth and the fifteenth of November.'

Easton shrugged. 'Fine, I can do that, no problem. I'll need to talk to Margaret and Emma though. Between them, they basically organise my whole life.'

'I take it Emma's your wife?' Frank asked.

He smiled warmly. 'She is.'

Out of the blue Lexy said, 'What sort of car do you drive Mr Easton, if you don't mind me asking?'

He seemed surprised at the question. 'I've got a couple of cars actually. I use my company Range Rover day-to-day and I've got a Porsche that I nip about in on sunny Sundays. And oh yes, and sometimes I drive Emma's car, she's got a Volvo estate. It's got the kids' car seats in it so it's our family go-to vehicle.'

'Thank you,' Lexy said.

'Aye, thanks for that,' Frank added. He paused then said, 'Okay Jack, I think we'll park Alison's case for a bit and move on to the Paul Davie thing, if you don't mind. From what we can make out, there's seems to have been some uncertainty about his movements during the last couple of days he worked here, and my forensic gurus are telling me they might be able to answer some of those questions if they could get a hold of the logfiles from your wi-fi system. Oh aye, and we need to make a plan of your office layout too,' he added, laughing. 'And before you ask, I don't understand any of this myself, I'm just the messenger.'

Easton's eyes seemed to harden. 'I don't know whether we have such a file,' he said stiffly, 'but I'll obviously check with my IT guys.' He paused. 'But I'll need to think carefully if it's something we should hand over to the police. Because as you can imagine, in our role as an IT provider we take data protection very seriously indeed. Our customers expect nothing less from us.'

Frank nodded. 'Sure, that's fair enough. But we can easily get a warrant if we need to, if it turns out to be a problem for you. Then you can tell your customers it wasn't your fault.'

The smile that Easton returned looked distinctly forced. 'No Chief Inspector, that won't be necessary. Assuming we do keep these files of course. As I said, I'll need to speak to IT to confirm that.'

'It would be great if you could,' Frank said. He turned and looked at Lexy. 'Well, unless you can think of anything DC McDonald, then I think we're probably done.'

Lexy shook her head. 'No, I think we've covered everything for now sir.'

'Good.' He stood up and extended a hand to Easton. 'Okay then sir, that'll do us for now. And thank you very much for your cooperation. It's inevitable that we will have a few more questions as the investigation progresses, but we'll let you know as and when they arise. Cheers for now.'

***

'What do you think to our Mr Easton then?' Frank asked Lexy as they walked back to the car. 'He's smooth, that's for sure. But is he being honest about everything, that's what I'm wondering?'

'I thought he was pretty credible when he was talking about Alison sir,' she said. 'I wasn't quite so convinced when you brought up that business about the wi-fi log file.'

'No, I felt exactly the same. And so did Maggie, when she spoke to him a couple of days ago. He's definitely hiding something, or maybe he's worried about something nasty emerging when we start digging into that file.' He sighed. 'Charlie Maxwell is going to have a bloody fit, but as soon as we get back to the station, I'm going to ask the DCS to organise a warrant. We need to get a couple of our IT forensic guys in there pretty damn sharpish before one of their geeks presses the delete button on that file.'

Chapter 20

Maggie hadn't thought twice about it when Frank had asked her if the agency could spend a few hours on the subject of Rebecca Christie's father, and more specifically, if they could try and find out who the man was. But now, as she sat with Lori in the Bikini Barista cafe sipping on a cappuccino, the sheer impossibility of the task began to strike her. At the time of her daughter's birth, Alison Christie had been living in a children's care home. The father could have been one of the other kids who were staying there, or more disturbingly, one of the adult supervisors. To complicate matters further, Maggie had discovered that the home, located in the east end of the city and privately-run but financed by the local authority, had closed more than ten years earlier.

'They call it a hospital pass, don't they?' Lori said, sounding amused. 'When you get given an impossible job. That's what we've got here, isn't it? That's what your lovely Frank's given you.'

Maggie laughed. 'Yes, not deliberately I hope, but that's what we've been given, no doubt about it. But to be fair, he doesn't want us to spend much time on it. It's just that he's worried there might be a bitter and jealous former lover in the picture who might have stored up enough hatred over the years to want to have murdered her.'

'That's totally and utterly nuts,' Lori said, wide-eyed. 'You're suggesting this mystery guy has stored up all this anger for twenty-six years or whatever it is and then he somehow discovers that the suddenly not-dead Alison is planning a wee holiday back in Scotland and decides to take his chance to strangle her and chuck her in the loch? I mean, can't you hear how totally ridiculous that sounds?'

'I know, I know, it *is* ridiculous. But we can't escape the bald facts. One, Alison Christie is dead, two, she was found murdered in Loch Fyne, three, that means someone killed her, and four, nine times out of ten the murderer is someone who was close to the victim.'

Lori shrugged. 'The idea that it might be Rebecca's mystery father is still nuts though. Maybe a bit less nuts after what you said, but it's still nuts.'

Maggie sighed. 'Yes, it is. But look, this isn't something we need to spend too much time on, because we've only got one option as far as investigating it goes, and even that's a long shot.'

'You're talking about social services?' Lori asked.

'Got it in one. We've asked the council's social services if they have records of who was at the children's home Alison stayed at. Assuming they do, we go down that list and do a few google and social media searches and see if we can track a couple of them down. We make a few phone calls, see if anyone knows anything or heard any rumours at the time, and chase up any leads that emerge. Simple.'

Lori laughed. 'Simple? You think so?'

Maggie gave her assistant a wry smile. 'Well, we'll find out in about half an hour when we meet them.'

'Where are we going exactly?' Lori asked.

Maggie glanced at her phone. 'My note says Glasgow City Council Social Services Department, Springfield Road, Parkhead. We're meeting a woman called Mary Clarke.'

'A lovely area,' Lori said. Maggie, not familiar with that part of the city at all, couldn't make out if her assistant was being sarcastic or not. 'Is it?' she asked.

Lori shrugged. 'Let's just say the social workers will be run off their feet over there. But that doesn't mean the people there aren't nice. It's just the area's a bit deprived, that's all. And just so you know, it's just two minutes from where the Celtic play.'

'That's a football team,' Maggie said confidently, 'and one's Protestant and one's Catholic but I can't remember which is which. Frank or Jimmy told me ages ago, but I can't remember what they said.'

'It's obvious you didn't grow up here,' her assistant said wryly. 'One, because you don't know which one is which, and two, because you've never asked me which one I support.'

'Is that important?'

'It is to some people,' Lori said. 'But no, not to me it isn't.'

'It's the area where Alison grew up, which says even more for her, doesn't it?' Maggie mused. 'That she managed to do so well, I mean. Anyway, we'd better get going, we don't want to be late.'

***

It was about a thirty-minute drive, the route being rather awkward, encompassing as it did both short stretches of urban motorway and traffic-light-plagued city streets. Thankfully, Parkhead social services office had its own car park right in front of the building, it being a sturdy and handsome red sandstone affair that looked as if it might once have been a school. The front doors opened into a large but drab waiting area, furnished with three or four rows of cheap red plastic chairs. A dozen or so people occupied the seating, presumably waiting to be seen by the officials hidden out of sight behind a dividing wall. A single receptionist sat at a desk, behind which a large printed banner warned that verbal abuse or violence towards staff members would not be tolerated, a statement that Maggie thought so obvious that it hardly merited saying. The receptionist momentarily looked away from her computer screen and shouted 'John Paton?'

'Aye, that's me, and about f*cking time too,' a voice occupying one of the chairs said. 'I'm a busy f*cking man you know. I've haven't got all day to piss about in this dump.'

The receptionist raised a finger and pointed at the sign behind her, then said dryly, 'Please, go through Mr Paton, Fiona's ready for you now,' nodding towards the double doors. 'Room four.'

Maggie and Lori walked over to her desk and introduced themselves. 'Maggie Bainbridge and Lori Logan from Bainbridge Associates. We're working with Police Scotland on a current enquiry and we've got an appointment with Mary Clarke.' She paused and grinned at the girl. 'That was another satisfied customer I assume?'

She gave a wry smile. 'Johnnie's a regular. He's trying to get access to his kids, bless him, but it would help his case no end if he didn't always turn up here reeking of drink. But I feel sorry for him. Him and dozens more,' she added dryly. 'Anyway, if you just go through these doors and along the corridor, you'll find Mary's office is fourth on the left. Her name's on the door.'

The sign on the door proclaimed not only the woman's name but her job title too. *Director of Social Services – Eastern Region.* Maggie knocked gently on the door then pushed it open.

'Miss Clarke?' she said, addressing the woman sitting behind her desk. 'Maggie Bainbridge and Lori Logan.'

Mary Clarke smiled at them and gestured at two chairs on the other side of her desk. 'Please, take a seat. And please, call me Mary.'

The other woman was about her own age, Maggie estimated, dark-haired and smartly dressed in a skirt and black round-necked jumper. She guessed Clarke's job was a position of great responsibility, dealing with the dissolute lifestyles of the many local residents who had been dealt a lousy hand in life's card game.

'You're here to talk about Alison Christie,' Clarke said. 'It's a very intriguing business, not to say odd. At least, from what

I read in the papers. She pointed at the buff folder that lay on her desk. 'But I've dug out the files. Paper-based,' she added. 'We weren't computerised in those days.'

'Yes, that's right,' Maggie confirmed. 'We're helping the police with their investigation.'

'More creeping privatisation then?' Clarke asked. 'They've tried to do that here and it ended in a total disaster. Our so-called outsource partner really didn't have the first clue what they were doing.'

Maggie wasn't about to get into a discussion about politics. She gave a disarming smile and said, 'Not really privatisation Mary. This is just a bit of administrative legwork that they would normally get their civilian support staff to do. They've been short-staffed because of illness, so we're just helping out. An extra pair of hands if you will.' It wasn't the whole truth, but she hoped it would serve to steer the conversation back to the matter in hand. She pushed on before Clarke had a chance to respond.

'As you know, Alison had her daughter Rebecca when she was only sixteen and when she was staying in a council children's care home. Springfield House, I think it was called. It's closed now I believe.'

Clarke nodded. 'Yes, about ten years ago. It was already well past it's sell-by date by then. The building was very old and hard to maintain. It had been a workhouse in Victorian times would you believe? Very gothic, but despite that, it had always offered the very highest standard of care over the years,' she added, in what Maggie thought was a slightly defensive tone.

'No, I don't think there's ever been any suggestion it offered anything but the best of care,' Maggie said. 'But I notice the home was described as a high-supervision environment. What exactly does that mean?'

'Exactly as it sounds. The children who were placed there generally needed round-the-clock care. In most cases, they would be children who had been unable to settle with foster parents. Springfield House was one of only two homes in the city that could care for these difficult kids.'

'And when you say difficult, what are we talking about here?' Lori asked.

'All sorts of behaviours,' Clarke said. 'A propensity to self-harm, a propensity to harm others, a propensity to abscond. These were generally the most difficult children in our care system.'

'And did they have a propensity to get pregnant too?' Lori asked.

'Yes, amongst the girls, there would often be a tendency towards promiscuity. But reading the file, this wasn't the case for Alison. Her pregnancy seemed a very calculated move on her part.'

'How do you mean?' Maggie asked.

'It's not so unusual with girls of this type,' Mary answered. 'And I'm sorry, I didn't mean that to sound as judgemental as it did. These girls have been starved of love growing up and many think that having a baby will fill that aching gap in their lives. Often, it turns out to be a disaster for both mother and child, but in a few cases, it's the making of them. Alison Christie fell into the latter category. She was a caring mother and of course her subsequent great success in life showed how brilliant she was at overcoming adversity.'

'Are you saying she chose to get pregnant?' Lori asked. 'Like she kind of engineered it?'

Clarke shrugged. 'Obviously I can't say for definite but I would say it is highly likely. The staff at the home would have been hyper-sensitive to their girls' emerging sexual maturity and would have made sure each girl had proper contraceptive advice and would have made sure they were on the pill too. So in many cases, yes, getting pregnant would be a conscious choice they had made.'

'I expect the file must say something about Alison's pregnancy?' Maggie asked. 'Because I suppose in some way it would have been seen as a failure of care and there would have been some sort of inquest.'

Clarke sighed. 'Trying to stop teenagers having sex is like trying to stop rivers flowing to the sea. But yes, it's not an outcome we would have welcomed.' She paused for a moment. 'But you can see the difficulty. We want our homes to be warm and caring sanctuaries for these young people who have been through so much. We don't want to turn them into prisons. There's a note in the file that says the management team considered whether they should lock the boys' dormitory at ten o'clock, but of course, how could you possibly reconcile that decision with your desire to provide as homely an environment as possible? In the end, all they could do was to redouble their sex-education program, to try and ensure young people of both sexes made informed choices. And twenty-five years on, I have to say that if I had been faced with the same situation, I would have made the same decision myself.' She paused again. 'What you have to realise is we're carers, not policemen or moral adjudicators. We try to steer the young people in our care in what we think is the right direction, but in the end, they're responsible for their own life choices.'

'Even if they're not capable of making them?' Lori said.

'Sadly, yes. As I said, we try to provide guidance, that's all we can do.'

'And what about the father?' Maggie continued. 'Was he ever identified?'

'No, Alison would never say. But it was thought highly likely it was one of the boys who were under care at the time.'

'There was never any suspicion that it could have been a member of staff?' Maggie asked cautiously. 'Because that sort of thing wasn't exactly unknown in the care system back then.'

'Absolutely not,' Clark shot back. 'For a start, there was only one male member on the team in the two years Alison was at the home, since the number of girls outnumbered the boys by about four to one. And as I have said, Springfield House had an unblemished record of care through all of its life. The staff were absolutely brilliant in the most difficult of circumstances.'

Maggie could feel her excitement rise. 'That means it *must* have been one of the boys then? And I presume you must have a list of those boys? In your little brown file there?' she added, pointing at the folder.

Clarke nodded. 'I do. There were five boys in care at the home during the time Alison stayed there.'

'Just *five*?' Lori blurted out. 'Bloody hell. Can we have the list right now then please, then we can look at it and find out who it was.'

The woman looked at them sharply. 'What are you going to do with it? Or more to the point, what are the police going to do with it? Because these boys were vulnerable young people and now many of them will be vulnerable adults, even as they approach middle age. Because even though it pains me to say it, it's an exceptional individual who emerges from the care system without some scars.'

Maggie nodded. 'I understand that Mary. But in a murder case, it's a matter of working to eliminate persons of interest as quickly as possible so that the real perpetrators are exposed. It seems highly unlikely that this man would be a suspect, but the police will want to talk to him just to be sure, and of course they will handle the matter with sensitivity, as they always try to do.' She paused. 'A woman has been murdered, and you'll agree with the importance of justice being done. And that by necessity means finding her killer or killers.'

'Very well.' Mary Clarke opened her folder and slid a single sheet of paper across the table, spinning it round as she did so such that it faced the two detectives. 'Here are the names that you want.'

Staring at each other open-mouthed in disbelief, it took barely a second for Maggie and Lori to realise they had, with ridiculous ease, got what they had come for.

Chapter 21

Maggie's revelation about the identity of Rebecca Christie's father had been, in Frank's opinion, nothing short of sensational. Had it really been Richie Whitmore, the autistic software genius responsible for the development of the Nurses Direct app, who had fathered Alison Christie's child? Whitmore, himself a damaged kid, who had been orphaned not long after his birth and then subject to cruel bullying through his childhood, before ending up in the relative sanctuary of Springfield House? In the research for his *Chronicle* article, Frank's journalist pal Yash Patel had tracked Whitmore to a care home in Helensburgh, to where he had been sent after being sectioned under the mental health act. But Patel hadn't uncovered that the man was the father of Alison Christie's daughter, and he was wondering whether or not to unveil the fact in their upcoming telephone call.

'Yash my old mate,' Frank said breezily as the journalist picked up his call. 'Plenty of political scandals to be chased up on? Has the prime minister been sleeping with his kids' nanny or has he accepted a stash of free cash from a dodgy donor?'

He heard Patel laugh. *'What have you heard? No, the Alison Christie thing is still making plenty of column inches, so that's keeping me busy right now. My editor wants it to run and run.'*

'Good to know. Anyway, you won't be surprised to hear that that's why I'm calling you. You know when you did your

Christie exposé a few weeks ago, you said you'd talked to a guy called Richie Whitmore?'

'That's right,' Patel confirmed. *'He was the guy who worked with Christie to write the Nurses Direct software. It was a bit of a sad case really. I think Alison basically shoved him out of the picture after she got what she wanted from him, and eventually he had a breakdown and ended up getting sectioned. Quite dramatically too.'* The journalist paused for a moment. *'I didn't write about that in my original article, but it's going into this weekend's piece, as it happens.'*

'What do you mean, quite dramatically?' Frank asked.

'I'm surprised you don't know, because it was all over the news up here.' Patel paused again. *'But I forgot, this was five years ago and you were still in London then. Anyway, it seemed he thought that Torridon Systems was cheating him out of money they owed him, so he erected a tent in front of their offices and did a kind of one-man protest for days on end. He stood at the front door with a placard, first thing in the morning and last thing at night, haranguing all the management as they came in and out, and waving a copy of the accounts at them. Eventually the police were called, but he got a bit violent and they arranged for the mental health services to do an assessment.'*

'And that resulted in him being sectioned?'

'Yes, it did, poor guy. But when I met him in his care home a few weeks ago, he was actually a lot better. He's allowed out now because they don't think he's a danger to himself or others any more. He goes fishing a couple of weekends a

month in fact. He's obsessed with it too. That's all he wanted to talk about when I met him.'

Frank nodded. 'I'm no expert, but you read that kind of obsession is often a characteristic with people who are on the spectrum, if that's the right terminology.'

'Yeah, I know what you mean,' Patel said. *'He's definitely a bit odd, you know, one of these people who won't look at you when they're talking. But he's pretty harmless now I would say. He seemed a gentle soul to me.'*

But *was* he harmless, Frank wondered? This was a man who once had issues with Torridon Systems and by default, that meant he had issues with Alison Christie too - issues that were serious enough for the police to be called and for the man to be detained under the mental health act.

'I assume you've got the name of the place Yash? Because me and Lexy are going to pay him a wee visit and have a chat.'

'Are you going to make it worth my while?' Patel said, his tone suggesting he was only half-joking.

Frank laughed. 'We're proper detectives. And how many care homes can there be in Helensburgh? Two, three at the most? A couple of phone calls and the mystery would be solved.'

'Point taken,' Patel said. *'Alright, I'll tell you. It's called Clyde View.'*

'Imaginative. And has it got one? A view of the glorious Clyde, I mean?'

'Don't know,' the journalist responded wryly. *'It was hammering down with rain on the day I went there and the mist was as thick as a thick thing'*

'Standard weather for that neck of the woods, but good for the fishing I expect. Talking of which, where does Whitmore do *his* fishing? Off Helensburgh pier I suppose? I used to go there when I was a boy to catch crabs. I caught millions of them.'

Patel laughed. *'Maybe he does, but he's also a member of a fishing club. He told me about it at length when we had our chat. It's in somewhere called Strachur, on Loch Fyne.'*

***

For the first ten minutes of their drive to Helensburgh, they sat in silence, each evidently immersed in their own thoughts. Then finally Lexy said, 'Are we going to ask Mr Whitmore for a saliva sample sir? Because we've got Rebecca Christie's DNA now and I suppose we really ought to see if there's a match.' She paused before continuing. 'But it's an unbelievably sensitive situation, isn't it? Because we have to assume he doesn't know he has a daughter and Rebecca, we assume, has no idea of the identity of her father. It could be devastating for both when they find out. We need to be really careful.'

Frank nodded. 'Aye, it's bloody tricky right enough. Maggie and Lori did a great job getting the list of boys who were at the children's home at the same time as Alison, and it was pretty remarkable to find out that Richie Whitmore was one of them, but it's not definite proof that he was the father, obviously.' He paused. 'But I did a bit of googling earlier and guess what I found out?'

She laughed. 'Do you really want me to guess, or is it a rhetorical question?'

'Yeah, it's one of them. What I found out is there's a high likelihood of autism being inherited. And do you remember when we spoke to Rebecca Christie on the phone? I don't know about you, but to me, she gave a lot of signs that she was on the spectrum too.'

'Yes, I agree sir, very much so. But I suppose that's just another piece of circumstantial evidence, strong though it is. We still need a DNA parental match to be sure.'

'We do, but I'm not sure we should go there today. Let's meet the guy and assess his mental state before we go steaming in with the hobnailed boots.' He paused and then grinned at his DC. 'But I need to tell you I've been doing a lot of head-scratching about Mr Richie Whitmore and I've come up with a theory that I'm going to have some fun testing out with Frenchie. Let's see if we can get him on the line.'

French answered the call on the third or fourth ring. *'Morning guv, how's tricks?'* he said brightly.

'All good here. I've got Lexy with me, I'll stick you on speaker-phone. I was wondering how you were getting on with tracing the identity of our mysterious fourth man in the pub?'

They heard French take a sharp intake of breath. *'It's been bloody hard work I can tell you guv, but yeah, I've finally got a name for the geezer. And you'll never guess who it was.'*

'Actually, I think I can,' Frank replied, adopting what he knew was an annoyingly smug tone. 'It wasn't a Richie Whitmore by any chance, was it?'

'Bloody hell guv, how did you work that out?' French shot back, evidently surprised.

Frank laughed. 'Nothing more than a bit of outstanding DCI-level deductive genius, if you must know. And I say that in all modesty. No, actually it was three things. One, you told me that Jack Thompson described the guy buying all the drinks as a bit weird, two, he said the guy had come down to Loch Fyne on a fishing trip, and three, we knew that Whitmore worked in IT at the hospital in Glasgow, because that – or so the story went until we found out more – that was where he supposedly met Alison Christie and helped her get her Nurses app off the ground.'

'Nice work I suppose,' French said grudgingly. *'But if you'd worked that out earlier you could have saved me a bloody trip up to Glasgow.'*

Frank laughed again. 'True enough Ronnie and for that I apologise. Anyway, what about you? Got a busy day ahead?'

'Run off my feet guv. That geezer who was on the golfing holiday is back today and I'm going to breeze round to his place and have a chat.'

'That's the guy who saw two men acting suspiciously in a van. The guy who might or might not have written down its registration number.'

'That's the one.'

'Oh, that reminds me,' Lexy interjected. 'And sorry to interrupt Ronnie. But sir, I checked out the number plates of that Audi that picked up Alison Christie at Oban airport. And you'll not be surprised they were false.'

'Cloned from another vehicle?' Frank asked.

'Not even issued to a vehicle. They were from a batch of numbers that weren't needed that year.'

He sighed. 'Fair enough. We'll just have to double-check CCTV footage around the town and see if that yields anything. Anyway Frenchie, sorry we cut you off in mid-flow. Have you got anything else to share with us before we ring off?'

This time it was French who sounded smug. *'Oh yes, I have guv. Something huge.'*

'Oh yeah? What's that Ronnie?' Frank said, his interest heightened. 'Come on, spill the beans.'

He heard French laugh. *'You're the DCI genius guv. Why don't you see if you can work it out and I'll tell you if you're right after you've had your meeting.'*

***

Clyde View care home was located on a quiet residential street at the high end of Helensburgh, set within spacious grounds that sloped away to the south, the gardens packed with lush rhododendrons that would burst into glorious colour as spring got into its stride in a few months' time. The two detectives had been shown into a spacious day room that looked out on to a wide patio. A few residents sat quietly in comfortable armchairs, whiling away the time, whilst a male nurse stood against a wall, arms crossed and looking all the world like a prison warden. Frank nudged his colleague and nodded his head towards the window. 'Look, there's that Clyde view they boast about. Right across the estuary to glorious Greenock, or is it Port Glasgow, I'm not sure which.'

'It would be lovely sitting out there on a nice summer's evening, watching the world pass by,' Lexy said. 'This is a nice place.'

'I still hope I don't end up in one of these places though, no matter how nice it is,' he said. 'But aye, it is nice.' He wandered over to the nurse and said, 'Morning, I'm DCI Frank Stewart. I take it you know Richie Whitmore? It's him we've come to see.'

The man nodded. 'Of course. What do you want to see him about, can I ask?'

Frank smiled. 'You can ask, but we can't really tell you. But I'm just wondering about his mental state, because what we want to talk to him about might be quite upsetting. What's your name, by the way?'

'I'm Stephen. Stephen McIntyre, I'm the senior nurse in the home. All our residents have vulnerabilities, that's why they're here. But Richie is doing well since he came to us.'

'Because he was sectioned a few years ago, wasn't he?' Frank said. 'And forgive my ignorance because I don't really know what being sectioned means.'

'It's when the state intervenes to protect a vulnerable individual from harming themselves and others. There are different levels of sectioning, but that's the one most people think of when they use the term.'

'And I assume Richie was somewhere else before he came here?'

The nurse nodded. 'Yes, he was in a secure unit at a specialist hospital in Glasgow for almost two years. But he improved greatly under their care. Which is nice,' he added, 'because I'm afraid there aren't too many success stories where mental health is concerned. That's a sad fact, but it's also true.'

Frank sighed. 'I didn't know that. But you say Richie is doing well, which is good to hear. And I've heard he can get out and about a bit, and even gets to do a bit of fishing. Is that right?'

McIntyre laughed. 'Yes, it is, and he loves his fishing more than anything. Which you'll find out if you get talking to him on the subject. I wouldn't exactly say he was obsessed, but he's not far off it.'

'I've heard he's a member of a fishing club over on Loch Fyne. Is that right, and if he is, how does he get there? And is he still allowed to drive? Because I know that sometimes people with serious mental health issues can't get insurance.'

'He doesn't drive, although he is allowed to. Actually, I take him over there because I like a bit of fishing myself. We go once a month on average, maybe a couple of times more in the summer. It's great and Richie really loves it. They often say that fishing keeps you sane but in Richie's case, I think that's literally true.'

'That's nice,' Frank said. 'And do the pair of you stay over?'

McIntyre shook his head. 'No no, it's only forty miles away, if that. Hardly takes an hour. We generally get there for nine and take one of the boats out for a few hours and see what we can catch. There's always a few more of the lads from the club out on their boats too. It's a nice sociable club. Afterwards we might grab a coffee and something to eat and then we head back.'

'So why Loch Fyne?' Frank asked. 'Because I imagine there's plenty of fishing just five minutes away from here on the Gare Loch.'

The nurse shrugged. 'Richie used to go there years ago when he was working for Torridon Systems, you know, the firm that Alison Christie started up.' He paused for a moment, as if unsure whether to continue with his chosen line of conversation. He lowered his voice then said, 'That's a crazy thing isn't it, her body turning up in that loch after all this time?' He paused again as something evidently dawned on him. 'Hang on, is that why you guys are here? Are you here in connection with Alison Christie's murder?'

Frank didn't answer the question directly. Instead, he asked, 'Is Richie aware that Alison's body has been found?'

McIntyre nodded. 'Of course. He's been pretty obsessed by it since the news came out, I would say. But of course, he knew her really well. They worked together at the Queen Elizabeth hospital and then he did a lot of the coding for her business. That's how they met, when he worked in the hospital's IT department.'

Lexy had now joined them. 'Is that what he told you Stephen? That he first met her at the hospital?'

He nodded. 'Yep, that's what he told me. To be honest, it was a bit of a no-go area conversation-wise. If you ever tried to go there, he would just clam up. But it was his one-man protests outside of Torridon's offices that got him sectioned in the end, so I don't think he was Alison's greatest fan, let's put it that way. And he still takes a copy of those financial accounts with him everywhere we go. Even when we go fishing. It's slightly weird to be honest. But harmless.'

'I'm sorry, what's that all about?' Frank asked, puzzled.

'That's what caused his breakdown,' McIntyre said. 'You see, I think Christie shafted him. There would have been no Torridon if it wasn't for his programming skills, but once she had the company up and running, she basically gave Richie the push. Sure, he was on some sort of commission that was based on the ongoing success of the business, but he maintained they were cooking the books to avoid having to pay him. That was what prompted him to erect that tent outside their front door.' He laughed. 'You've got to hand it to him, he was a determined sod. He was there for nearly three weeks until you guys moved him on.'

Frank gave a wry smile, 'Not us personally. I was in London with the Met and DC McDonald here was still at school. But yes, he must have felt sore about it.'

It occurred to him that Stephen McIntyre had gone quite a way to providing much of the information they intended to talk to Whitmore about. It was evident too that the nurse had a close and probably trusting relationship with the man. He hesitated for a moment then said, 'Actually, do you think it would be better if you sat with Richie whilst we talked to him? Because we're very sensitive to his condition, obviously. We don't want to upset him unduly.'

'Yeah, I could sit with him,' McIntyre said. 'But wouldn't I then be finding out what you want to talk to him about? Although I think I can guess already,'

'I'm sure you will respect the necessary confidentiality sir,' Frank said wryly. 'But yes, it would be good if you could sit in on the meeting. Thank you.'

McIntyre nodded. 'One of my colleagues will be bringing him through in a minute. We can grab these chairs over there,' he said, indicating a group of armchairs circling a coffee table in a corner of the room. 'No-one will overhear us there.'

A few minutes later, a female nurse entered the room, trailed by a tall and gaunt looking man who looked to be in his early-to-mid-forties. 'There we are Richie,' the nurse said in a kindly tone. 'That man and that lady want to have a wee chat with you. Stephen will stay with you and I'll be back in a quarter of an hour to make sure you're okay.'

Whitmore was tall and painfully thin, with a shock of greying hair brushed back from his forehead. He looked at McIntyre and then at the detectives before giving a tentative *'Hello.'*

'Hello Richie,' Frank said, smiling. 'I'm DCI Frank Stewart and this is DC Lexy McDonald. We've got a few wee questions to ask you, if that's all right? Shouldn't take too long. Come on, let's grab a seat. My colleague DC McDonald will get us started.'

'We'd like to ask you a few questions about Alison Christie,' Lexy began, 'because Stephen tells me you're aware of what's happened to her, and obviously we want to find out who was responsible for her tragic death.'

He gave her a suspicious look. 'Yes, I do know what happened, but so does everybody in Scotland. It's been on the TV every day.'

'You knew her very well, didn't you? Right back to when you were both at Springfield House, isn't that right?'

'She told me not to talk about that,' Whitmore shot back, his voice dropping to a whisper. 'And I promised I wouldn't.'

'I'm sorry, what's this about?' McIntyre intervened.

'Alison and Richie were in care together for two years,' Lexy explained. 'They were in a children's home in the East End of Glasgow. A nice home,' she added. 'They were well looked after.' She turned back to Whitmore. 'That's where you became friends, wasn't it? You and Alison?'

Whitmore didn't answer immediately. After a considerable pause he said, 'Yes. I was lonely and confused back then and she helped me. She said I was clever and I could do great things. But that's all I'm going to say about that time.' He folded his arms tightly across his chest and looked away from them.

'That's okay Richie,' Frank said in a kindly tone. 'We're fine with what we know already.' He paused. 'And now, if we come forward twenty-five years, did you have any idea that Alison was suddenly going to turn up back in Scotland after supposedly being dead for five years?'

Whitmore looked at McIntyre again as if seeking guidance. 'No, I didn't, of course I didn't. I was the last person she would tell if she was going to do something like that. She hated me.'

The nurse stepped in before Frank could say anything. 'No, she didn't hate you Richie. She was just a very thoughtless person who was very careless with her relationships.' He then gave the detectives a sharp look as if to warn them off this line of questioning.

'That's why you carry these accounts around with you?' Lexy said gently, nodding towards the plastic folder he had laid on the table as he had sat down. 'You think she treated you unfairly, after all you had done for her? Because you wrote the Nurses Direct software and there would have been no Torridon Systems without you. That's right, isn't it?'

Ignoring her question, he said, 'I was to be paid a royalty, and I needed it after I left the company. I was suffering with my mental health and I just wanted enough money to buy a small lodge in a forest somewhere and to be able to go fishing every day. But they said the business wasn't making any profits and so they couldn't pay me.'

'And is there something in these accounts that made you think they weren't being truthful?' she asked.

He didn't answer at first, but then finally said, 'Yes, there is. That's why I keep this copy. In case they go back and try to erase history.'

'Can they do that?' Lexy asked. 'And that's a genuine question. Because I always thought that once a company had filed its annual accounts, that was it. That the numbers were carved in stone so to speak.'

He gave her a conspiratorial look. 'Oh yeah, they can do that alright. But I'm watching for it, make no mistake. They won't get away with it if they try it.'

'Would it perhaps be possible to take a copy of your document?' she asked tentatively. 'Then at least there would be another copy in circulation, which might help you if any future issues arise.'

He considered the point for a moment then nodded. 'Yes, I suppose that would be useful. They've got a copier in the office. Just as long as you give me it straight back.'

'Of course we will,' Frank said. 'But how did it make you feel, these issues with the accounts? Were you angry with Alison? *Very* angry perhaps?'

'I was very angry and very sad at the same time,' he answered. 'I did my stupid protest and then I had a breakdown. That was all Alison's fault so yes, I was angry with her.'

Frank looked at him evenly. 'And a few weeks ago, did you find out she was coming back to Scotland and that she was going to be in your favourite place in Loch Fyne, and did you decide to finally take your revenge?'

'Wait a minute,' McIntyre said, his voice raised. 'That's just not on. Shouldn't Richie have a lawyer present if you're going to ask that sort of question?'

'It's a reasonable enough question when we're conducting a murder enquiry,' Lexy said. 'And Stephen, you can probably help with this question, because we believe Alison may have been killed on around the ninth or tenth of November. Were you and Richie on one of your fishing trips at that time, can you recall?'

McIntyre shrugged. 'I don't know, we might have been. But I don't see why that matters, because Richie didn't kill Alison Christie. And neither did I for that matter, just in case you're wondering,' he added acerbically.

'Well, we need you to check your diaries and let us know please,' Frank said, 'And if you were both here, we'd want independent corroboration from one of your colleagues. Just routine you understand.' He paused for a moment then said slowly, 'There's just one last thing Richie. I need to take you back ten years, to the Noble Stag bar on the other side of Loch Fyne. You know it, I take it?'

Whitmore stared at the floor. 'No,' he said. 'I don't know it, and I've never been there.'

'Are you sure about that Richie?' Frank asked. 'Because I think you went there to meet your pal Jaz Davie and you got him and his mates pissed on your tab. I wouldn't have thought that was something you would forget in a hurry.'

Whitmore didn't look up. 'I wasn't there and I don't know anyone called Jaz Davie. I don't know what you're talking about.'

Frank sighed. 'It doesn't mean you're going to be in any trouble, but lying about it isn't going to help you, Richie. So why don't you tell us what happened back then? For your own good.'

'I'm telling you, I don't know what you're talking about,' he shot back, obviously distressed. 'It's rubbish. I don't know why you're making all this stuff up. It's really upsetting me.' He looked at the nurse and said plaintively, 'Do I have to stay here Stephen?'

'Right, this has gone far enough,' McIntyre said, looking at Frank and getting to his feet. 'I think this meeting is now over.'

Frank shrugged. 'Stephen, I know you're trying to help Richie and that's to your credit, but we're investigating a murder and that's often unpleasant for folks who might be involved. And the thing is, there's a landlady and a guy who survived the boat accident who will both be able to identify Richie, so we're only putting off the inevitable.' He paused then said. 'But to be fair, we've probably done enough for now.' He looked at Whitmore and smiled. 'Richie mate, it would be better for everyone if the truth came out, but it's probably best that we give you some time to mull that over. So we'll leave it for now and we'll see you another time.'

Just at that moment, the female nurse came back into the room. Evidently recognising the situation, she said, 'Come on Richie, we'll take you back to your room and we'll get you a nice cup of tea.' Placing a gentle hand on his elbow, she led him away.

Frank got up and started towards the door, but half-way across the room, he suddenly remembered something.

'Stephen, you said earlier that Richie liked Loch Fyne because he used to go there when he worked for Torridon. What was that all about?'

'They owned a house, in Strachur, right on the loch. Employees and their families were given free use of it as a reward when they had done good work.'

'Really?' Frank said, sensing this might be important. 'And do they still have it do you know?'

The nurse shrugged. 'No idea, I only know because Richie told me about it. But it was years ago. He hasn't worked there for more than eight years.'

He nodded. 'Aye, point taken. Well thanks for that Stephen, that's something for us to take a look at. Come on, DC McDonald, we'll leave this gentleman in peace.'

***

'He was scared, wasn't he sir?' Lexy said as they walked back to the car. 'Richie, I mean. But do you think *he* could have killed her?'

He shrugged. 'I think he's angry enough with Alison Christie to be a suspect, definitely, but I'm not sure that I see him as a cold-blooded killer. But I'm more interested in why he's lying about being at the Noble Stag on the day these boys died.'

'Haven't you just answered your own question sir? Two boys died, and he was the man who got them so drunk that they fell overboard. That's not something you would want pinned on you.'

'Aye, you're probably right Lexy.'

'And what about these accounts that he won't let out of his sight?' she continued, brandishing their copy of the document. 'Is there something in them that might give us a clue to this crazy case?'

'Possibly. But can *you* read a set of company accounts?'

She laughed. 'I can *read* them, but I can't make sense of them. They're all gobbledegook to me.'

'Maybe I can get Maggie to look at them. She did loads of financial fraud cases when she was a barrister, so she knows her way around a balance sheet. Anyway, let's get Ronnie on the line and see what he's got to tell us.' He pulled his phone out of his pocket and swiped to French's number.

'Are you going to make a guess about what he's going to tell you?' Lexy asked, grinning.

He shook his head. 'No, I won't steal his thunder. Besides which, I can't think of anything.'

'Hi guv,' French answered, perky as usual. *'How did your interview with the Whitmore geezer go?'*

'Informative. So how have you got on?'

'Brilliant guv. I've got two things to tell you and I'll keep the best for last. First one is my chat with the guy who'd been off on his golfing trip. Derek McKenzie's the guy's name by the way. Anyway, I wandered down to his gaff earlier and he told me what happened, and apologies if I've told you some of this stuff already.'

'Don't worry, I'll tell you if you're boring me. Push on.'

'Okay guv. So, apparently five days before we found the body in the loch, a guy turned up in their shared courtyard area in a big van, a Transit, Derek thinks, and went into the house next door. The thing is, Derek said he'd never seen anyone in the place in the four years he'd lived there, other than the cleaners who went in once a month.'

'This was unusual then,' Frank said, interested.

'Apparently so guv. So our man Derek wandered out to have a chat with this guy, to make sure it was all kosher and such like.'

'And?'

'The guy said they were maintenance men working for the owners and they'd been asked to check the place out because it had been without electricity for over a week.'

'Plausible,' Frank said, nodding. 'They were without power for nearly a fortnight up there after that big storm took the pylons down.'

'Yeah, that's what Derek told me. He said that him and his wife had got by fine because they've got oil-fired central heating and he also has a solar battery set-up that's enough to keep his lights on. But he said a lot of the folks in the village depended on diesel generators and it was impossible to get refilled during the power cuts because of demand. And he said that they normally could hear the neighbour's generator when it kicked in but he realised it hadn't been running for a day or two.'

'And you said men. There was two of them then?'

'That's right guv.'

'And what time was this?'

'About seven o'clock at night. It was dark obviously. He chatted for a minute but the guys seemed anxious to get on with whatever they came to do, so he left them to it. They disappeared into the house and he went back inside.'

'Is that it?' Frank said, mildly disappointed.

French laughed. *'No guv, there's more. About an hour later, Derek sneaks out with a torch and takes a note of the van's number. And before you ask, yes, I've got it. But here's the thing. He heard them leave, and it was at three in the morning, which you have to admit is suspicious. But he didn't look out the window to see what they were up to unfortunately.'* He paused for a moment. *'Oh yeah, there was something else as well. Derek said a couple of days later one of those council refuse trucks turned up on the drive. You know, the type they send out to take away old sofas and such like. The guys told him the house was going up for sale and they were clearing away some old stuff. A couple of chairs, a table and a big fridge they said.'*

'Bloody hell,' Frank said. 'Are you thinking what I'm thinking?'

'I don't know what you're thinking guv. But I'm thinking that we need to get a warrant to search that property.'

'Exactly, because you know what, maybe we've just found our murder location,' Frank said, feeling his excitement rise. 'I'll get Andy McColl down there right away and see what he digs up.'

'Nice work Ronnie,' Lexy interjected. 'But can I try a quiz on *you?* Because I think I might be able to guess what that registration number of that van is. Hang on a minute.' She took out her phone and swiped to her notes. 'Is it AN72 URC by any chance?'

'Bloody hell, how did you know that?' French said, obviously surprised.

'Wait a minute,' Frank said. 'That's the same number that was on that Audi that picked up Alison Christie at Oban Airport?'

Lexy nodded. 'One and the same sir.'

He gave a smile of satisfaction. 'Is it now? Well, I think we'll find out soon enough that that was a schoolboy error on the part of the bad guys.'

'And who exactly are they sir?' she asked.

He grinned. 'Right now, no idea. But I feel we soon will.'

'Excuse me guv,' French interrupted, *'but you've still not heard my sensational news. And you've still got a chance to guess what it is.'*

'No, give it to us straight Ronnie,' Frank said. 'We're fed up waiting.'

'Right-oh guv. What it is, the hospital finally got me the list of attendees on that outward-bound course, and you'll never guess whose name was on it.'

Frank laughed. 'We're already done with the guessing game. Just give us the bloody name.'

'It was Alison Christie guv. Alison-bloody-Christie was on that course.'

Chapter 22

With every passing day it was becoming apparent to both Maggie and Frank that the three overlapping matters – Alison Christie's murder, Jaz Davie's drowning, and the disappearance of his brother Paul – were becoming inextricably linked. But what was also annoyingly true was that the recent blizzard of startling revelations had if anything made their cases more confusing rather than less, a point Frank was bemoaning as he sat in the Bikini Barista cafe with Maggie and Lori, awaiting a call from Eleanor Campbell.

'I mean, the whole thing is beyond comprehension, isn't it? Take my murder case for a start. Okay, so maybe there's an outside chance I've found my murder location, but other than Richie Whitmore, I've haven't a bloody clue who would have wanted to kill Alison, and even Whitmore's a bloody long shot. And then there's that crazy thing with the number plates, and these two guys with the van too. Not to mention Whitmore's obsession with Torridon's accounts from five years ago. I mean, what's that all about?'

Maggie laughed. 'Yes, but we know from experience that the old jigsaw cliché that they always use in murder mystery novels is actually true. First, you need to have all the pieces, then you fit them into place, and not until then do you see the full picture. Right now, we're still at the gathering pieces stage, but I think you'll find we've actually got more of them than you imagine. And it's been gathering pace nicely in the last few days, hasn't it?'

'And we've found out a lot of things about your three men in a boat case too,' Lori added. 'Jimmy told me that the instructor guy had been shagging a woman when he should have been inspecting the dinghy, and now we're hearing that Alison Christie was on that course too, and that Richie Whitmore was the fourth man in the pub. I mean, that's a lot of stuff, isn't it? Good stuff.'

'See?' Maggie said. 'As I just said, it's gathering pace nicely.'

He sighed. 'I suppose so. Anyway, what's so urgent with wee Eleanor?'

She shrugged. 'I don't know. She sent me a message this morning saying she had some news about the Torridon wi-fi logfiles, and that she needed to talk to me right away but that you had to be there too, and she would call at ten o'clock.'

He laughed. 'She'll be wanting some technical advice from me no doubt. Anyway, let's call her to save time,' he added, glancing at his watch. He picked up his phone and swiped down to her number.

'You're seven minutes early,' was her opening line as she answered his call.

'Aye well, we're on an efficiency drive up here. Time is money and all that. Just so you know, I've got Maggie and Lori with me, and I believe you've got something interesting to tell us.'

'They must think we're like idiots,' she blurted out, sounding angry. *'As if we wouldn't notice what they did.'*

He grinned. 'By *they*, I assume you mean the geeks at Torridon Systems and by *we*, you refer to the splendid IT gurus of our forensic service, with particular reference to yourself. So, tell us what's happened. We sit here with our breath baited.'

'They redacted the file. I know they did because the file is date-stamped from two days ago and yet it was supposed to be the file from six weeks ago. And there's no wi-fi booster data from the basement level of the building, which is ridiculous. They must think we're idiots,' she repeated.

'What does that mean exactly?' Maggie asked.

'I've got the plan of the building and it's got four levels,' Eleanor explained. *'There's the ground level and a first and a second floor with offices.'*

'Yes, we've seen them,' Maggie said, nodding. 'Been in them in fact.'

'But they've got a humongous basement too,' the forensic officer went on. *'That's where their server farm is located, where they run their online service. And it's massive. That's why their office is beside the river,'* she added. *'Because computers generate huge amounts of heat and they can cool the room by pumping river water through pipes. It's like standard practice for server farms.'*

'Good to know,' Frank said. 'Go on.'

'Okay. So according to the logfile, they don't have any wi-fi boosters at the basement level. Which is ridiculous.'

'How's that?' Lori asked.

'Because lots of staff will be working down there,' Eleanor said. *'And those staff need access to the network, probably more than anyone.'*

'Sorry, are you saying Torridon have deleted some of the data in the file they gave you?' Maggie asked.

'Exactly. But they're really stupid. Like, seriously dumb. Because the file header shows its path.'

Frank frowned. 'What does that mean?'

Lori laughed. 'It means she can access their server and go straight to the folder where they store those logfiles.'

'Is that right Eleanor?' he asked.

There was a silence, then she said, *'Like yeah. That's what I've done.'*

He took a sharp breath. 'What, you've bloody *hacked* them?' he said, not sure he could believe what he was hearing. 'Already?'

'I did,' she gushed. *'I thought it would be okay because it's an official missing person case, and I knew we had a warrant too, and Maggie said it might turn into a murder case once we have more information, so I thought it was really important and I was worried they might delete the proper file before I could get to it, so I had to work fast in case they did.'*

'Eleanor-bloody-Campbell,' he said admiringly. 'Two years ago, you wouldn't blow your nose for me unless you had all the forms filled in in triplicate, and now you've gone completely rogue. What an excellent transformation. So did you get this file you were looking for?'

'I did. It's on my laptop.'

'And have you had a chance to look at it?' Maggie asked with growing excitement.

'Yeah, I've looked at it.' Then silence.

Maggie exchanged an amused look with Frank. It seemed as if this was going to be a typical *I've-done-something-clever* conversation with the often-curmudgeonly forensic officer. As was usual, the information would need to be dragged out of her line-by-line, with each nugget only being extracted by deploying an appropriate expression of sweetening praise.

'That's amazing,' she said, getting the ball rolling. 'And have you been able to find out anything?'

'Like yeah. I was able to track his phone on the last days he worked there and it was mega interesting.'

'You're dead clever Eleanor,' Lori said, evidently keen to get in on the act. Maggie gave her a thumbs-up, although she hoped her assistant wouldn't go too sickly with the eulogies.

'What was interesting Eleanor?' she asked.

'The movements of his phone. So, it was at his desk all day Wednesday, which was his last day working there, and it was there until after seven o'clock. Seven-eighteen to be precise.'

'That *is* interesting,' Maggie agreed. 'Friday was his normal day for staying late but I guess he couldn't do that if a Wednesday was his last working day.'

'But then it was in a corridor in the basement and it didn't appear back on his desk until the next afternoon. And then it was switched off.'

'A corridor?' Frank said. 'How do you know it was in a corridor?'

'That's the whole point of using geo-location with wi-fi technology,' Eleanor retorted, in the withering tone she seemed to reserve for interactions with him. *'It's like super-accurate.'*

'And it was in the corridor overnight then?' Lori asked. 'Yeah, of course it was,' she added, answering her own question.

'So we can assume he had gone down to the basement to find something or do something?' Maggie said, thinking out loud. 'Maybe something in that server farm thingy you talked about.'

'No, he was never in the server room,' Eleanor said. *'Only in the corridor. Or at least, his phone was there. Maybe he dropped it there. I can't tell that, obviously.'*

Maggie was silent for a minute as she thought through the possible implications of this new revelation. Then she said to Frank, 'This is quite disturbing, isn't it? Do you think it's grounds for you and Lexy to go back in there and question Jack Easton again?'

He nodded. 'Aye, definitely. But to be honest, I'm going with Eleanor's simple explanation. That he went down there for some reason and dropped his phone out his pocket. Next day, he realised what he'd done, went looking for it, then went back to his desk to pick up a few things before leaving. But yes, we'll go and talk to Easton and see if he can shed any further light on the situation.'

Maggie noticed that Lori was wearing a sceptical expression and shaking her head slowly. 'That's not what happened, no way. But I can't work out what did. But I will. Trust me, I will.'

***

Frank had returned to New Gorbals police station, leaving Maggie and Lori to enjoy another coffee in their favourite little cafe. In ten minutes or so, Donnie Pollock would be joining them – it had only been two days earlier that Lori had discovered the surname of the amiable IT wizard – to report on progress with fathoming the purpose of the computer code he had discovered on Jaz Davie's laptop. But now, they were looking at the open pages of a photocopied A4 document that Maggie had laid on the table in front of them.

'It's a while since I've done this,' she said, staring at a dense table of figures. 'When I was a hopeless barrister at Drake Chambers, the public-school boys got all the glamorous criminal cases and I got dumped with the dull commercial stuff. But it taught me how to read a set of accounts, worse flipping luck.'

'I did some of this at school,' Lori said brightly, 'and I've helped Stevie here at the cafe with his books when I worked here. It's quite easy in principle, isn't it? Add up how much cash you've brought in, take away what you've spent, and what you're left with is your profit.'

'Hmm yes,' Maggie murmured. 'If only it were so simple. I learned very early on about the dark arts of creative accounting, when revenue doesn't come with cash attached and liabilities can stretch years into the future, and ownership is in the hands of shady offshore companies that you can't trace.'

'And what about these ones?' Lori asked, pointing at the document. 'You had a look at them last night, didn't you?'

She gave her assistant a wry look. 'Yes, during the hour or so I spent rocking Isobel to sleep. Or *trying* to get her to sleep more like, the little minx.' She paused. 'This is Torridon Systems' annual report for the financial year 2018. So about five years ago. And these were the last published accounts before Alison disappeared.' She flicked backwards through the document until she reached the first page. 'This is all pretty standard stuff. It starts with the Chief Executive's review of the year, which is optimistic in tone, as is par for the course with these. Alison writes that it's been another year of great progress – they always say that – despite strong economic and political headwinds.'

'What does that mean?' Lori asked.

'That's where they blame external factors outside their control for any problems the business has had during the year,' Maggie explained. 'They always say that too.' She paused for a second. 'Now here's something that's interesting. Because in the last paragraph, she mentions they have had exploratory talks about a merger with Hudson Medical Staffing, which she says has the potential of delivering great synergies and opportunities for both.' She laughed again. 'They always say that about mergers too.'

'But what about the profits and stuff?' Lori asked. 'Were they making any cash?'

'I'll come to that in a minute. Before we do, there were a couple of notes in the document that were very interesting. First, as is required by company law, you have to disclose any future liabilities the firm may have, and the royalty payment to Richie Whitmore falls into that category. Hang on, I'll tell you exactly what it says.' She cleared her throat and began to read. *'The company has in place a royalty agreement with Richard David Whitmore which will pay an annual cash royalty of two-point-five percent of audited revenue, providing audited nett profits in the preceding financial year exceed half a million pounds.'*

'I think I understand that,' Lori said. 'If Torridon makes more than a half a million quid in profits, he gets two and a half percent of it.'

'No, it's better than that. He gets two and a half percent of *revenue*, not profits,' Maggie corrected. 'Which means if their turnover was say twenty million, he would get half a million. A very tidy sum indeed.'

'But he thinks they cheated him out of it,' Lori speculated. 'By some creative accounting I assume?'

Maggie shook her head. 'Actually, I looked at the income statement and I didn't see any direct evidence of that kind of skulduggery.' She paused. 'But what was interesting was two things that Richie had circled in red ink, and I think it's those items that are at the heart of his beef with them. Look, I'll show you.' She flicked over a couple of pages and then pointed to a circled paragraph.

The paragraph was headed *Director's Renumeration.* 'Company law says they have to declare what they pay their directors. And Torridon at the time had only two directors, Alison herself and Jack Easton. And do you see what it's telling us?'

Her assistant studied the page then said. 'Is that right? That Alison was only getting fifty thousand a year but Jack Easton was making four hundred and fifty thousand?'

Maggie nodded. 'It must be right, because it's here in black and white. Remember, Alison was dedicated to her company and always wanted to plough back as much of its profits as she could, which is why she only took a relatively modest salary. And Easton's situation isn't actually unusual in my experience. He was Alison's principal advisor when she was setting the company up. And then he moved from the accountancy firm to become Torridon's financial chief, on what we now can see was a very lucrative package. That happens all the time with new and exciting companies. But of course, such a high salary has a significant negative effect on company profits. You can see why Richie Whitmore might have felt sore about it. He was the software genius behind Nurses Direct, but this bean-counter seemed to be the one who was reaping the most benefit.' She paused. 'But that's not the most interesting thing in this document, not by far.'

She turned over a few more pages and then stopped. 'This is the nitty-gritty,' she said. Torridon's income statement for the financial year 2018. I'll let you read it, to see what you make of it.'

Lori studied the document for nearly a minute then sighed. 'I see what you mean Maggie, it's bloody complicated. But if I'm reading this correctly, they actually made a *loss* that year despite all of Alison Christie's public razzamatazz about how brilliant the company was doing. I see Richie circled that bit too.'

Maggie nodded. 'Yep, and it was quite a significant loss too, nearly three hundred grand. But look at this section here.'

'What, the one headed *operating expenses*?'

'That's the one. And look at this line, another one that Richie's circled in red. Read it out.'

'Okay,' Lori said. 'It says *Recurring business consultancy and licence fees to Blue Mountain LLP.*'

'And how much are these fees?' Maggie asked.

'Bloody hell,' Lori said, open-mouthed. 'Five hundred and fifty thousand. Now *that's* a lot of money.'

'It is,' she agreed. 'And *recurring* means it's a nice fat sum which is due every year. That tells me that poor old Richie Whitmore would have been waiting a long time to get his royalty payment.' She paused. 'So who the hell are these Blue Mountain guys? That's something we need to find out. *Urgently*.

***

They were surprised that Donnie arrived carrying only a hard-backed notebook, having evidently left the Jaz Davie laptop at his shop.

'You've come empty-handed,' Maggie grinned. 'We better push a coffee into one them, and quick. Skinny latte, isn't it?'

'Yeah, brilliant,' he said. 'With oat milk too please.' During this brief exchange she noticed to her satisfaction that he hadn't taken his eyes off Lori for a second. She raised an arm to attract proprietor Stevie's attention. As ever, he responded instantly to the summons.

'What can I get youse guys?' he asked brightly, notepad in hand. 'Must be getting near lunchtime, that's all I'm saying. And today's special is mac and cheese with the crispy toasted cheddar topping.'

Maggie laughed. 'Sounds delightful, but we'll have another injection of caffeine first Stevie. A skinny latte for Donnie here with oat milk – I assume you do that?'

'This area's student-central,' he said in a sardonic tone. 'You'd be ostracised for life if you ordered real cow's milk with your drink. So aye, I do oat milk by the tanker-load. Same again for you ladies?'

He scribbled down their order and departed. 'Right then Donnie,' Lori said, 'What have you got for us?'

Donnie sighed. 'Good news and bad news I'm afraid. The bad news is I couldn't get the software running on Jaz's laptop. That's why I didn't bring it. But the good news is, that doesn't matter, because I've been able to work out what it does by reading the code.' He hesitated for a moment. 'To be honest, I've been a bit worried about this meeting.'

'Worried?' Maggie said. 'How come?'

He looked sheepish. 'It's dead technical and it might be really difficult for you guys to understand what the hell I'm talking about. I don't want to come across like a big show-off and I really don't want you to think that I'm trying to make you feel stupid, because I'm not. But I've thought about it, and there's no way I can explain it without getting at least a wee bit technical.'

Maggie laughed. 'Don't worry, we're used to being made to feel stupid by a certain technical wizard of our acquaintance. Give it to us straight and we'll expect to feel really dumb all the way through. We're tough, we can take it.'

He smiled. 'Okay, you asked for it. So the gist of it is that Jaz's code is a super-efficient search algorithm that would allow you to do really fast searches and matches. It's really clever stuff. It kind of approaches the search problem in a way I've never seen before. I don't know how to explain it, but maybe you could describe it as an early example of AI technology. But forget all that,' he added. 'All you need to know is it lets any application using it do lightning-fast searches and matches. It's brilliant, it really is.'

'It's brilliant and it's lightning fast. That's all we need to know,' Maggie said, giving a thumbs-up.

He nodded. 'Got it in one. So now we go to the code snippets that I found on Paul Davie's USB stick.'

'You found they were the same, didn't you?' Lori said, a smug expression briefly crossing her face.

Donnie shook his head. 'Well, that's what's dead interesting. Because, no, they're not the same.' He paused. 'But if you were to reverse-engineer them into pseudo-code, then yes, they would be the same.'

Maggie laughed. *'Now* you've got us. I didn't understand a single word of that. Except that they're not the same, but they *are* the same.'

He gave her a rueful smile. 'Yeah, that's what I was afraid of. But I promise, I'll only be horribly technical for another minute and then it will all become clear to you.'

'That's called hope over experience. But please, carry on.'

'Okay, but brace yourself.' He paused for a moment and furrowed his brow. 'So when you're writing programs, you have to hold certain bits of data that you want to use later in the computer's memory and you hold that data in what's called variables. And you give each variable a name so you can retrieve it later when you need it.'

'Like *Donnie* for example?' Lori asked mischievously.

He laughed. 'Aye, you could call one Donnie if you wanted to, but they're normally just given letters like a and b and so on. They look like a maths formula, if you remember them from back at school. Anyway, when I looked at the code on the USB stick, all the variables had been given different names. That would be like Donnie being called Johnny in your example. But it was still holding the same data, and I'm pretty sure the pseudo-code analysis would show that the program logic was identical.' He hesitated then laughed again. 'Actually, I don't know why I bothered telling you all that rubbish. All you need to know is that yes, it's basically the same code but that someone's gone to a lot of trouble to disguise the fact.'

Maggie was silent for a moment. 'You mean someone has *stolen* that code from Jaz and then tried to hide the fact?'

Donnie suddenly looked crestfallen. 'Bugger, that's something I hadn't thought of. You see, I don't think there's any way of telling which came first. So, yeah, one has copied the other, definitely, but which came first? I'm not sure you could say.'

'But the USB code,' Maggie asked, thinking out loud. 'Do you think it's part of the Nurses Direct system?'

He nodded. 'That I *can* say for definite. There's a header block at the top of the file and it's got a version name and number on it. *NursesDirect V7.5.1* it says if I remember rightly.'

'So they copied it,' Maggie said slowly. 'No, scratch that. They *stole* it. They bloody stole it.'

And as she said it, it was as if half the pieces of the jigsaw had been sprinkled with a magic fairy dust and had miraculously popped into place. Sure, there was still another five hundred pieces to find and fit together in this most complex of puzzles, but at that moment she was experiencing the surge of excitement that always appeared when the end game was coming into view.

It wouldn't be long now.

Chapter 23

They had been summoned, by email, to the major incident room at New Gorbals police station for what Frank had humorously described as the most humongous brainstorm in the history of crime-fighting. A three-line whip had brought Jimmy down from Braemar and Eleanor Campbell up from London, and they were joined by Maggie, Lori Logan, DC Lexy McDonald, DC Ronnie French, DI Andy McColl and of course Frank himself. Not invited but present nonetheless, as was his prerogative, was Detective Chief Superintendent Charlie Maxwell, who had been growing anxious because of the seeming lack of progress in what was one of the highest-profile murder cases to come across his desk in years. Maggie knew that as much as Frank liked Maxwell, he would have been wishing that the senior officer had stayed in his executive office on the top floor. It was inevitable that when a big dog like the DCS was in the room, it constrained what the more junior ranks might contribute to the proceedings, they being understandably reluctant to look foolish in front of such a senior figure. Mind you, she thought, with Eleanor, Jimmy and Lori in the room, not to mention Frank himself, there would be no shortage of outspoken voices giving their two penny's worth.

But the real problem, she realised, was that of the three interlinked cases they were working on, it was the murder of Alison Christie that was showing the least progress. Other than Richie Whitmore, Frank had no real suspects, and even Whitmore looked an unlikely candidate to say the least. Not only that, the search for a clear motive had proved elusive with only the aforementioned Whitmore bearing an obvious grudge against the murdered businesswoman. Frank hadn't admitted it to her directly, but from the tone of their frequent discussions on the matter, she could tell that a hint of desperation was beginning to creep in to his demeanour. This, above anything, was the reason for bringing the extended team together in this room, in the hope that from somewhere, a flash of game-changing inspiration or insight would emerge.

Tasked with getting the session underway, it was DI McColl who was standing at the front of the room once more, marker pen in hand, with his back to the investigation whiteboard. 'Right guys, before we start, I've got a bit of late breaking news,' he said. 'A couple of snippets in from the US. First, I managed to talk to that ski lift attendant who was on the blue-rated piste the day Alison disappeared. Julia Gomez is the girl's name, and she confirmed that she saw Alison do her run two or three times and then she never saw her again. Secondly, I spoke to someone at Hudson Medical Staffing and they confirmed that on the day of their meeting, Alison and Jack Easton flew into Westchester County Airport in a private jet and were picked up by a limo that took them to Hudson's offices, where they met with James Hudson the owner and founder of the company. They had various discussions and lunch with him whilst the lawyers dealt with crossing the T's and dotting the I's. They shook hands on the deal and she went off to Colorado and Easton flew home.'

Frank nodded. 'Aye, that's what he told us too. And it's good to get confirmation of her last known movements over there from the ski attendant. Nice work Andy.'

From the back of the room Maxwell shouted out, 'Yeah, it's all very nice Frank, but if you don't mind me saying so, your whiteboard looks a bit sparse to say the least. I doubt if there's more than half a dozen mugshots up there and one of them is of the bloody victim. As far as I can see, this is a murder investigation with an absence of suspects. Which, as you well know, is never good.'

'Quality not quantity sir,' Frank responded, the quip making Maggie wince a little. But her husband evidently knew Maxwell well, so maybe he wouldn't take it the wrong way.

'If you don't mind me saying so Chief Superintendent,' she intervened, 'it's the absence of motive rather than the absence of suspects that's the real problem with this case. Plus, the fact that we've no idea what Alison Christie was doing between disappearing off the face of the earth in Colorado then turning up in Oban airport of all places.'

'Which wasn't exactly her smartest move, given what happened to her after she got here,' Maxwell observed.

'Well let's just walk through what we know, out loud, and see if that produces any eureka moments, shall we?' Frank said. 'Who's going to start?'

'I will if you want sir,' Lexy said.

Frank nodded. 'Go ahead.'

She took a breath. 'Okay. So, around eight weeks ago, Alison's body was pulled out of Loch Fyne by a fishing boat. The body was examined by our pathologists, and it was found she had been strangled and then perhaps no more than a day or two later, she had been dumped into the loch. Her last known movements were some three days earlier, when she arrived from the US at Oban airport on a private jet, having previously been declared dead in Colorado five years earlier. She was picked up at the airport by an Audi wearing false plates, and that was the last sighting of her. That sighting was on the airport CCTV by the way.'

'And who was the last person to actually eyeball her in person? Maxwell asked.

'That would be the Border Force agent who checked her passport,' Lexy said. 'And it's worth pointing out that her passport hadn't been cancelled after her supposed death.'

'Why not?' the DCS barked.

'It's a hole in the process sir,' she said. 'The process actually relies on the relatives sending the password back, although there are some systematic checks across the government IT systems to provide some element of fail-safe. But that falls down where the deceased person has been declared dead outside of the UK. And that's what happened here.'

'Okay, I think I understand,' Maxwell said, nodding. 'Carry on.'

'Okay sir. Our first step was to interview a number of individuals who were close to the victim, those being her estranged husband, the actor David Stirling, her daughter Rebecca Christie, who's a landscape artist and now lives in Australia, and Alison's close business colleague Jack Easton, who had been with her right from the start of Torridon Systems. All had strong alibis for the time of death and none appeared to have a compelling motive to kill her.' She paused and pointed at the board. 'And they're all up there sir.'

'Pretty sharpish, we checked the CCTV and APNR around the vicinity where the body was found,' Ronnie French said, 'but that drew a blank, because there ain't many cameras in that neck of the woods. Next, me and a couple of the local uniforms did the door-to-doors. That was in a place called Strachur. We were obviously hoping that someone might have seen something suspicious around the time of the murder.' He paused. 'Just one thing turned up. A couple of geezers in a van arrived at a lodge that hadn't been used for years. The neighbour thought it was a bit strange and he collared them for a chat.' His voice tailed off. 'The van was on false plates, but would you believe it, they were the same false plates that were on that Audi that Lexy mentioned earlier. So that made that lodge interesting to say the least.' He stopped then looked at DI McColl. 'And Andy, you and the forensic squad have been down there these past couple of days, haven't you?'

McColl nodded. 'Yeah, we have. And we've found nothing so far. The place had been lying empty for years and in fact the council had recently been contacted to clear out a few remaining items of furniture. We hoped – no, that's not the right word, but you know what I mean – we suspected it might have been the murder scene. But it's clean, although we're still going over the place with a fine-tooth comb just to be sure.'

'And I assume you've checked who owns this place?' Maxwell asked. 'Because someone has to.'

'We did. According to the land registry, it's owned by a company. An outfit called Blue Mountain LLP.'

'What?' Maggie blurted out. 'Andy, did you say Blue Mountain?'

McColl nodded. 'Yep, that's what the land registry entry says. And the company's registered in the Cayman Islands, so we've no information on directors or anything like that.' He nodded towards Eleanor. 'Frank's just asked Miss Campbell to do some further investigation on that aspect.'

'It will be mega-tough to find anything,' Eleanor said sourly. 'That's like the whole point of the Cayman Islands.'

'Yes, it will be,' Maggie said. 'As Eleanor said, that's the whole point of offshore ownership, to keep the real owners' identities hidden.'

'But the company really does exist,' Lexy said. 'Because I talked to the council refuse guys and the collection was booked online and paid from an account in that name.'

'An offshore account?' Jimmy asked.

Lexy nodded. 'Yeah. But it was a current account, and you can pay stuff using them from anywhere, so long as it's registered in the worldwide payment system. Which this one was.'

'So why are we all so interested in this outfit?' Maxwell asked.

Maggie held up the document she had brought into the room with her. 'Because according to this set of company accounts, Torridon Systems have been paying Blue Mountain more than half a million pounds a year. That was one of the main factors that caused the suspect Richie Whitmore to have his mental breakdown. He thought they were using creative accounting to deny him the considerable royalty payment he was due.' She paused for a moment. 'And until two minutes ago, that's what I thought too. I suspected that Blue Mountain was an artificial vehicle created to reduce the published profits of Torridon Systems so that the royalty could be avoided.' She hesitated before continuing. 'But now Andy' discovered it's a real company and it owns a valuable property on Loch Fyne.'

'So what does that mean for our case?' the DCS asked.

Maggie shrugged, furrowing her brow at the same time. ' don't know, I really don't know.' Sighing, she stood up an took a step forward so that she could get a better look at the whiteboard. 'But the answer is up there somewhere, if only could see it.'

For the next ten minutes, Frank invited each person in turn t give their views on the case, and there were valuabl contributions from Jimmy and Lori in particular, wh benefited from being detached from the main polic investigation and therefore could take a wider view. But through it all, Maggie didn't hear a single word, as she stared at the board with an unnerving intensity. *The answer was up there, somewhere.* She knew it *had* to be, but no matter how hard she looked, it simply refused to leap out at her.

And then suddenly, completely out of the blue, she saw it. *The accounts. The private jets. The blue-rated ski-run. The house by the loch. The refuse truck. And the photographs on the board. Above all, the photographs.*

'It's there,' she shouted, pointing at the board. 'It's there. Staring us right in the face. It's so *obvious*, I don't know why we didn't see it before.'

'What the *hell* are you talking about?' Frank shot back. 'Are you saying you know who did it? Do you know who murdered Alison Christie?'

She nodded vigorously. 'Yes, I do, and I know the motive too. And I know everything else as well. *Everything.*' She paused for a second. 'Except there's just one thing I need to confirm, to be absolutely sure.' She paused again then said quietly,

'Jimmy, you need to take me to Helensburgh. Right now.'

Chapter 24

'I know you're probably not going to tell me until we get there,' Jimmy said, 'but why in hell's name are we going to Helensburgh? And all that other stuff on the phone a minute ago? What was that all about? Because I'm seriously confused, I don't mind telling you. And this thing about the private jets and the photographs,' he added. 'That makes it even more unfathomable.'

They were hurtling along the dual-carriageway that skirted the northern bank of the Clyde, the sat-nav suggesting they were less than twenty minutes from their destination.

Maggie shrugged. 'I need to confirm something, something critically important to my theory, and I can only do it where we're going.' Which, she admitted to herself, was not strictly true. Her mission could probably have been accomplished just as easily on the phone, but adrenalin was coursing through her and she needed to be doing *something* otherwise she felt she might have a minor nervous breakdown. Besides, she hadn't wanted to be in that room if her theory had turned to dust in front of her eyes.

'And as to the phone call, I asked the police to dredge the river beside Torridon's offices because I very much fear that's where the body of Paul Davie will be found. And as to the involvement of the New South Wales police, that may only be precautionary but we'll find out for sure when we get to our destination.'

They travelled in virtual silence for the rest of the journey, Maggie staring resolutely out the passenger window and ignoring any of Jimmy's attempts to engage in conversation. As they passed the sign indicating that they had now entered the town, he laughed. 'You're going to have to speak to me now. Because I need directions, otherwise we'll be driving around this place all bloody day.'

She glanced at her phone's sat-nav. 'Of course. Second left and then it's third right and then straight on for half a mile. But I'll shout it out when we get to each turn. Just two minutes away is what it's saying.'

And two minutes later, they were there, a large sign at the entrance proclaiming it to be the *Argyll, Bute & Lomond District Refuse and Recycling Facility.*

'You've brought us to the *dump*?' Jimmy said incredulously.

'Can't you work out why?' she asked, frowning. 'I should have thought it was obvious. Remember, the council did a pick-up at the lodge on Loch Fyne just a few days ago.'

He laughed. 'What, do think you might find some cash or a winning lottery ticket stuffed down the side of the old sofa?'

'It's not a sofa I'm interested in, believe me.'

They pulled the car up in a designated parking bay and jumped out. Immediately, Maggie ran towards one of the workers, a lanky youth in regulation hard hat and hi-viz jacket.

'Hi, we're with the police. Can you take us to the site manager please?'

'Whit's it aboot?' the youth asked.

'That's private and confidential pal,' Jimmy said in a faintly menacing tone. 'Just get the manager, okay?'

He shrugged. 'Aye, alright then. Wait here.' He spun round then shuffled off across the yard at a languid pace. A few minutes later, another man appeared, he also hard-hat-and-hi-viz equipped, but his rank was signalled by the fact he was also wearing a collar and tie.

'Hello, I'm Paddy West, site manager,' he said pleasantly. 'What can I do for you? You're the police, are you?' he added.

Maggie nodded. 'We're investigators working with the police on the Alison Christie murder case. I'm Maggie Bainbridge and this is my colleague, Jimmy Stewart.' She had figured that mention of the Christie case would overcome any reluctance the manager might have to cooperate, and immediately it was apparent that the tactic had worked.

'Man, that's a bloody crazy affair, isn't it?' he said. 'Have you got anybody for it yet? Because from what I read in the papers, it's all a bloody mess and you guys haven't a clue who did it. No offence of course,' he added quickly.

Jimmy gave the man a sardonic smile. 'You shouldn't believe everything you read in the papers Paddy.'

'No, probably not,' he said. 'Sorry. Anyway, how can I help you guys?'

'I'll cut straight to the chase, if you don't mind,' Maggie said 'A few days ago, you did a pick-up from a property over in Strachur, on Loch Fyne.'

'That's right, I remember,' he said. 'A couple of the lads popped over there in the wagon and collected an old sofa and a big freezer from a shed round the back of the house.'

Maggie could feel the hairs bristle in the back of her neck. 'Have you still got it? The freezer I mean?'

He shrugged. 'That? Oh aye, we'll still have it. It's a very specialised job dealing with these old-school fridges and freezers you know. You can't just chuck the refrigerant down the drain, although between you and me that's what we used to do before all this environmental malarkey became fashionable. Nah, it takes nearly a month before we can get the metal in the crusher nowadays.'

'Can you show us it please?' she asked excitedly.

He shrugged again. 'What? Aye, I suppose so. Follow me guys.'

He led them to an enclosed area in the far corner of the yard, stuffed to capacity with discarded cookers, washing machines, fridges and freezers. He pointed to an appliance near the front of the patch. 'That's it there. Looks like it's not been processed yet.'

'It's an upright,' she said, surprised. 'A tall one.'

'Aye, so what? Anyway, take a look if you want. I've got some things to do.' He started to walk off, but Maggie said, 'No please, just wait a minute. It could be important. We might need you to move it.'

'Fair enough,' he said, thrusting his hands into his pockets. 'But don't take all day.'

She and Jimmy walked over to the appliance then stopped exchanging glances. 'Better do this I suppose,' she said. With evident trepidation, she extended an arm, pulled open the door and looked inside. Then she beamed a huge smile of satisfaction.

'Look Jimmy, do you see?'

He nodded. 'Yeah. Pristine. Someone's done a right job on this.' As they continued to gaze at the sparklingly-clean interior, an unmistakable odour hit their nostrils. *Bleach*. And now she knew her crazy theory was right, one hundred percent. *This appliance had been the final resting place for poor Alison Christie these last five years.* Whoever had done this to her had taken considerable measures to erase the truth but Maggie knew it would all have been in vain.

Because you could scrub and scrub and scrub, but no amount of scrubbing would prove a match for modern forensic science.

Chapter 25

The next day, the group had been reassembled in New Gorbals' major incident room, but this time they had been joined by a small team of lawyers from the Procurator Fiscal's office. Jennifer Grant, head of the prosecution service for the Glasgow and Strathkelvin area, was in charge, and would have the ultimate decision about how the multiple prosecutions would be brought. But first, she and her team had to hear the full facts of the three cases, and to that end, Maggie was now on her feet and holding court in front of the whiteboard.

'I'm not quite sure how to approach this,' she began uncertainly, 'because although the three crimes certainly overlap, only two of them are directly connected, and the perpetrator of one of them is already dead.' She paused, chewing on the end of her marker pen before continuing. 'I suppose it's probably easiest to go through them in chronological order. Which takes us back ten years, to the shores of Loch Fyne, where a group of staff from the Queen Elizabeth hospital in Glasgow were on an outward-bound team-building course. Of the fifteen or so participants, two were of great significance to this affair, one being Alison Christie, who at the time worked as a senior nurse at the hospital, and Jaz Davie, who was a member of its IT department. And as part of our wide-ranging investigations, we discovered that it was actually Jaz Davie who had the idea for the Nurses Direct app and had indeed written an early prototype.' She paused. 'Whereas the legend spun around the meteoric rise of Torridon Systems had always claimed the software genius behind the app was a man called Richie Whitmore. Not so, ladies and gentlemen. But we'll be hearing more about Mr Whitmore in just a moment. Quite a bit more,' she added. 'And his, I'm afraid, is a rather sad tale.'

'The next part of our story can only be supposition, but we must imagine that at some point, Jaz Davie had shown his software to Alison and at the same time, revealed his idea for the Nurses Direct business. Immediately she would have seen its enormous potential, and consumed with ambition and avarice, she determined that she must have the idea for her own. To do that, she had to get rid of Jaz Davie, and the outward-bound course gave her the perfect opportunity. She knew that as part of the programme, participants had to sail a dinghy across the loch, not a huge distance for an experienced sailor, but a significant challenge for a beginner, which is why the course organisers insisted on participants being accompanied by an experienced instructor.' She paused and smiled ruefully at the group. 'Enter stage left, Richie Whitmore and stage right, Willie Armitage. As I said a moment ago, Richie's is a particularly sad and tragic tale. He's on the spectrum, quite markedly so, and like Alison, spent a portion of his older childhood in the care system, specifically in an institution called Springfield House, which is where they first met. And where they had the relationship that resulted in Richie fathering Alison's child Rebecca.'

'He fathered her *child*?' Jennifer Grant said incredulously.

Maggie nodded. 'Oh yes, and it was very calculated on Alison's part. She badly wanted a baby and she chose Richie because even then, he was hopelessly devoted to her.'

'But I've read about it, and she never revealed who her daughter's father was, did she?' the lawyer said.

'No, she didn't, and Rebecca certainly never discovered who her dad was,' Maggie agreed. 'In fact, I'm not sure if Richie ever knew either. He does now of course,' she added, 'and it seemed to come as a huge shock to him.' She paused. 'Anyway, coming back to the events on Loch Fyne. Richie and Jaz worked together in the hospital's IT department and were friends - or at least close acquaintances, because Richie didn't and doesn't really make friends as such. We think Alison would have suggested Jaz and his two boat-mates should visit the Noble Stag bar to down a stiffener before their sailing expedition, at the same time arranging for Richie Whitmore to turn up at the bar claiming it was his birthday and wielding his credit card. In parallel, she had induced the weak Willie Armitage to abandon his supervisory duties in return for an afternoon of sex with her. And of course, the inevitable happened. Tragedy on the loch, and Alison now had her hands on the embryonic Nurses Direct app.'

Jennifer Grant was silent for a moment then said, 'Goodness, this is a tough one, isn't it Maggie? Can I ask you, as an experienced barrister, what would have been your take on the chances of a prosecution had Alison Christie still been alive?'

She gave the senior prosecutor a rueful look. 'Honestly, I don't know Jennifer. Alison obviously planned the whole thing very carefully, but ultimately, the death of the two men was an accident. All she had to do was claim she knew nothing about it, knowing it would be virtually impossible to prove otherwise.'

Jimmy spoke up. 'And I interviewed Willie Armitage and he definitely wasn't aware of the big picture. He simply couldn't believe his luck that a beautiful woman like Alison Christie wanted to go to bed with him. For him, it was a once-in-a-lifetime chance he wasn't going to pass up on.'

'I don't think Richie would have been in on the scheme either,' Maggie said. 'You ask for my opinion Jennifer? I don't think we would have stood a cat in hell's chance of getting any charges to stick against any of the three. Which is why the scheme was so fiendishly clever.' She paused then smiled at Frank. 'But at least there's one person in the room who's pleased with the outcome.'

He held up his hands in a submissive gesture. 'Aye Miss Grant, I was the dumb cop who did the initial investigation and I don't mind admitting that I made a right balls of it. But I suppose I can take some satisfaction from the fact that it probably wouldn't have made any difference if I'd got to the truth back then. Not much satisfaction, mind you,' he added. 'It was still a monumental screw-up on my part.'

'You're forgiven,' the prosecutor said, laughing.

'And I forgive you too my darling,' Maggie said fondly 'Anyway, next we come to the murder of Alison Christie. As Detective Chief Superintendent Maxwell has pointed out on more than one occasion, this crime suffered from a distinct absence of suspects, but a distinct absence of motive too Frank's team pursued the case diligently, but it seemed tha anyone who might remotely have had a motive to kill her hac a cast-iron alibi. That was before I realised that we were al the victims of a deception, a deception that was ultimately exposed by the unexpected arrival of the ferocious Storm Kitty on these shores. But before we come to that, we must go back five years, to when Alison Christie really met her end, and it's back to that period too when we must look for our motive.' She stretched over and picked up the document that was lying on an adjacent desk, then held it aloft. 'Here's where we'll find our motive. In the 2018 annual account of Torridon Systems, where we find that Chief Financial Officer Jack Easton was in receipt of a salary of four hundred and fifty-thousand pounds and that the company was paying a consultancy fee of more than half a million pounds to Blue Mountain LLP. Many of you will know the Blue Mountains National Park is one of the most beautiful areas of New South Wales in Australia, where Alison's daughter has made her home and I'm sure we will eventually trace the ownership of that company back to Rebecca Christie.'

'I already did. This morning,' Eleanor Campbell piped up.

'I thought you said it was going to be mega-tough to do that?' Frank said sardonically.

'And it was, off-the-scale difficult,' the forensic officer replied contemptuously. 'But I never said I couldn't do it like mega-fast.'

'It's very good work Eleanor,' Maggie said soothingly. 'Thank you for that important confirmation of the ownership of the firm.' She paused again. 'So, to the motive. This was the period when Alison was driving forward with her plan to take over Hudson Medical Staffing – her plan for world

domination, as several people have described it to us. Thi
was a plan that was driven by Christie's huge ego, he
burning desire to be not just the UK's most famou
businesswoman but to be a serious player on the global stag
too. But Hudson were several times the size of Torrido
Systems and the takeover was going to require a huge fundin
package, provided by a consortium of UK and US banks. /
leveraged buyout is the technical term I believe, and the resul
would have been to shovel a massive amount of debt ont
Torridon. Those debt repayments would have meant th
company would no longer be able to pay the annu
consultancy fee to Blue Mountain, a company set up b
Alison purely for the benefit of her autistic daughter. At th
same time, the plan was to move the headquarters of th
combined operation to New York State, meaning that a UK
based financial chief would no longer be required.' Sh
paused. 'So we had, at a stroke, two people who would suffe
a catastrophic loss of income if the takeover plan was to g
ahead. There, in a nutshell, is your motive.'

'Jack Easton and Rebecca Christie conspired to carry out th
murders?' Jennifer asked. 'They are our killers?'

Maggie nodded. 'They are.'

'What I want to know is how the hell you worked it out'
DCS Maxwell asked. 'And why you and your pal had 1
gallivant off to Helensburgh yesterday.'

She laughed. 'Yes, I suppose that wasn't strictly necessar
but it was a vital piece of evidence I wanted to see with n
own eyes before I was confident enough to share my theo

with everyone. As to how I worked it all out? Well as I said yesterday, the solution had been always there, right in front of our eyes, right from the start.' She pointed to the whiteboard. '*Look*. Look at Alison and Rebecca Christie. They could be mistaken for twins rather than mother and daughter, couldn't they? Remember, there was only sixteen years difference in their ages.' She paused. 'And yesterday, it all suddenly clicked, when I thought about the private jets and when DI McColl told us about his conversation with the ski-lift attendant.'

Maxwell laughed. 'I'm sorry Maggie, but you've bloody got me there. What the hell have these two things got to do with it?'

She smiled. 'Allow me to explain. Firstly, the thing about private jets is they can fly into small airports, and the thing about small airports is, they don't have iris scanning and facial recognition technology like the big airports have. At the smaller airports, immigration is handled in the old way, where an agent simply looks at your passport then looks at your face and if that matches, you're in.'

'Are you saying that Rebecca Christie impersonated her mother?' Maxwell asked.

She nodded. 'Exactly that. Let me try and explain the chronology. Torridon Systems owned a luxury lodge on Loch Fyne, mainly so they could reward their staff for good work, but it was used often by the directors for their own leisure too. We believe that Alison, Rebecca and Jack Easton were staying there the weekend before Alison and Easton were due to fly to the States to complete the Hudson takeover deal. And on that weekend, as they had planned, Alison Christie was strangled and her body placed in the freezer that we believe was specifically bought for the purpose. The one that Jimmy and I found at the refuse facility yesterday.'

'Bloody hell,' Maxwell said.

'For the next part of the plan, Rebecca became Alison. She and Easton flew from Glasgow to the US in the private jet they had hired, landing at Westchester County Airport in upstate New York, where they were manually processed through immigration. With much of the negotiation of the deal having been conducted by the respective companies' lawyers, James Hudson and Alison Christie had never before met face-to-face, so the meeting proceeded without any hint of suspicion on their part. The next part of the subterfuge was that Alison Christie had to die in a skiing accident, so that the takeover deal could never go ahead. Rebecca, posing as her mother, flew to Colorado whilst Jack Easton flew home.' Maggie paused and then smiled. 'But it turns out Rebecca is nowhere near as accomplished a skier as her mother was, which explains why the ski-lift attendant saw her traversing the resort's big wide blue run several times. A really fanatical skier like Alison would never have wasted a precious day's skiing on such unchallenging slopes. When I heard that, I was ninety-nine percent certain that my crazy theory was right. And for five years, no-one suspected a thing. That was, until Storm Kitty came along and threatened to ruin everything.'

'Bloody hell, don't tell me there's *more*,' Maxwell groaned, an intervention that caused laughter around the room.

'She's nearly finished Superintendent,' Lori said brightly. 'Just another couple of hours and she'll be done.'

'Oh God, I hope it won't take that long,' Maggie said. 'At this point, you might be wondering why they decided to store Alison's body in the freezer, rather than disposing of it, because it is rather macabre to say the least. But the thing is, it's far from easy to dispose of a body, and if they *did* that and it should be subsequently discovered, then of course the whole scheme falls apart. Instead, they mothballed the lodge and installed a generator to cover for power cuts, knowing that sometime in the future they would have to face the problem of what to do with the body, but thinking that *sometime* could be postponed almost indefinitely.'

'Until that bloody great storm flew in from the Atlantic,' Frank said.

'Yes,' Maggie said. 'They must have panicked when it became apparent that the lodge would be without electricity for at least two weeks and it would be impossible to get diesel for their generator once it ran out. So the private jet subterfuge was dusted down once again, and Rebecca Christie made a desperate flight from Sydney to the US – we assume she did this on her own passport but we'll have to confirm that – then, posing as Alison, she flew into little Oban airport, where a Border Force agent manually processed her details. Then she was picked up by Jack Easton in Bill Warren's Audi, that car wearing false plates to avoid detection. Where she went afterwards is still to be determined, but our thoughts are she stayed overnight in Oban, then caught a train, ending up at Heathrow where she flew back to Australia as Rebecca. The idea of course was to lay a false trail, so that should the body be discovered, the police would be investigating a current murder rather than one that had been carried out five years earlier.' She paused. 'And yes, it was pretty desperate, but they must have hoped the body would be lost in the loch forever. The flight from the US was just part of a contingency plan – a plan which very quickly unravelled.' She paused again. 'Anyway, a day or two later her mother's body was removed from the freezer by Easton and Warren, wrapped in polythene sheeting and dumped in the loch, the body being moved by a van wearing those same false plates. That was a stupid mistake on their part, as was disposing of the body in the loch. Because just three or four days later, and no doubt to their great dismay, she was fished out by that little boat.'

'Aye, and we we're there to see it,' Jimmy said. 'Setting off a great wild goose chase.'

'On that point, don't our forensic pathologist friends have some questions to answer?' Jennifer asked.

'Do you mean, how did they miss that the body was frozen? Frank said.

Eleanor jumped in, evidently anxious to defend her forensic colleagues. 'If a body is frozen immediately after death, and there haven't been any injuries which would have caused a loss of blood, then it stays almost perfectly preserved. It's like all these crazy rich dudes freezing themselves after they die. When they're like brought back to life, they're in perfect condition.'

Frank laughed. 'I don't think the boffins have *quite* perfected that bit of the technology yet, but I get what you're saying.'

'And when the body was submerged in that freezing water,' she continued, 'it would have defrosted like *ridiculously* slowly. That also would have stopped it suffering any serious damage.' She paused. 'Obviously, if the path lab guys had *known* the body had been frozen, they might have been able to find some evidence of that. But they didn't.'

'Yes, that makes sense,' Maggie said.

'But I just can't believe that any daughter would be involved in killing their own mother,' Jennifer said. 'It seems so cold-hearted. No, worse than that. It's evil.'

'I can understand why you would feel that way,' Maggie said, 'and I'm not trying to defend her actions, but Rebecca, like her father, is heavily on the spectrum. Her only focus and indeed interest in life is her painting. It started as an escape when she was a child and quickly became a total obsession. In her mind, it would have seemed perfectly logical that anything that prevented her from pursuing her passion would have to be eliminated, and losing that huge annual allowance from Torridon Systems would have done just that. And of course, Jack Easton was all too aware of her condition and would have cynically exploited that fact. We're pretty certain that the whole thing will have been his idea.' She paused. 'And, as we're about to discover, once Easton had committed one murder, he had no compunction in committing a second one.'

'Oh God, there *is* more,' Maxwell said, shaking his head in mock disgust. 'Right, we're going to take fifteen minutes to grab a tea or a coffee or, in my case, a quick fag, then we'll brace ourselves for the final act.'

***

Back in the major incident room, Maggie waited for the gentle hubbub of conversation to die down before continuing 'Okay guys, I hope you're all suitably refreshed. So finally we come to the disappearance of Paul Davie. He's the brother of Jaz, who we heard about earlier. Just so you have some background, let me tell you that Bainbridge Associates was approached by Paul's partner Ruth a few weeks after he had disappeared. No foul play was suspected at first because he had allegedly been having an affair with a work colleague, an Indian software contractor, and the initial evidence seemed to be suggesting he had left his partner and daughter and ran off to India with his lover, a woman by the name of May Mishra.' She paused. 'Plausible on the face of it, but a few things didn't seem to stack up. Firstly, his partner Ruth was adamant that Paul was completely devoted to his little daughter and would never have left her, no matter how rocky her parents' relationship had become. Secondly, Paul had vigorously denied that he was having an affair, even going so far as to suggest that the sexually-explicit texts that Ruth had discovered on his phone had been some crazy type of conspiracy or fraud. Thirdly, and perhaps the most significant fact was that after years of pursuing a steady and boring career working for the council, Paul Davie had handed in his notice and, out of the blue, had decided to become a sel employed software contractor. And of course, this latter fact was even more notable because the firm he went to work for was Torridon Systems.' She paused again. 'Not long after, it emerged that what seemed to have triggered this uncharacteristic and risky change of career path was the sad death of his mother, and specifically, something he had discovered when he was clearing out his mum's house.'

'Aye, he found his brother Jaz's laptop,' Lori chipped in.

'That's right,' Maggie said. 'We now know that it was Jaz Davie, not Alison Christie or Richie Whitmore, who had first come up with the idea for Nurses Direct. And when he was looking at his brother's laptop, Paul discovered, no doubt to his total surprise, that it contained what looked like an early version of the application. He knew that Jaz had for many years worked at the same hospital as Alison Christie and it didn't take him long to put two and two together. Crazy though it seemed, it appeared that Christie had stolen the idea for Nurses Direct from his brother, and at that moment he decided he must find proof of that fact.'

Lori made a face. 'Paul was a bit of a boring wimp and his partner Ruth was always nagging him to do something with his life. She's seriously beautiful but a right dragon. And a bit of a bitch too,' she added, triggering a laugh in the room.

'That's right,' Maggie said. 'I don't think he had the plan completely worked out in his head, but I believe he had this vague idea that if he could prove the software had been stolen from his brother, he might be able to negotiate some big compensation payment so that Ruth would be proud of him again. So, he got a contract at Torridon and started digging.' She paused again. 'Now we come to the USB stick. It turned out that Ruth Davie had found a USB memory stick in a pocket of a cycling jacket that Paul had been wearing on one of his last days working at Torridon. Naturally we were anxious to discover what was on the device, so we took it to a chap called Donnie Pollock, who runs a computer repair shop just up the road from our own offices.'

'Lovely Donnie,' Lori said, beaming a seraphic smile.

'Yes, he is lovely,' Maggie laughed, 'and super-smart too. We'd already given Donnie the laptop and he had managed to crack the password and gain access to it, and we hoped he could do the same with the memory stick. But when we handed it over, he told us something interesting, something we didn't know. It turns out that many large organisations have security software that detects if someone inserts a USB device into any computer on their network.'

'That's right, they do,' Jennifer Grant interjected. 'We have it on the Procurator Fiscal systems, because the last thing we want is someone stealing case files and leaking them to the press, or worse, using them to intimidate witnesses. If anyone tries it, alarm bells ring all over the place. And it's immediate dismissal if you're caught doing it of course,' she added.

'Yes, and I think unfortunately it was that capability that ultimately led to Paul Davie's murder.' She smiled at Lori. 'Donnie confirmed to us that what was on the USB stick was code that proved beyond doubt that the live version of Nurses Direct contained the code that had been written by Jaz Davie years earlier. We think Jack Easton and Bill Warren had become suspicious of Paul Davie's motives, particularly when he had asked to be transferred onto their Legacy Code project, a project that had been specifically launched in order to obliterate any traces of Jaz's original code. They knew it would have been catastrophic for the reputation of the company if the truth about the origins of the app had emerged.' She paused and smiled. 'I spent nearly twenty years prosecuting these kinds of cases when I was a barrister. And to use a crude Americanism, I would be suing the ass off these guys if it was my case, and I wouldn't be settling for anything less than ten million.'

'What, we're saying someone in Torridon *murdered* him?' Maxwell said.

'That's our belief, yes,' Maggie said. 'We think that when Paul used his USB stick to copy a chunk of the Nurses Direct code to use as evidence, it triggered an alarm in their security systems. We believe he was then confronted and then forcibly dragged down to the basement level, where he was probably strangled. During the struggle, it seems his phone fell out of a pocket and lay undetected in a corridor for more than twenty-four hours. We know this fact due to very clever work by our colleague Eleanor Campbell.' She pointed towards the forensic officer, who accepted the praise with a modest if seraphic smile. 'Of course, I accept this version of events is only conjecture,' Maggie sighed, 'but if and when we retrieve the body from the river, I'm confident that the cause of death will be confirmed as by foul play.' She paused again. 'Afterwards, the phone was discovered and the killers used it to try and set a false trail. First it was placed on his former desk to make it look as if he had returned to the office the day after he had left their employ, then three days later it appeared at Heathrow, to support the story that he had run off to India with his lover.'

'Yes, what of this aspect of the case?' Jennifer asked. 'Was he really having an affair with this woman?'

Maggie shook her head. 'No, we don't think he was in a sexual relationship with Maya Mishra, but there is some uncertainty around her exact involvement in the case. When Lori and I talked to Jack Easton and Bill Warren about it, they suggested that Paul may have been the victim of an immigration honeytrap, with Mishra trying to ensnare him so that she could obtain British residency. To be honest, we weren't sure what to make of that suggestion, and I'm not sure we'll ever know the truth of it. It's very possible that Easton or Warren or both may have put her up to it, but unless she confirms it herself, we won't know for sure.' She shook her head, sighed, then addressed the prosecutor. 'And I'm afraid Jennifer, that's a problem shared by this entire case. Because although the motive strongly points to Easton and Warren being responsible for Paul Davie's murder, we don't as yet have a shred of evidence to support our theory. And even if we find Paul's body, I very much doubt that will change.'

'I wouldn't be so sure,' Frank said. 'Somebody in Torridon must have witnessed what happened. We'll interview every single member of staff and we'll keep doing it until we get to the truth.'

'I wish I shared your confidence,' she said ruefully. 'We'll just have to see how it pans out.'

'You know better than anyone that the law is an imperfect affair,' Jennifer said. 'But we'll be charging Jack Easton with the murder of Alison Christie, and Bill Warren will be facing a perverting the course of justice charge at the minimum. They will be both going to prison for a very long period. For life, in Easton's case.'

'And what of Rebecca?' Maggie asked.

'We will extradite her of course,' the prosecutor said, 'and then I guess she'll have to face a mental health assessment. But I'm pretty sure we'll charge her with murder and let the sentencing judge worry about any mitigating circumstances.'

The group fell into silence, as each member reflected on a job well done, whilst wondering whether justice would ever be fully served in the cases of the Davie brothers. But as Jennifer Grant had said, the law was indeed an imperfect affair. The outcome of this whole thing had been *far* from perfect, Maggie thought, but the bottom line was that a callous murderer had been brought to book, and that at least had to be counted as a success.

Epilogue

It had been as complex a case as any they had worked on, but the celebrations afterwards were muted. A few of the team had repaired to Great Western Road's Horseshoe Bar for drinks, but Maggie, feeling as if she had been immersed in evil for the past goodness-knows-how-many days, had been desperate to get back home and be with Isobel, Ollie and Frank. Besides which, there had been a development to be discussed, a development which had every prospect of turning their family life upside down, although possibly in a good way – only time would be able to judge that. It had been announced that Frank's former and short-lived government minister boss, the now-opposition politician Katherine Collins, was to be made a Dame in the upcoming New Year's Honours list, and that she was to be made head of a resurrected cold case unit. This time around though, the unit's scope was being extended to encompass an anti-corruption remit, and it was to be relaunched with a new title, the Government Anti-Corruption in Public Office Agency. It hardly tripped off the tongue but at least it made it plain what it was all about. Yesterday, Collins had called Frank to offer him the job of Director of Investigations, the senior operational role in the new unit. But the catch was two-fold. One, he was to be given no alternative; either he accepted the role or he would be given a euphemistically-titled 'package' to ease his departure from the police service, a fate she knew would destroy him. Two, the new role would be based in London, in an expensively-upgraded Atlee House, and in parallel with directives going out across the civil service, there would be no option for remote working. For Frank, it was a choice between London or no job at all.

Thinking it through for the umpteenth time, after Ollie had been tucked up in bed and Isobel had settled in her cot, Maggie began to realise it wasn't the move back down south that was concerning her. After all, she had lived there for twenty years after her move from Yorkshire, and it was where her adored son Ollie had been born and where she had had that first life-changing encounter with the Stewart brothers. She would miss Scotland immensely of course, but it wasn't going anywhere, and she could visit any time she wanted to. No, it was the thought that she would have to close down the Byres Road office and let the wonderful Lori Logan go. How was she ever going to find the right words to break the news to her, and how would the girl react? Lori had been a revelation, turning out to be super-smart, crazily hard-working and brilliantly loyal to boot. She wondered briefly if the girl might want to move to London with them, but she doubted Lori would want to leave her family, and even if she did, how could Bainbridge Associates possibly pay her a salary that would allow her to rent even a one-bedroomed hovel in the capital? But then, in a flash of inspiration, the solution came to her, a solution so obvious she wondered why she hadn't thought of it straight away. Maggie Bainbridge might be moving to London, but that didn't mean that Bainbridge Associates must follow. Why not keep the Byres Road office and maintain a Scottish branch of the firm? Lori was more than capable of vetting potential clients and, with Jimmy's help, running all but the most complex of cases. Allowing herself a brief smile of smug satisfaction, she stretched over to Frank, sitting on the sofa alongside her, and silently planted a warm and lingering kiss on his cheek, which he returned with interest.

And once again, all was well with the world.

A BIG THANK YOU FROM AUTHOR ROB WYLLIE

Dear Reader,

A huge thank you for reading *The Argyll Murders,* and I do hope you enjoyed it! For independent authors like me, star ratings are our lifeblood, so it would be great if you could take the trouble to post a star rating on Amazon when prompted. And if you did enjoy this book, I'm sure you would also like the other twelve books in the series -you can find them all (at very reasonable prices!) on Amazon. Search for 'Rob Wyllie' or 'Maggie Bainbridge'

Also, take a look at my webpage - that's **robwyllie.com** - where you can download a free Maggie Bainbridge mystery for you Kindle. It's called 'Murder of the Unknown Woman, and it's one of my favourites. Thank you for your support!

Regards, Rob

p.s. that thing in Chapter 9 about Google maps and timeline history – I didn't make that up, that's one hundred percent a feature of the app! So, if (heaven forbid) you're planning on murdering your other half, or are intent on executing an audacious multi-million pound jewel heist, I'd turn that feature off at your earliest opportunity. Go to 'Settings' and see if you can find out how to do it. (Or for a very reasonable fee, I'll show you how). And by the way, on Android phones the default setting is 'on'. Which means you've got an Android phone and you've already committed your heinous crime, it's probably too late. Expect a knock on the door any day soon.......

Printed in Great Britain
by Amazon